An Unconventional Family

By

Roberta B. Bombonato

ISBN: 978-0-578-01628-3

Published by AGB Productions

Printed in the U.S.A. via Lulu Press
(www.lulu.com)

For Pappa Bear, Mami, and Hot Patootie...

Thanks for never giving up on me
(When I thought you should)
And for always loving me
(When I thought you shouldn't)

One: Marvin alias Azrael

"Listen, I just can't hang out tonight, baby." I said lying like a conniving snake.

"I know. Every time we start getting closer, you get that itch---no, that urge to fuck someone else. We've been doing this dance for ten years now, Marvin. I hate to break it to you, but you're not some great mystery to me anymore." Carmen said holding her anger in like the seconds of silence before a nuclear bomb explodes. *I better get out of here before she blows.*

"I'll call you, O.K.?" I said after taking in a deep breath. I kiss her gently on her forehead that is hot as if she had a fever, but I know the heat is just a result of anger instead of sickness. She holds her breath and avoids eye contact while I gracefully exit her apartment.

The elevator doesn't have its usual "out of service" sign, but I feel like walking. Step after step, I walk down the hallway followed by going down the stairs and out the door of her decrepit building. The sun's heat touches my face and the city air enters my nostrils, but it isn't long until I find myself feeling the coolness of the shade the subway tunnel provides. After I swipe my subway card and join the various people waiting for their transportation, I take a seat on an empty bench when suddenly; Carmen's face pops into my head. *Have we really been a part of each other's lives for ten years?* Yeah, I guess we have. *I'm not some great mystery to her anymore?* I seriously doubt that. *She still doesn't know what I do for a living. She doesn't know about my past.* My train got here and I followed the herd inside. *When did I even meet Carmen?*

I was about twenty-one...no, twenty-two. I had just finished a job and I was drowning my sorrows with tequila shots at a bar I adopted as my home away from home. I smelled her sweet scent before I turned around responding to her tap on my shoulder. She instantly mesmerized me. Now I knew why she smelled so sweet; her skin was the color of milky caramel candy. Her angelic face quickly drew me in and my eyes were directed to her perfect, big lips as she asked me: "What's wrong?" *What a weird pick-up line,* I thought to myself and then I noticed how genuine she seemed. She actually cared about what my answer would be. Of course, I never answered her honestly that night...or any other night, for that matter.

"Excuse me, Sir? Do you have the time?" A vivacious blonde with legs for days asked me crashing my train of thought. I brought my left wrist closer to my face and checked the time.

"It's fifteen past." I responded with almost a musical tone to my voice.

"Fifteen past what?" She confusedly asked the way a blonde should.

"Fifteen past one, dear. Where are you headed?"

"I have an audition at three at a studio on sixteenth and Broadway." She smiled as if I should be impressed by yet another aspiring actress in New York.

"That is very close to my place. I'd love to help you burn off the nerves." I said hypnotizing her with my charming smile.

"How sweet! I am very nervous...what did you have in mind?" She looked deep into my blue eyes and I could tell she was already mine. I took a step into her welcoming personal space and wrapped my right arm around her tiny waist. Her lips quivered and like a magnet, her lips joined mine. She melted into me and let out a great big sigh.

Minutes later, we were at my loft fucking Carmen out of my head. We had sex on my kitchen counter where Carmen often cooked at, on the coffee table Carmen got for my twenty-fifth birthday, and finally in the shower. She moaned like an amateur porn star as I played Beethoven's Ninth Symphony in my head. The shower was a nice finale to our aerobic performance. She left for her audition shortly after she wrote her number down on the notepad I have next to my phone. "Call me," she said already hoping for the encore that would never happen. I locked the door behind her and walked toward the notepad where I ripped the sheet she wrote on. The paper went in my pajama pant's pocket as I went up the stairs to open my safe located behind my closet. After punching in this week's code, I got my dirty Beretta 92FS with AAC Evolution-9 silencer. I hadn't cleaned it since using it last night before going to Carmen's. Now is a good a time as any. It's funny how a simple task can have such a calming and soothing effect. My cell phone started to ring yanking me out of my peaceful state. I took it out of my pocket and placed it on my ear.

"Yeah?" I answer knowing only clients and potential clients have this number.

"Hi, I got your number from Vanessa." A gay man's voice said with a slight lisp.

"And?"

"Well, isn't it obvious? I want to hire you to do a job." His smart-ass tone irritated me.

"Meet me at the corner of forty-third and Broadway in thirty minutes."

"Oh, I don't know if I can make it in thirty minutes. I— "

"If you don't show up, don't bother calling me again. I'm a busy man." I cut him off and hung up the phone. *Why is it people always think I give a damn about their schedules?* No, the only thing I give a damn about is if the people they want gone truly deserve such a harsh end. The last thing I want is to kill an innocent person. I put on a white t-shirt, jeans, and a Yankees hat after I tied my sneakers. Then I took out the paper with the blonde's number on it, lit it with my butane lighter, and with the burning paper, I lit my menthol cigarette. The ashes fell down on my hard, wooden floor and quickly disappeared with the brief memory of the blonde with nice legs. As the inhaled smoke filled my lungs, the nicotine ran through my veins and everything was right in the world. Seconds later, I was out the door and dialing Vanessa's number.

"Hello?" She answered in almost a whisper.

"Hi, it's Azrael." I said in a firm tone.

"Is something wrong?"

"Did you give my number to anyone?" I asked as I activated the lie detecting voice scanner on my phone.

"Yes, I gave it to Theo. Oh, I hope that's all right. I figured it would be since I got your number from Beth and all. You get your clients by word of mouth, don't you?" She asked while having an internal panic attack. In this case, I didn't need the technology; but I double checked anyways. She was telling the truth. I hung up the phone as soon as I had the information I needed. I put the cell phone in my pocket and kept walking toward the subway. *Theo, Vanessa cleared you. Who are you going to need me to kill?*

In the subway, I started to surf the internet on my iPhone and looked up the number from which Theo called me from. From then on, it was cake finding out what he looks like, how old he is, his social security and etc. I was even able to round up a list of people in his life that he could potentially want dead. My guess is on the stepfather. It's always the stepfather.

Two: Carmen Moreno

"Nina, I can't believe he needs time from me again!" I scream into the phone.

"You really can't believe it? I can believe it...it happens *all* the time." She patronized into my ear.

"You're right. It *does* happen all the time, so why does it still bother me? Shouldn't I be immune to this agony by now?"

"You should, but you're not. I think you're kinda masochistic. Why don't you let Jose take you out on a real date?" She said starting to push my buttons. *I was wondering how long it would take for her to mention Jose.*

"Really, Nina? That's all you have to say? Don't you know by now I'm just gonna say no?" I hissed.

"After all this time all I want is for you to open your eyes and realize that this toxic man will never be the man that you deserve. Are you sure he's not secretly married?"

"Yes, Nina. I'm sure."

"Did you figure out what he does for a living yet?"

"No, I haven't. And even if I did, what would it matter in this situation?"

"I guess it wouldn't matter, but I'm still curious. Ten years and you still don't know what he does. That baffles me. How can something like that never come up? And if it does...how does he always manage to weasel himself out from answering the damn question!"

"Nina..."

"I'm sorry...continue bitching and moaning please."

"Thank you. Well, this time it's almost like everything was going *too* good. Like, we haven't fought in a really long time about anything. I was spending the night almost every night and we were finally getting into a routine as if we were an old married couple. It makes *no* sense why he pulled away this time!

"Last week, he even told me to bring over some clothes to leave over! He's never said anything like that before! I mean, I always brought stuff over anyways, but he never gave me permission like that. And I was so used to being at his loft...remember how at first I felt strange being there because it was so fancy?"

"Yeah, I remember..." She almost sounded bored...

"I'm sorry I'm talking so much. It's just that this time, I thought he was finally going to ask me to move in!"

"Hey, quick question...is that why you always buy him furniture for his birthdays and Christmases? Are you decorating his house because you secretly want to live there?" She read me like a book. Her discovery stung a little.

"No, I just want him to have a nice home to come home to. Did you know that when I first met him he only had a laptop by a beanbag, an inflatable couch, and a mattress on the ground?" I lied about the first part. Secretly, I am only decorating it because someday I truly believe I will live there. Someday, I really do think he will open his eyes and see that we belong together. The loft is just beautiful. It has hardwood floors, a huge kitchen with granite kitchen tops and Brazilian cherry cupboards, an enormous living and dining room, a bathroom downstairs right next to the spare bedroom which he now uses as an office (but it could easily be turned into a baby nursery), and finally, the stairs that lead you to the master bedroom/bathroom which you can see into from the kitchen.

"Then you sure did turn it around, chica. But just because you change the loft that doesn't mean that you will change the man that lives in it." She killed my buzz.

"You are such a downer." I accused.

"Hey, I just call it like I see it. You performing today?"

"Yeah, I have a show at four fifteen, one at six, and one at eight fifteen."

"Cool, do you need a ride after work?"

"That would be great."

"O.K. then, I'll come watch your eight fifteen show. I gotta go. See ya tonight." She didn't give me a chance to say goodbye, but that was Nina. I looked into the refrigerator for some comfort food, but found nothing. I had already opened it three times before with no luck, but I keep opening it because I truly believe a bucket of fried chicken will magically appear if I will it so.

My apartment is so small that I don't even have a wall between my bedroom and my kitchen. Well, actually my bedroom is my living room. I have a pull out couch that becomes my bed at night. I share a bathroom with three other tenants in my building. Every floor has a bathroom, and everyone that lives on that floor shares that bathroom...get it? It's awful. I'm a belly dancer. I just recently landed a job performing at a local pub, which is nice. I'm saving up to buy a studio, so I can teach dance someday. That's why I'm living in this crappy apartment...so I can save money. But, I've been saving money my whole life. Seems like as soon as I have a good lump sum, something big happens and I have to spend it. Seven years ago, my brother needed bail money. Do you think he paid me back? Six thousand dollars don't come easy either. Then last year, my mom got really sick. The hospital did everything they could, but she still passed on. I, of course, had to pay for the hospital bills and funeral arrangements. My brother didn't even bother to show up at the funeral. Anyways, now I'm just saving.

I started getting ready for my show when the Marvin box called out to me. The Marvin box is just a box where I put pictures and little things that remind me of some good times we had together; the best times, actually, and the best memories. Maybe I should have a bad Marvin box and a good Marvin box. That way, when I feel like this, I can only look at the bad box to convince me that I am better off without him. I couldn't manage looking at just the bad box, though. The good box would win, so scratch that. I got the box down from my closet and placed it on my couch/bed. I sat down and started going through it. Marvin is such an attractive man. He is about six foot four, blonde, blue eyes, and tan skin. He dyes his hair blonde. I only know that because I've seen the dye boxes in his bathroom's trash can. He never lets his true colors show. I mean that literally and metaphorically. He has a washboard for a stomach and the infamous "v." His arms are very muscular too, but not to the point where he can't put his arms down. They're the perfect size. And he doesn't have chicken legs either. He is very proportional unlike those guys that go to the gym just to work out their arms.

I have an egg shell from the first time he made me breakfast in bed inside the Marvin box. I wrote the date on it with a sharpie; April eighth, nineteen eighty four. That was a good morning. I also have Broadway tickets from all the shows he's taken me to over the years. He always gets the best seats. He met my mom once and took us out to dinner. She told him a good wine tells a story inside your taste buds. I kept the carry-out paper menu from the restaurant that I swiped when he wasn't looking. My mom knew just what I would do with it, so she distracted him while I hid it in my purse. Then when she died, he brought over a bottle of wine to drink with me. He quoted my mother and said it was time to tell stories with our taste buds. I told him nearly all the fond memories I had with my dear mommy. I kept the cork from that wine. With the exception of that night, we always drink tequila. I have a label from the bottle of his favorite kind. I looked over at the clock and it was almost four. The smile that was on my face faded away abruptly when the reminiscing stopped and the "Oh, shit I'm gonna be late," started.

I ran out the door as soon as I gently put all the memories and good times back in the Marvin box. I ran until it felt like my throat was burning with the oxygen/carbon-dioxide exchange. But it didn't matter; I like working there enough not to have them replace me just yet.

Three: Keiko Akashimi

"Daddy, I want to put in this CD." I said handing him one of my various Disney CDs.

"Now, Honey, you know very well that today is Sumi's turn to pick the music. Tomorrow will be your turn again." Daddy said and though I understand what he is saying, it doesn't mean I have to like it.

"Fine." I said while putting my CD safely back in my Disney princess CD case. I turned my head to look out the window at the landscape passing by fast to avoid Sumi's victorious glare. *I hate her taste in music.* I see her hand daddy a Marilyn Manson CD and seconds after it was in, she started head banging. *Teenagers suck.* She used to play with me all the time when she was twelve, but now that she is thirteen I'm too young all of the sudden. *I'm eight years old!* Jia is eight, but since she's an advanced eight year old in the same grade as Sumi, she doesn't have to be excluded like me. I swear, the moment I met Jia I knew that I had been replaced.

"Why do we have to go to school during Spring Break?" Sumi asked trying to sound sophisticated.

"Because we want you to learn as much as you can so you can go to college and become something great." Mommy said smiling at daddy.

"But all my friends are going to Cabo!" All the sophistication left with her brief, whiny statement.

"We have to work, sweetie." Daddy lamented.

"What do you do again, Daddy?" I asked.

"I specialize in trades and business transactions. Mommy helps out in the office. She's like my co-pilot." Daddy took Mommy's hand and kissed it making her smile.

"Trading what?" Sumi asked making their smiles wipe away.

"Whatever needs to be traded. Who's ready for breakfast?" Daddy asked and changed the subject at the same time like he always does when Sumi's or my questions about his work get too specific. He always misses career day, too. Sumi and I think he does illegal stuff. Lately, she's been bugging him a lot. I don't blame her. Last Christmas, these bad guys dressed in all black came over and beat him up pretty bad. They also broke dishes, tipped over our beautiful tree, and took all our presents. He promised nothing like that would ever happen again, and it hasn't; but Sumi feels like it might. That's why she wants some answers.

We parked at the gas station we stop at every morning to buy breakfast and get gas. While Sumi, Mommy, and Daddy got out, I tried to be sneaky and switch out Sumi's bad CD with my good one. As I pressed the eject button and put her CD on the center console, I felt a presence that gave me chills up and down my spine. I turned my head to the right and suddenly I was face to face with a big, creepy Hummer with black tinted windows. I don't know why I felt so scared, but I tried crawling into the backseat forgetting that Sumi's CD was on the center console. I broke it with my knee which made me gasp at the same time that the Hummer's window started to roll down. The driver looked right at me! He looked so mean. His eyes were as dark as death, his hair was blue, and his lip had a nasty scar on it. As he looked at me, my skin prickled and my hands started to moisten. After the longest two seconds of my life, he creepily drove away. I quickly got out of the car and ran to Mommy feeling that if I hugged her hard enough, she would protect me from everything; like somehow she would become my shield.

"What is it, Keiko?" Mommy asked placing her loving hand on my back.

"What's wrong, honey?" Daddy chimed in.

"She's shaking. What's the matter, Keiko?" She asked now with a more serious and concerned tone to her voice.

"The bad man was here," I finally confessed.

"Who's the bad man?" Mommy asked.

"The bad man is the person she blames everything on. She broke my gold eye shadow the other day and blamed it on him. What did you do now, you little punk?!" Sumi yelled as she squeezed my arm extra hard and firm. Daddy looked in the car where I was seconds ago and noticed Sumi's cracked CD.

"Is that what the bad man did?" He pointed at the CD and raised his eyebrow while he spoke in a deep, stern voice.

"Not with his own hands..." I admitted.

"What, Keiko? He made you do it with your hands?" Sumi sarcastically asked rolling her eyes.

"Technically, with my knees." I replied.

"Keiko Akashimi, I am very surprised at you! I've taught you to take responsibilities for your own actions." Mommy yelled and stopped hugging me at once.

"But the bad man scared me, Mommy!" I pleaded.

"What was my CD doing out of the CD player?" Sumi asked. My stomach dropped. *Now they really won't believe me.* Sumi went to the CD player and pressed the eject button. My Disney CD popped out.

"I thought so." Sumi dryly said.

"That's it, Keiko. No breakfast for you. You sit in the car with your seatbelt fastened and think about what you've done!" Mommy yelled. I lowered my head and did as she said. *There really was a bad man this time!* I haven't lied since Mommy said that lying destroys people, families, and civilizations. I promised I would never lie again, and I haven't! *They should've believed me.*

After ten minutes of solitude, my family returned and the smell of breakfast filled the air. They put on their seatbelts and we started driving to school. My stomach growled and I knew it would be a long day. I knew I would be looking at the clock counting down the minutes till lunch. Sumi noticed my agony and turned to me licking the jelly slowly from her jelly doughnut. *How evil.* My mouth watered involuntarily.

When we got to school, I didn't bother to say goodbye to Mommy and Daddy. They didn't say anything either. Sumi walked in front of me and I followed looking at my feet. Jia was at the top of the steps waiting for Sumi. I wish I only had to see her at school because when she comes over the house, my parents always hint toward me being more like her. I really *dislike* her only because I know it's not right to hate.

"What's up Sumi? Hi, Keiko." Jia cheerfully said.

"Yo." Sumi replied. I said nothing. I walked to my class after they walked away without saying bye to me. I sat down on my desk and put my head down. The desk felt cold against my chin. Miss Estefana told us to take out our books and read silently. *Even the teachers don't wanna be here during Spring Break.* I raised my hand and asked for a bathroom pass. I wandered the empty hallway that almost looked haunted. When I walked into the bathroom, I immediately smelled smoke. Then I saw Sumi and Jia smoking cigarettes.

"Sumi, Mom's gonna kill you!" I yelled unaware of how loud my voice had gotten.

"How's she gonna find out?" Sumi asked full of attitude.

"Yeah, Keiko, how's she gonna find out?" Jia chimed in.

"Smoking is bad." I sheepishly said.

"Whatever. Are you done, Jia?" She asked nonchalant.

"Yeah, let's go." Jia replied. They put out their cigarettes with the faucet water in the sink and then they left. I went in the first stall and sat down on the toilet. I looked at my watch and it was only nine fifteen. I took a deep breath and decided it was time to face the music and go back to class. I looked at myself in the mirror as I walked out of the bathroom. That's when I saw the bad man pointing a gun at Jia and Sumi. I quickly hid behind the door leaving a sliver of it open to witness what was happening. They looked so scared! He told them not to speak. Then he grabbed Sumi's arm and brought her close to him. She yelped quietly trying to follow his instructions. He took out a photo of our family and carefully started examining and analyzing Sumi's face. He looked back and forth from her face to the picture and from the picture to her face. My pupils dilated as soon as he unexpectedly shot her right between the eyes at close range. Her body limply fell down like a puppet whose strings were cut by its puppet master. My tear ducts started to burn and tears started to come out of them almost instantaneously. Jia's mouth opened and as soon as sound was faintly starting to come out, he swiftly broke her neck silencing her forever. Before he dropped her body next to Sumi's, he studied her face next to the picture. And then his phone rang.

"Hello?" He answered with a raspy voice while dropping Jia's flimsy body. I cupped my mouth and my knees gave out.

"I got the older one...Yeah, I'll get the youngest after school...No problem." He closed his flip phone and walked outside. If I didn't see him walking, I wouldn't have heard him. He almost moved like a cat; a bad and evil cat. I couldn't believe how silent his gun was. It was so unlike any movie I saw against my parent's permission when they thought I was asleep. When the tears lessened and I felt a little more composed, I walked toward the bodies. *Poor Sumi.* Her body was surrounded by a crimson red blood pool. *And poor Jia.* Her head was turned all the way around. I cried by Sumi's body uncontrollably when suddenly a scary thought came into my head. *I'm next. I want my mommy! I need to get out of here!* I went to the double doors and peeked outside noticing that the bad man was parked right in front of the school. I started walking toward the back where the playground was. I knew exactly where the fence was cut; it's how the big kids leave school unnoticed.

It was easy to go through the fence since I was much tinier than the high school kids. As soon as I was off school grounds, I started running as fast as I could. I was running so fast that I stumbled and fell down scraping my elbow. It started to bleed and sting, but I couldn't cry knowing that the bad man was so close by. Our house is only ten minutes from here by car, but running takes longer. I got home at ten. The door was wide open which was weird to me. I walked into the kitchen and noticed mommy was sprawled out on the floor surrounded by a pool of blood just like Sumi! *Mommy...*

I needed mommy's comfort desperately, but that was something that would never happen again. I dropped down to her side and pulled her arm over me trying to find the comfort in her touch. Even though it felt the same way my teddy bears hug me, just the knowledge that it was mommy's body helped. When I stood up, there was no doubt in my mind that Daddy was dead somewhere, too. I went up the stairs and sure enough, there was his body hanging by a rope on the ceiling. There was a gun next to his shoe. It looked just like the one the bad man used at school today. I cried some more at this sight and when I couldn't bear it any longer; I went to my room to start packing. I knew I couldn't stay here. I've seen Annie. Kids that get taken to orphanages have to clean and instead of kisses, they get kicks. *No, thank you. Plus, the bad man would find me.* Then I went into daddy's room and took the emergency cash from his sock drawer. *I can't believe my family is dead. This has to be daddy's fault.*

I looked around everywhere one last time and then with one deep sigh, I ventured into the outside world looking for a new home. I walked and walked until my little feet hurt in such a way I never felt before. *How long have I been walking?* Then, I saw a building with a sign reading "condemned." I noticed that the people on the sidewalk were passing by it as if it didn't even exist. *That's what I need; to be somewhere that doesn't exist.* Two seconds later, I crawled inside an opening and was faced with an elevator that was clearly broken. It leaned like the Tower of Pisa. I opened the door and crawled inside feeling safe at once. I closed the door as much as I could. The darkness of being inside the elevator was as dark as the darkness I felt inside of me. I felt my eyes start to close, but as soon as they did, the faces of my now dead family acted like a slideshow behind my eyelids. I started to cry and shake uncontrollably. It was as if my body wanted to show my soul how much despair it was feeling, but my soul already knew it...felt it. I started to hiccup and after a while, my chest started to hurt. *What is to become of me now?*

Four: Marvin

I arrived at the checkpoint precisely nine minutes before said meeting. I sat down on a bus stop bench, waiting for Theodore Remi. Eight minutes later, I saw him wearing white shorts, white sneakers with pink socks, and a pink polo shirt. *Very gay indeed.* He looked so nervous and I couldn't resist catching him off guard. Plus, intimidation in my line of work is key.

"Follow me, Theo." I startled him and almost laughed at how high he jumped.

"Azrael?" He foolishly asked.

"What's wrong with you? I said follow me, not talk to me." I snapped. *Is he stupid? Why would he say my alias out loud like that?*

"Yes, Sir." He saluted me as if he was in the army and I was his commanding officer. *Yes, he is stupid.*

"Shh." I silenced him before he could get any dumber. I took him to my "office," which just happens to be an abandoned warehouse. It's perfect to meet new clients.

"Achoo!" He sneezed and took out a pink hanky from his back pocket. *Just my luck; he's probably allergic to the dust. He's already high maintenance.*

"Now you can talk, Theo." I allowed.

"How do you know my name?" He fidgeted.

"It's my job. Why did you contact me?" I rebutted.

"I need you to kill my stepfather." *Two points for me.*

"Why?" *Don't lie, Theo...I don't like liars.*

"It's so hard to say to a complete stranger..." He fidgeted once more. This time he almost acted like something disgusted him. *He was molested or raped.*

"I've often heard that it's much easier to speak to a complete stranger. Take comfort in the fact that after this meeting, we won't see each other again."

"Vanessa did tell me you needed to know a valid reason...May I ask why you need to know?" Behind his eyes there was a shame you could only get from being sexually assaulted.

"These are my requirements. I'm sure Vanessa told you that I do background checks on all my hits and clients. I don't off the innocent. If you won't comply with my terms, you can kill him yourself." Terror jumped out of his eyes like I've never seen before. And I've seen a lot.

"Oh Mr. Azrael, he's just a horrible man," he paused and took a deep breath like he was about to unload the weight of the world on me, "When I was ten, he started molesting me. And then when I was thirteen, he raped me. Every time mom would be gone, he would invade me. We went to court once, but he won. Now my mom doesn't believe me anymore. I just want him dead! He belongs in hell and I just need you to make his departure sooner rather than later!" He broke down and started crying into his hanky. *Two more points for me. How do I always know? Have I done this for too long?*

"What's his name and social security number?" I finally asked when his hysterics calmed down a bit. He handed me a folded piece of paper with the information I needed. Vanessa probably told him of everything I would ask for.

"Do I pay you now? Will you call me when he is finished?" He felt at ease to ask.

"I will text you an account number tonight for you to deposit the amount that I will send you in the same text message. I won't proceed with anything until the whole lump sum is deposited in the account I supplied you with. And no, I won't call you when the job is done. You will know when your mother calls you up bawling her eyes out."

"O.K., Mr. Azrael. Thank you so very much." He said misty eyed.

"You're welcome. Now get out of here." I abstained from eye contact because I can always tell who the huggers will be. He was definitely a hugger. As soon as I noticed he was gone, I alleviated my fury by punching the dry wall. It really chops my balls to hear stories like Theo's. *Why do things like this happen?!*

"Achoo!" I heard and felt stupid for losing it in public; though, in my defense, I thought I was alone.

"Didn't I tell you to get out of here?" I turned around, but was surprised that Theo was nowhere to be found. Instead, there was a little Asian girl standing there with possible blood stains on her t-shirt and skirt.

"Hi." She said looking up at me with her squinty eyes.

"Um...hi." I replied uneasily.

"What are you doing here?" She asked with curiosity spilling out of her eyes.

"Working." I replied still confused at the situation. *What is a little girl doing in a warehouse? Where are her parents? What the hell is going on?!*

"Oh. Working is good. I haven't seen anybody here in six days!" She said sounding glad to have human contact. *Six days without supervision?*

"Why have you been here for six days?"

"I haven't been living here." She gave herself away sounding so defensive.

"You've been living here?" *Why was I even concerned?*

"No, silly, I just said I *haven't* been living here." She annunciated the "haven't."

"Where are your parents?" I interrogated.

"In a better place." She vaguely said.

"What's a better place than New York City?"

"Heaven." *Shit.*

"Oh." I managed to spit out.

"Wanna play tea party?" She asked unaffected by the conversation.

"Um...no. I'll catch you on the flip-flop, kid. Be safe." *Must...Get...Out.*

"What does that mean?" She curiously asked again taking a step closer to me.

"It means I'm leaving and I'll see you later."

"When is later?"

"I don't know." *Are kids always this curious? Aren't they supposed to not talk to strangers or something?*

"Well, I need to know these things. I have to look presentable." She smiled showing the cutest dimples I've ever seen.

"How old are you, kid?"

"Eight." She looked down and hugged her teddy bear. I hadn't realized she was holding one until now.

"What do you know about looking presentable?" I chuckled.

"I'm a lady. That's what ladies do."

"What's your name?" I asked after laughing a bit at her seriousness of the lady comment.

"I'm Keiko Akashimi. What's your name?"

"Az---Marvin." She didn't need to know my alias.

"Azmarvin? That's a strange name." She said without inhibitions. *What a lady.*

"No, just Marvin." I corrected.

"Nice to meet you, Mr. Marvin." She extended her tiny hand for me to shake it. I carefully took her hand in mine feeling how soft and brittle it was. *Was I ever this tiny?*

"Kid, be honest with me. Have you been living here?" I honestly wanted to know.

"Are we friends?"

"Sure."

"Friends never lie to each other, right?"

"Right..."

"Then yes, Mr. Marvin, I have to admit that I've been living here for six whole days."

"Don't you have aunties and uncles? A grandma...maybe, that would take you in?" I asked truly feeling concerned about this little girl who was no kin to me.

"No, they are all in Japan. Daddy broke their hearts for doing something bad and now they don't ever wanna see us again. Well...there is no 'us' anymore. I guess they don't wanna see *me* anymore." She said for the first time sounding sad since our chance encounter.

"Are you hungry?" I inquired.

"As a matter of fact, I am." *As a matter of fact...she's such a funny little girl.*

"Come on, I'll take you to get a happy meal and then I'll drop you off at the police station."

"The police station? Why?"

"Because you can't live here. It's dangerous." She looked deep in thought for thirty seconds.

"You can take me to get the happy meal, but I must decline to the police station proposition."

"You must decline?" I asked chuckling. *This kid is hilarious. Who talks like this?*

"Yes, I must decline." She smiled in a serious manner as if nothing was negotiable.

"What if I say it's not up to you?"

"Hey, I thought we were friends. Friends don't pressure friends to do things they don't wanna do like drugs, or dangerous stunts...or going to the police station." She counted the reasons on her miniscule fingers and looked deep into my eyes when the police station reason came out of her mouth.

"I can't let you stay here, kid."

"Why don't we go eat and talk about this later?"

"Quit being a smart-ass and get your things," she gasped at me and looked flabbergasted, "What?"

"You said the 'a' word." She whispered making me speechless. After a minute of us looking at each other she scrunched up her forehead and sighed.

"I won't tell." She finally decided.

"Thanks." I smiled. She walked toward the elevator and opened it with a mop. In it, was an air mattress, a pink pillow that said "princess" on it, and a pink backpack. She also had drawings hung up on the elevator walls. Some of the drawings had stick figures lying on the ground surrounded by blood. She was actually quite talented. I took the drawings down without wrinkling them and shoved them under my arm.

"You ready?" I asked.

"No, I need a minute to say goodbye to my home." She said. I nodded. She then bowed down to the elevator with her hands joined together in prayer position. *What a strange kid!* With her head bowed down, her shiny black hair curtained the sides of her face. I just now noticed her bangs. I also noticed how skinny she was. I guess she looks like a typical Asian kid, only cuter in the face if that makes sense.

"I'm done." She said as she put her backpack on her back and held my hand. I cleared my throat immediately feeling uneasy and strange. I never held a kid's hand before. I don't even hold Carmen's hand in public. I took my phone out of my pocket and looked at the time so I could have an excuse to stop holding her hand. We walked to the nearest McDonald's side by side. I opened the door for Keiko and she seemed to like that I acted like a gentleman. She walked up to the line and looked up at the menu. When it was our turn, the cashier seductively smiled at me.

"May I take your order?" She asked.

"Yeah, I'd like a number two with no pickles or mustard large sized with a coke, no ice." I winked at her when I was done talking. She blushed which made her seem more intriguing through my eyes.

"I would like a happy meal, please," Keiko said politely, "And I would like the cheeseburger prepared with only mayonnaise." She specified.

"What do you wanna drink, sweetie?" The cashier asked.

"I would like an orange soda, please."

"That will be ten fifty four, Sir." I reached for my wallet and paid for it. When the order was up, I carried the tray to a booth as Keiko got us some napkins and straws. On the tray, I noticed that the cute cashier had written her number on our receipt with a smiley face next to it. I looked back at the register and smiled at her making her blush again. I made sure she saw me put the receipt in my jeans pocket before I sat down. Keiko started inhaling her food like she hadn't eaten in days.

"Slow down, kid." I ordered. She listened. As I ate, I started looking through her drawings carefully analyzing each of them to put together in my mind exactly what this kid witnessed. I could clearly see that the four people were killed in two different locations. And then one drawing jumped out at me.

"Who's this, Keiko?" I sternly asked.

"That's the bad man." I knew exactly who he was. She did a good job with the drawing; especially the scar on his lip. I gave him that scar long ago. *Her family was assassinated!*

"Is this the man that sent your family to the better place?" I asked already knowing the answer. She nodded much too preoccupied by the food in her mouth.

"Did he see you?" She shook her head still chewing like this was the best meal she's ever had. I lost my appetite and started to contemplate whether or not the police was the best route to take. Bram is ruthless. He kills whole families and there's no doubt in my mind that he is looking for this one. He never leaves a job unfinished. *No, he wasn't trained that way.* I decided this kid was going to be a pro-bono case. She can stay with me until I have a chat with Bram. I looked at Keiko and noticed she had swiped my uneaten French fries. *She must've been so hungry.*

"Keiko," I said in a serious tone, "What happened to your family was very bad. I'm sorry for your loss." I was surprised at how much I sympathized. She looked at me and her eyes started filling up with tears. *Oh no, please don't cry.*

"Thank you for dinner, Mr. Marvin." She said as she wiped her almost tears with the sleeve of her shirt.

"You're more than welcome. Keiko we're friends, right?"

"Most definitely." She nodded animatedly.

"Friends let friends be a guest in their homes." I said.

"I can't."

"Why not?"

"Because the bad man will find me."

"No, he won't. I'll protect you."

"He's looking for me, Mr. Marvin." She said with a hint of fear.

"How do you know that?" I wondered.

"Because I heard him on the phone. The elevator was a good hiding place...I don't think your house will be." She honestly said.

"I found you, didn't I?" She nodded.

"It will only be a matter of time until he finds you there, too. He won't even think to look at my house, though."

"Will I get my own room?" Her eyes sparkled.

"Kind of. You can sleep in the pull out couch in my office. Is that all right?"

"Yeah. Mr. Marvin, can I have an ice cream cone?"

"Sure, there's a good ice cream place by my house." She quickly stood up and threw the trash away. She was eager for that ice cream and it only made her cuter. We walked along the sidewalk for a few blocks and when it was time to cross the road, she tried holding my hand again.

"What's your deal with the hand holding?" I asked half annoyed.

"I can't cross the street without holding your hand." She innocently said.

"How did you cross the street when you were alone?"

"I held my own hand."

"Then do that. I'm right beside you." We walked to the subway and rode it to my street. There, I bought her the ice cream I promised. When we got to my place, she politely asked to take a shower. I showed her the bathroom she would be using while I gave her a clean t-shirt and a pair of Carmen's clean volleyball shorts. While she showered, I made up the couch/bed in my office with flannel sheets.

"That was nice. I hadn't showered in six days, you know?" She said after she yawned. My shirt looked like a dress on her, and the volleyball shorts that looked so tight on Carmen were practically falling off her tiny body.

"Mr. Marvin, will you tuck me in?" I went over to the bed and pulled the blanket over her without touching her when she unexpectedly hugged me tight. My heart dropped and I felt myself pushing her away with my hand making her lay flat on the bed without touching me.

"Good night, Keiko." I finally said walking toward the door and softly closing it behind me.

"No! Don't close it all the way..." She begged.

"O.K." I opened it halfway and just like that, she drifted into the sleep world without a care in the world. While she slept, I washed her clothes removing all the blood stains so she could wear it in the morning. *Today was insane. How can she act like Pollyanna when her family is dead?* I need to get a hold of Bram, but this will surely be difficult. The last time we talked face to face...things didn't end well. And we pretty much agreed to not look for each other again; kind of like a treaty that would be best if it weren't broken.

Five: Carmen

"You were real good tonight, Carmen. If you keep this up, you will be headlining in no time." Hector, my boss, said as he handed me my paycheck. When I first came in for a job interview, he tried talking me into becoming a stripper. You see, after my eight o'clock show, this bar becomes a strip club. *I refuse to take my clothes off for money.* My mom didn't raise me like that. He soon realized that he wouldn't be able to change my mind about showing my ta-tas, so he gave me three time slots for my belly dancing routine. Standing your ground pays off sometimes.

"When that time comes, I'll be ready." I said flashing my pearly whites. I saw Nina sitting by the bar where the lesbian bartender admired her from afar. I've told Nina before that she leads her on, but as long as she gets free drinks...

"Chica, you were on fire tonight!" Nina proudly said before hugging me tight.

"Thanks, I'm beat!" I admitted.

"A dance like that deserves a celebration! Let's go out to dinner."

"Nowhere fancy though...I'm too sweaty; maybe even a little stinky." She laughed.

"How about some pub-subs?" She knows me all too well.

"I'm in love with that idea." We walked to her car which was double parked with a ticket under the windshield wipers as usual. Like a creature of habit, she took the ticket and littered the sidewalk before unlocking the doors so we could get in the car and hit the road. She drives like a maniac with a death wish, but somehow, I know I'm safe with her. Her stereo blared as the engine roared to life. I could feel the bass and each beat made my body unconsciously start dancing. Nina put her '68 Dodge Charger into first gear and the tires squealed as we pealed out toward the busy streets of New York. She restored this car herself. I almost don't believe it's the same car she saved from the junkyard. That's where she goes to hunt for new projects.

"I see you finished the car." I noted.

"Yeah, I'm almost sad to see it go..." She said with a slight melancholy tone to her voice.

"You already found a buyer?" *She just finished yesterday! I guess next week we'll go back to driving around in her ordinary Honda Civic.*

"Of course, wanna go to the junkyard with me tomorrow?" No trace of melancholy could be heard as she excitedly asked.

"Maybe..." I stared off into space as I pictured myself going to Marvin tomorrow to talk. I always wait for him to come to me after he's gotten over whatever he needs to get over...but this time, I'm going to break tradition. We pulled into the Publix parking lot as if we were being chased by the cops. As she sped between the lanes, she looked for the perfect parking space. I knew she made a choice when the car started to do a three sixty and a quick reverse. Adrenaline pumped through my veins as I held the "oh, shit!" handle tight and had an internal conflict as to whether or not my eyes should be open this time. Before I knew it, we were perfectly backed into a parking spot symmetrically between the lines and the engine was shut off.

"You can relax now, Carm." She laughed as she patted my back and rolled her eyes.

"Nina! That was awesome!"

"You closed your eyes in the best part." She disappointedly pouted.

"I don't think you're ever going to make me into a thrill seeker like you." I said as I always do after she does her stunts.

"A girl can still hope." She said. We got out of the car and admired it.

"Is this the same type of car Vin Diesel drove in The Fast and The Furious?" I asked.

"Yeah, it is. Oh, I forgot to tell you. Tomorrow I'm leaving for Cali. I got a gig and I'll be gone for three days." Nina said. Did I mention she's a stunt driver?

"Congrats. You will be missed." I put my arm around her and we walked inside toward the Deli section. We ordered our usual (Nina always gets a meatball sub on white with Swiss and parmesan cheese while I always get a turkey sub on wheat with provolone, mayo, honey mustard, onions, lettuce, and black olives) and filled our cups with fountain drinks. Today was a lemony day, so I decided to get a Sprite, with no ice; the only thing I order with ice is water because only water can't get watery. I have a philosophy: the point of a meal is to get to dessert. I walked over to the bakery and looked over their selections. The Tiramisu looked divine! I grabbed the prettiest one and we walked to the cash register. We paid separately though I offered to pay for hers. When we got to the car, I saw the melancholy I heard earlier in her eyes.

"You're really attached to this car, aren't you?" I mused. She sighed.

"Not exactly, but... my dad used to have a car like this one and I don't know. When I was working on it, it almost felt like he was there with me. I just miss him, that's all." She said looking away before she seemed too vulnerable. Her dad died before I met her, but the wound was still fresh as if it happened just yesterday. We got in the car and drove in silence; no music or conversation. When we got to my place, she parked and as we climbed up the stairs, she was back to her old self joking around and being hilarious. I unlocked my door and took my shoes off at once. Nina went over to my DVD stack by the TV and predictably picked Bride and Prejudice. Seconds later, we were snuggled next to each other eating our store bought dinners and watching our favorite movie. I've tried making Marvin watch this movie so many times, but he always seems to fall asleep. He's so tired all the time, unless there's sex involved. *Hmm, it would blow his mind if I came over and pretended as if nothing happened the other day; pretended as if I was coming over for just sex...*

After the movie, I took a shower. Three shows really take a toll on my sweat glands! When I got back, I noticed Nina had cleaned up by throwing all the trash away. I also noticed the couch had been transformed into a bed and Nina was sprawled out on it looking like she's been sleeping for hours. I moisturized my body and brushed my hair before putting on my pajamas. Then I walked toward the bed and pushed Nina to make a little room for me. It's funny how she lives in a penthouse, but she's here four nights out of the week like she has no better place to go.

Six: Marvin

I heard the wooden floor creak and I felt a presence coming closer toward me. The creak was quick which suggested the person was oddly small. Somewhat confused, I reached for the dagger under my mattress avoiding as much movement as possible and kept my eyes closed. I concentrated on the presence, now coming closer and closer to me. Precipitously, I rolled off the bed and got behind the tiny person restricting their arms and holding my dagger on their throat. Gradually, I came out of warrior mode and hid the dagger. *Keiko...I could've so easily hurt her...*

"Mr. Marvin, are you all right?" She asked tilting her head and looking at me inquiring about my well-being as if I didn't almost just kill her.

"Keiko, you mustn't take me by surprise *ever*. Announce yourself if you're about to enter my room!" I scolded. Tears started welling up in her eyes and a single one streaked down her face.

"I just came to tell you that your kitchen is on fire." She warned wiping her tears away.

"*WHAT?!*" I sprung into action running down the stairs three steps at a time. The fire was small and fairly contained to the eggs burning on the frying pan. I speedily threw the pan into the sink and turned on the water to put out the fire causing smoke to set off the smoke detector. *Oy vey, it's too early for this*. I turned to Keiko, who was woefully sitting on the last step of the stairs.

"Were you allowed to make breakfast at your parent's house?" I asked.

"No..." She said in a sheepish, small voice.

"The same rules apply here, O.K.?"

"I never had to announce myself before going into mommy and daddy's room..." She mentioned. I looked at the ceiling as if an answer would be written there. I took a deep breath and sat down next to her on the stairs.

"I'm sorry about earlier, Keiko. This is a very different kind of household that you will temporarily be living in," another deep breath, "Regardless, the same general rules apply. No cooking by yourself and...what are some other rules your parents had?"

"Don't go swimming without supervision?"

"We don't have a pool here, so that one doesn't really apply. What else you got?"

"Don't play with your sister's make-up?" I laughed. She giggled.

"Let's modify that one to no snooping around my room. Lay another one on me."

"Make your bed and wash your face before breakfast." I looked over inside the room and noticed the bed was already made.

"I don't mind if you don't make your bed since I never make mine."

"Really? Didn't your mommy teach you that your room reflects the kind of person you are?" Her words stung. My mother *did* teach me that. Making my bed always hurt me too much because it always reminded me of her. *Everything reminds me of her.*

"Mr. Marvin, are you O.K.?" She sweetly asked touching my stubbly cheek.

"Yeah, I'm fine. How about we go out for breakfast?" I changed the subject and stood up.

"Yay!" Keiko yelped and started jumping up and down with joy.

"All right, then. Get dressed. Your clothes are inside the drier." I pointed toward the laundry room by the kitchen. She walked toward it at the same time as I went up the stairs to get dressed. I took my dagger out of my pocket and dug it under the mattress where it belonged. I brushed my teeth and put on some basketball shorts with sneakers and a basketball jersey. I reached for my wallet on my night stand and started walking toward the stairs. *Marvin, it takes two minutes to make your bed. Don't you like making me happy?*, my mom's voice said in my head. I turned around and looked over at my bed, then reluctantly made it. *See? That didn't kill you, did it?*, her voice said again this time making me smile. *No, mom, it didn't kill me...*I winced at the word *kill.*

"I'm ready, Mr. Marvin!" Keiko screamed from downstairs.

"All right, I'm coming. Hold your horses." I said as I went down the stairs. I need a little time to unwind in the mornings. *How is she already full of energy like this?* I opened the door and was face-to-face with Carmen who was standing with her arm ready to knock on the door I just opened.

"Carmen...hi." I said surprised. She noticed the guilty tone in my voice right away.

"Marvin! If you have a girl in there I'm gonna perfórela y aplástela como una cucaracha!" Carmen defensively said with tons of aggression. A smile flashed across my face. *She's so cute when she's angry.*

"Carmen, it's not what you think." I finally said.

"When have I heard *that* before?! Where is she?!" She stormed inside and automatically looked up at my room assuming a woman would be up there half naked; except this time, her assumption was wrong.

"Hello, are you coming to breakfast with us?" Keiko said making Carmen's mouth fall all the way down to the floor.

"Who's this?" Carmen asked disoriented at the surprise.

"I'm Keiko Akashimi."

"Oh, hi. I'm...er...Carmen." Keiko extended out her hand and Carmen shook it still confused at what was happening. Then she looked at me as if demanding answers.

"Why don't you join us for breakfast?" I smugly asked. We walked together to Denny's. On the way, I noticed that every time we crossed a street, Carmen would take Keiko by the hand. Keiko smiled at me as if rubbing it in my face. The hostess sat us in a booth and handed us menus. Within the same minute she left, our waitress arrived.

"Hi, my name is April and I'll be your server today. What can I get you folks to drink?" She asked as she handed Keiko a kid's menu with three crayons.

"I would like some chocolate milk, please." She smiled as she asked; the waitress and Carmen smiled in awe at her politeness and celestial smile.

"Coffee." Carmen and I said in unison. The waitress left to get our drink orders while Carmen's eyes burned a hole on my forehead.

"Keiko, do you like arcade games?" I asked as I reached in my pocket.

"Yeah! Ms. Pacman is my favorite." Her eyes glittered.

"Why don't you go play then? The grown-ups have to chat for a bit." I added. She took the quarters and didn't hesitate as she jogged to the Ms. Pacman game.

"Who *is* that, Marvin?" She asked.

"That's Keiko Akashimi." I answered like a smart-ass.

"I'm serious."

"It's complicated, baby." I hit a nerve and right away regretted my choice of words.

"Why is everything about your life so complicated? I can't know what you do for a living. I can't move in. I can't get a commitment from you...just tell me why you're suddenly baby-sitting a little Asian girl?!" She said hurt and aggravated at the same time.

"I'm not baby-sitting her."

"Is she *living* with you?!"

"Sort of..."

"Did you impregnate some girl...? Is she *yours*? Is this why you had to have a break from us? Did you think I wouldn't understand?"

"Carmen, this isn't about us. The two things are completely separate."

"Look, I just don't understand. Remember Thursday night? We made love all night long and I even let you smoke inside my apartment. Then you have the *nerve* to tell me you need a break as soon as I wake up?! Well, I don't even think you were gonna say anything if you hadn't dropped your lighter on the floor and woken me up, right? You were just gonna leave without saying a word! What did I do wrong this time, Marv?! Everything was going so great..." I could see the heartache in her eyes.

"You didn't do anything wrong. It's just..."

"Complicated?" she cut me off, "Marvin, I'm tired of everything being so *complicated*. Maybe I just need to accept that we aren't gonna work. Why don't we just stop this once and for all? It's over." She put on her coat, got up from the table, and just when she was about to start crying, she stormed off. I got up to run after her, but something held me back and I sat back down. Keiko then stomped her way over to the table and crossed her arms in front of me infuriated.

"What did you do to Ms. Carmen?!" She snapped.

"Nothing." *Nothing, I just broke her scarred heart...again.*

"But you made her cry! Friends don't make their friends cry...not on purpose anyways. And you didn't even go after her to apologize!" The waitress came to the table with our drink orders.

"Is your friend coming back?" She asked before she took the other cup of coffee from her massive tray.

"No." I replied.

"Are you guys ready to order?"

"Keiko, tell her what you want."

"I'm not hungry anymore." She sat down beside me still with her arms crossed.

"She'll have a grilled cheese with hash browns and I'll have some scrambled eggs, grits with cheese, and bacon." I said as I handed her the menus. She went to put our order in and I looked at Keiko.

"Why do grown-ups fight?" She asked uncrossing her arms and taking a gulp of her chocolate milk.

"Did your parents fight?" I deflected.

38

"All the time."

"About what?"

"Money." We sat together in silence. Keiko did the crosswords and games on her kid's menu while I pondered the termination Carmen placed upon our messed up relationship. When the food got there, Keiko refused to eat. I knew that if she didn't eat now, she would bug me later about being hungry.

"What can I do to make you eat?" I finally asked.

"Apologize to Ms. Carmen." She negotiated. I pictured Carmen's face crying like she was before she left. It pained me to see her that way. And I know it would be best for her...safer for her, if she was done with me. On the other hand, maybe it's time for her to know the man she's been with for the last ten years. Maybe it's time she knew the truth.

"How about we bring her breakfast after we eat?" That did it. Keiko started eating right away. I smiled. *I wonder if she always got her way with her parents.*

It's definitely time to tell Carmen the truth about me. I've wronged her so many ways over the years...one time, I even hit her. It was back when I wasn't used to having her spend the night; back when the nightmares were strong and hard to ignore. The night I hit her, all she was trying to do was pull me closer to cuddle; but instead of it being the romantic gesture it should've been, it woke me up in fight mode and as a result I elbowed her on the mouth. When I heard her voice crying out in pain, I remembered she was over. I felt like the scum of the world. I wanted to vomit when I saw her bleed. *I* made her bleed. I haven't been able to fully trust myself to sleep with her beside me since, but I don't mind. I like watching her sleep. It baffles me that she still feels safe with me after that night. That's why people in my line of work don't have girlfriends...wives...families. It's not safe. I shudder at the thought that someday he can find me. I couldn't live with myself if he hurt her trying to get to me. And yet, I keep endangering her because I can't make myself stay away. The truth of the matter is: I love her. *Holy shit, I love her.*

Seven: Carmen

"I can't believe he has an Asian girl living with him." Nina's tone of voice contradicted her sentence.

"No, Nina. I don't think you understand. This Asian girl is little." I tried to explain.

"What? Like anorexic?"

"No," I chuckled, "Like eight or nine years old little."

"Oh, I see. Like a little kid? I knew eventually something like this would catch up with him. I mean, if you spread your seed around, you're bound to grow something...somewhere." *Why did he have to grow something in Chinatown?*

"I snapped today and I finally just ended it."

"Yeah, that will last."

"I've never ended it with him before, Nina. This time, it's different." *This time it's different all right. Usually the girls I catch him with are eighteen or older...* I turned toward the door when I heard the knock.

"I gotta go, Nina. Someone's at the door."

"Ten to one it's him. Call me later." She said and then hung up. I opened the door and sure enough, it was him.

"We brought you breakfast, Ms. Carmen. I hope you have a microwave to heat it up." Keiko said as she handed me a Styrofoam box from Denny's.

"Thanks, honey." I said. I turned to Marvin and he mouthed the words "I'm sorry." I've only heard him apologize once...and it was eight, no nine years ago when I woke him up wrong and he accidentally hit me. I knew it wasn't his fault, but it was nice seeing him walk on eggshells around me for a week. It felt like he really cared. I raised my eyebrow and skeptically let them in.

"Keiko, do you like puppies?" I asked.

"Do I ever! Whoever doesn't like puppies has issues. They're so cute!" She said making Marvin and I smile.

"Follow me." I said as I took Keiko's hand and walked to Ms. Gregory's. She lives three doors over from me and breeds pug puppies. I knocked three times on her door.

"Oh, hi Carmen." She said as she opened the door; her bloodshot eyes surprised it was only me.

"Hi, Ms. Gregory, can Keiko look at the puppies?" I asked.

"Who's Keiko?" She asked making it obvious that she was stoned... again.

"I'm Keiko." She said pointing at herself.

"Sure, come on in." She opened the door wider.

"Can you watch her for ten minutes?" I asked while Keiko fawned over the puppies. Ms. Gregory looked past me and gave me a look I didn't understand.

"More like forty minutes, but...O.K." I turned around and saw Marvin by my doorway. *Oh, the look makes sense now.*

"Thanks." She closed the door and I took a deep breath. *I need to resist Marvin's charm. I need to break this vicious cycle.* I walked toward the apartment and didn't say a word while I looked for a fork to start eating my breakfast. Marvin looked pensive. After I found a clean fork, I sat down at the dinner table and started eating. *I'll be damned if I speak the first words.* Three bites later, he graced me with his presence.

"Do you want the truth?" He asked shocking the hell out of me. I almost dropped the box of food.

"Yes." *I've wanted the truth for ten years...* He sat down on the chair across from me at the table looking down at his hands. *I've never seen him like this before.* He inhaled deeply three times as if he was meditating in yoga class before he looked up at me. His blue eyes penetrated through my anger and turned it into utter curiosity.

"I'm a hit man." The words floated in the air for what seemed like an eternity; and then they hit me.

"You're a hit man?" I asked. *Yes, estúpida, that's what he just said!*

"Yeah, you know...a hired killer."

"I know what a hit man is!" I defensively hissed. He pulled back still sitting on the chair. *This makes sense. This is why he has wounds and bruises he can never explain. This is why he's always tired and why I sometimes don't hear from him for a while...*

"How does Keiko fit in to this?" I asked after I processed the information.

"I found her at a warehouse after meeting a client. Her family was killed by a hit man, a guy I know. This guy is hardcore. He will go to the ends of the earth to find her, and he won't rest until he does. That's why she's gonna stay with me for a while." *I think I liked what I thought better. Why couldn't he have just fathered her with a random girl from Chinatown? It would be so much easier to hate him.*

"Why didn't you get the police involved?" I asked.

"Because she wouldn't be safe with the cops."

"What about her extended family? You should tell them she's at least O.K. If she was my niece or granddaughter, I'd be worried sick."

"There was a rift between the extended family. For now, we're all the kid's got." *Did he say we're all the kid's got? We?*

"We?" I echoed.

"I was hoping that maybe you could watch her while I do some digging around for Bram." *Ah, he said we because he needs a favor.*

"Bram...that's a fitting name for a hit man." I ignored his request and articulated my observation.

"It's just his alias." He added.

"Still...clever. What's your *alias*?"

"Does it matter?"

"No, but for honesty's sake..."

"Azrael."

"The angel who separates the soul from the body at the moment of death." I thought out loud.

"Precisely."

"So, what? Is Keiko gonna be your adopted daughter now? How does this work?"

"This is all just temporary. We'll figure it out when she's safe."

"Just make sure she knows that," I paused, "Girls get attached, you know..." He knew I wasn't only talking about Keiko. *What does all of this mean? He finally opened up to me after all these years. But I can't go back to him. Not this time. I need a commitment. I'm done with this dance of ours. I'm ready to be in a grown up relationship. No more high school drama.*

"Are we O.K.?" He asked.

"Yeah, we're O.K., but we should just cool it for a while." I replied.

"Cool it?" His eyes looked bluer than the sky, but I stayed strong. *I can resist. I can.*

"Yeah, as in: let's be friends. Just friends."

"I suppose I'll have to live with that. Are you O.K... with what I do, I mean?" *Don't look at his perfect lips moving flawlessly. Don't think about kissing him.*

"It was never about your job, Marv. I could care less if you're a hit man or a doctor...all I cared about was us." I said. He looked down at his palm apologetically. We sat in silence across from each other.

"I can only watch Keiko until three thirty. I have a show at four." I finally broke the silence.

"You're the best, Carm," he said as he jumped up from the chair and walked toward the door, "And I mean that." He closed the door behind him, and my heart started to hurt. *Am I doing the right thing? Will he ever be what I need him to be?* My internal conflict can wait. Keiko is waiting and I'm sure Ms. Gregory's ten minutes are up. I looked over at the clock and almost smiled. *She was right. Our conversation took forty minutes exactly.* I walked over to her door and knocked.

"Come in!" I heard through the door. I opened it and closed it behind me. Keiko was sitting on the sofa with a puppy sleeping on her lap.

"He's cute." I admitted as I sat down next to her.

"I named him Snoopy." She petted him tenderly.

"Snoopy's a beagle, hon." I called into question.

"Not my Snoopy." She corrected.

"Mr. Marvin had to run some errands so it's just me and you for a while." I said.

"Can we stay here and play with Snoopy?" She asked. I looked at Ms. Gregory and she was practically kicking us out with her eyes.

"Ms. Gregory has to get back to work and since she works from home, we would be interrupting her." I diplomatically answered.

"Can I come back and visit him?" She asked. *Maybe bringing her here was a bad idea.*

"Do you want him?" Ms. Gregory asked.

"Do I ever!" She hugged him tight.

"Wait a sec, hon. How much?" I turned to Ms. Gregory. *Nice selling tactic, get the kid hooked and then make me break her heart when we can't afford it.*

"I can't charge for that one. He has lazy eyes." She said disgusted.

"I'll be the best mommy you ever had, Snoopy." Keiko promised as she kissed his forehead.

"Thanks." I said as we walked out. *I hope Marvin isn't allergic.*

Eight: Marvin

I took the subway back to my place. Listening to the sporadic metal clanks, I thought of Carmen. *Were we really going to be just friends? Does that mean she will be dating...doing other guys?* Thoughts were spinning inside my head until I felt sick to my stomach. I walked to my loft feeling the pressure change outside through my rib; I broke it three years ago doing a job, and now I'm the first to know when it'll rain. *I have a lot of work to do in a short amount of time. When did Carmen say I have to pick Keiko up? Three?* I looked over at the clock and started to hustle. *I only have four hours.* I turned on my computer and typed in my next hit's name, Joe Leoni, along with his social security. The search engine brought up some old cases, but not enough details. I decided to hack into the FBI mainframe. *There we go.* Information flooded the computer screen.

I found out that when he was eleven, he had to go to therapy for touching his sister inappropriately. Then, when he was eighteen, he was accused of molesting his friend's eleven year old brother. The charges were dropped. When he was twenty, he was charged with raping a fraternity brother. Those charges were also dropped. And these are only the things he was caught doing. The list kept going on and on until the last case popped up; it was Theo's. The information backed up Theo's story. Next, I tracked the stepfather down. Turns out he works on Wall Street, and his company is due for a maintenance call on their computer network. *Perfect, I couldn't have planned it better myself.*

I called his company and confirmed their one o'clock appointment. Then I called the computer company and canceled the maintenance call. Soon after the phone calls, I checked the bank account to see if Theo deposited the said amount. *Good boy, Theo.* His part was done and it was time to comply with mine. I went upstairs and dressed myself as a computer technician. Two minutes later, I was down the stairs and out the door walking to the parking garage where my van is parked at. In the van, there is everything I need to pull off this dinky, but necessary, part of the job.

Lunch hour traffic was actually not too bad today. I got to Joe's company ten minutes before one. Stacy, the lobby receptionist, was surprised that not only was I promptly on time for the appointment, but I was early. She informed me that Mr. Leoni was gone for the day, but that his office was open. *Could this be any easier?* I walked to the elevator carrying my trusty duffle bag. I pressed the button for the thirteenth floor once inside. The elevator dinged in acknowledgement closing the doors and promptly opening when we reached the destination thirteen floors later.

His office was easy to find and I was amazed at how much privacy I was blessed with today. The thirteenth floor was completely empty. I unhooked the surveillance cameras before entering his office so I could remain anonymous. *Amateurs.* I sat on his desk and started looking through the internet history. *What a sick bastard.* The selection of porn was disturbing. I sifted through the hard drive and copied all the files I needed. I then installed a program that acts as a spy; if he changed anything on his schedule, looked at porn, wrote a memo...whatever, I would be the first to know.

I looked at the clock and noticed it was already two forty five. *Shit, Carmen is going to kill me.* I logged off and left the computer the same way it was when I came in. I gathered my stuff and put everything back into my duffel bag. I plugged the cameras back on once I was out, and entered the elevator. As I started walking toward the entrance, I noticed I had a swagger to my steps. *This was extremely easy to pull off. Everything was my side. That's never happened before...* I drove to Carmen's as fast as I could, but traffic was not cooperating. My laptop beeped. *Joe's using his computer.* I pressed the space bar and noticed him booking a conference room downtown. All of the sudden, my eyes were drawn to one of the many names that would be attending the conference.

The nape of my neck started to sweat due to anger and fear. The fear left and the anger remained, getting stronger and stronger every second I looked at the screen. I felt as if my blood heated up a thousand degrees and started to boil inside of my veins. My heart pumped the blood lava and I felt as if my skin was melting off turning me into a monster. *Julianni Romero.* Not only is he the head of the most notorious mob in the world today, he is also the man that assassinated my family in cold blood. Car horns started blaring behind me and I noticed I was holding everyone up. I took a deep breath and tasted sweet revenge on my tongue. I've been waiting for the perfect opportunity to kill him with my bare hands for years... *This is my chance. Julianni, your days are numbered. Theo, I could kiss you for this!*

I drove to Carmen's scheming in my head, thinking strategies, visualizing the terror in Julianni's eyes when he saw little Marvin Costa alive and well (against his best efforts of putting a hit on me) about to kill him slowly. *He will suffer. He will pay.*

Nine: Carmen

Where the hell is he? I guess I should just take Keiko to my show with me. No, kids aren't allowed in the pub. Can I leave her here? No, kids need supervision. I'm going to kill Marvin! And if I lose my job, I don't know what I'll do to him.

"Are you O.K., Ms. Carmen?" Keiko asked while petting Snoopy, who was on her lap, once again asleep. I just noticed I was making her nervous by pacing back and forth.

"Marvin should've been here by now, that's all." I sat down and crossed my legs.

"He'll be here soon. You'll see." *I remember when I had faith in him like that.*

"I sure hope so." I said. I started tapping my fingernails on the dinner table. Each tap was equivalent to every second he was late. *Tap, tap, tap...* Three forty. *Tap, tap tap...* Three fifty. *Tap, tap, tap...* Four o'clock. My phone started to ring and there was no doubt in my mind that it was Hector. *Tap, tap, tap...* Four ten! *Knock, knock.* I opened the door and took one look at him. The rage suddenly burst out of my body through my mouth and my thoughts started being verbalized involuntarily through my mouth.

"¡Voy a matarle! Voy a tocar mis manos alrededor de su pequeño cuello perfecto y apretón como un constrictor de boa hasta que su cuerpo tire la lucha para el aire que sus pulmones nunca sentirán otra vez..." I pointed at the clock angrily and then, without another word, I left.

"Bye, Ms. Carmen!" I heard Keiko's adorable voice as I ran down the stairs. If my fury was controllable, I would've replied; but when I'm this angry, it's best to not say anything to innocent bystanders.

I arrived at the pub at four thirty five. My lungs were burning from running the whole way, but the minute I stepped foot in the pub and saw Hector, I jumped on stage and started my routine. The DJ played my song and I danced proving my worth to Hector and differentiating myself from any other dancer anyone's ever seen. Since I was so late, I decided I was going to combine my shows into one long one if for anything, to prolong the inevitable lecture. Something happened halfway through my show. I've heard of out-of-body experiences before, but never had one until today. I saw myself dancing and I watched the crowd watching me. Men wanted to *fuck* me and women wanted to *be* me. The minute I danced my finale routine, my soul re-entered my body and all I could hear was the applause. It's never been this loud. I bowed gracefully and went backstage. No matter what Hector had to say, I was content. I was drying off my sweat with a towel when Hector tapped my shoulder.

"Carmen..." He said. I looked into his eyes and was sure he was about to fire me.

"That was insane! You dance like that from now on! Whew! You just earned yourself a headlining spot. Now get out of here. I'll call you when I set up a photo shoot for the new posters." He shocked me and I was speechless.

"Go home, before they ask for an encore!" He said. I knew I couldn't do an encore even if I wanted to, so I floated home on a cloud.

The first thing I did when I got home was take a shower. As the water washed the sweat off my body, I shook my head. *Even when I think Marvin has ruined my life, he makes it better. Why can't I ever just stay mad at him? All I wanna do now is see him...hug him...kiss him.* I got dressed and French braided my hair. Then I packed some Disney movies into my purse and I took a taxi to Marvin's. I couldn't wipe the smile off my face. I knew that headlining would help me reach my goal sooner because the raise was enormous. Soon, I would buy the dance studio. Soon, I would be my own boss and make my own hours. I paid the taxi driver and ran to knock on Marvin's door. The look on his face when he saw me was priceless.

"Hey, Carm. Are you here to kill me?" He asked smiling that irresistible smile.

"Hi, I just got a promotion. You're buying me pizza."

"Yay, pizza!" Keiko ran towards me and hugged my legs. Snoopy followed her and wagged his tail.

"Are you who's to blame for Snoopy?" Marvin asked raising one eyebrow.

"Consider us even." I said. He shrugged his shoulders and we didn't speak more on the subject.

"What kind of pizza do you want?" He asked.

"Pepperoni!" Keiko and I said in perfect harmonizing unison.

"Pepperoni it is." Marvin said chuckling softly to himself as he dialed the number to Mario's Pizza Palace.

"Look, Keiko, I brought movies. Which one do you wanna watch?" I asked as I opened my purse for her to pick. She pointed at Brother Bear. I took it out of my purse, out of the case, and then put it the DVD player as Keiko picked Snoopy up and sat on the couch in front of the TV. I sat down next to her and pet Snoopy's tiny head once before reaching for the remote and pressing play.

"Come on, Mr. Marvin. It's starting." Keiko said.

"I gotta get some work done, but I'll come back when the pizza gets here." He said.

"O.K." Keiko disappointedly said. We watched forty five minutes of the movie before the pizza got here. I heard Marvin's movements and then his footsteps, so I didn't move from the couch when the doorbell rang.

"Hey man, how much do I owe you?" Marvin's beautiful voice asked.

"Twenty nine thirty seven, Sir." A young man's voice said. Marvin paid him and closed the door. Then I heard him getting plates and cups in the kitchen before he set the table.

"It's grub time, you two." He called. We ate while watching the end of Brother Bear at the dinner table. When the whole pizza was devoured, Marvin did the dishes while Keiko and I put in Cinderella. Marvin took a seat next to me after he turned the dishwasher on. The faint scent of his Old Spice deodorant went up my nostrils when he put his arm around me. I abstained from smiling with my mouth, but I couldn't control my heart starting to beat faster. He leaned in close to me almost as if in slow motion. I made myself keep looking at the TV. Then I felt the hot air from his breath on my neck and shortly after, his soft lips kissed right below my ear. I closed my eyes and nearly surrendered, but my will was stronger than ever when my eyes opened. I lightly pushed him away and his eyes gazed at me playfully. I turned to look at Keiko, who was spread on the couch like butter on toast, fast asleep.

"We should put her in bed." I said. He got up and carried her to bed. *I wonder if my dad ever carried me to bed this way.* I picked up Snoopy and brought him to lay with Keiko on the bed. The two of them didn't wake up and looked so divinely peaceful dormant on the bed. Marvin and I walked to the living room. He closed the door halfway and read my expression.

"She doesn't like it when the door is all the way shut. I think she gets scared or something." He answered.

"I used to be like that when I was little." I admitted. I almost expected him to say that he was too, but he held his tongue like he always does when the past is brought up.

"So, did you find your...*colleague*?" I queried.

"Ha, you mean Bram?" He chortled.

"Yeah..." I felt silly at my choice of words.

"Not exactly, but I found his boss." There was a flash of emotion when he said 'boss,' but I can't be certain of why. He leaned against the wall looking as fine as can be and I leaned on the counter. Both of us were looking at each other, not saying a word. The room seemed to be closing in on us and the silence kept getting louder and louder. I desperately wanted to say something...but nothing came out. We then started conversing with our eyes. He was saying how much he wanted to kiss me and I was saying we can't and he knows why. I was almost expecting this to get awkward, but it didn't. Instead, it felt like we were both in junior high wanting to kiss each other, but being too nervous about it at the same time.

"Say something in Spanish..." He broke the silence.

"What do you want me to say?" I asked.

"Something...anything."

"Usted me irrita." I blurted out. He came closer to me as if I had just invited him.

"This whole friends thing you want us to try...does it come with any benefits?" He said as he ran the back of his finger on the bare spot between my tank top and low rider jeans.

"If it did, nothing between us would change." *Good answer, Carmen.*

"Hm." He said now with his palm on my hip under my tank top.

"So, how long have you been a hit man?" I asked trying to change the subject, but not pushing him away.

"Since I was fourteen." He answered while he picked me up and sat me on the kitchen counter.

"Wow, that long?" I asked as he took a step closer and stood between my legs. The space between us became really hot really fast and I started having to remind myself to breathe.

"Uh huh." He said under his breath and then wrapped his arms around my waist and looked into my eyes. My heart started beating fast pumping my blood and making me blush.

"Who's Bram's boss?" I asked. His jaw tightened and he started to pull away. *Not this time.* I reached for him and hugged him tight with my arms and my legs. Even with me being on the counter, he was taller than me.

"Please don't pull away..." I whispered in his ear. His body relaxed and he hugged me back. We held each other for what seemed like an hour. I could hold him like this forever.

"He's the man that made me an orphan..." He said in a tone of voice that made him sound like a boy instead of a man; the vulnerability manifested through his body.

"Oh." *Oh? Is that all you're going to say? Here he is opening up to you, and all you can say is "oh"?!*

"Remember the night I took you to watch Rent?" He asked.

"Yeah..." *How could I forget? That was the night you left to go to the bathroom and I didn't hear from you for three days.*

"He was sitting across from us on the opposite side. That's why I left...because I couldn't stay and not kill him," He admitted, "I didn't mean to hurt you, but if I had stayed, there was no way for me to not get caught..."

"Why couldn't you just be honest with me?" The words escaped my mouth.

"I'm being honest with you now..." *That doesn't make up for the time I was lied to... I thought knowing the truth would make everything better. I didn't count on being so mad...so heated; almost on the verge of spontaneous self combustion.* I got down from the kitchen counter and got my purse.

"Where are you going?" He asked.

"I need to get home. It's late." I said dryly.

"Crash here. I'll take the couch." He said. I nodded and went up the stairs. He didn't follow me. I lay on the bed awake for a long time. After a while, I could even hear Marvin snoring downstairs. *I suppose I shouldn't look to the past anymore. Maybe I should stay focused on the present. He's being honest with me now...* It was four in the morning when I finally started drifting off to sleep...

Ten: Keiko

"Look! Santa came, everyone!" I yelled to wake everyone up so we could open presents. Outside the white snow looked fluffy and I was anxious about playing with the new sleigh I asked Santa for.

"Do you have to be so loud?" Sumi asked with her teenage attitude.

"Aren't you excited at all?" I wanted to know.

"Who wants hot chocolate with marshmallows?" Mommy asked. Sumi's unenthused face finally cracked a smile.

"We do!" Sumi and I said at the same time.

"Honey! We're getting ready to open presents." Mommy yelled up the stairs. Daddy is always the last one down. Mommy always reminds me that some people are not morning people like us. Sumi is halfway between the two. I started counting how many boxes had my name on it and trying to figure out which box was big enough for a sleigh.

"Hot chocolate for my girls..." Mommy said handing Sumi her green cup and then handing me my pink cup.

"She has more marshmallows than me!" I protested instead of thanking her.

"No, you both have six. I counted." Mommy promised. I was still skeptical, but when I tasted it somehow it didn't matter anymore. Daddy finally graced us with his sleepy presence. He scratched his eyes while he walked and we all laughed at the fact that he only had one slipper on. The minute he sat on the couch, he started to snore. At least he's here. Mommy doesn't let us open presents unless we are all in the same room...sleeping or awake.

"Keiko, why don't you pass out one present for each of us and we'll open them together?" Mommy asked. I started picking out the ones with pretty wrap paper when the doorbell rang. Mommy went to open the door. When she came back, there were four men wearing black suits with her. I noticed that they tracked in dirty snow on the carpet and that one of them was holding a baseball bat.

"Haro! Wake up!" Mommy sounded frantic. Daddy opened his eyes just in time to get a fist in the face. I hid under the couch. Daddy cried out in pain and his nose started to bleed.

"Mr. Romero sent us. Do you have his money?" One of the men asked.

"I will have it before New Year's." Daddy's voice was shaking. Then the man with the bat came closer to him and started repeatedly hitting him with it.

"Stop!" Mommy shrieked. He didn't listen. Sumi crawled under the couch with me and put her arm around me. Daddy's leg made a popping noise and his bone ripped through his pajama pants. I put my hands over my ears because his screams were so loud. The man with the bat hit our Christmas tree once and it fell over breaking a lot of ornaments. Then he pulled mommy by the hair and threw her on the ground.

"Don't hurt her!" Daddy screamed unable to stand up because of his leg. The men looked at each other and laughed. Then they started gathering the presents and loading them in their car.

"This is now Mr. Romero's property. You'll have till the first to come up with the rest of the money. Don't even think about leaving town." The man with the bat threatened daddy before he broke the coffee table in half scaring Sumi and I to death. I screamed at the top of my lungs and woke up drenched in sweat. Though I was now awake, I kept seeing Sumi's dead body then mommy's and then daddy's in the darkness. Tears poured out of my eyes and my body was vibrating all over. The lights finally turned on and I saw Mr. Marvin. I jumped from the bed and ran to him.

"It's O.K." He said patting my back. Ms. Carmen kneeled down beside me and held me like mommy would if she was here.

"Aw, honey, it's O.K. Shh, I'm here. It's O.K." Ms. Carmen made my body stop vibrating and the tears stopped coming out of my eyes.

"Um...the dog is jittery. I'm gonna walk him." Mr. Marvin said. Ms. Carmen nodded and then she carried me to the kitchen. She poured water in a cup and handed it for me to drink.

"Did you have a bad dream?" She asked as I drank the water till the last drop.

"I had a bad memory." I corrected.

"What do you mean?"

"I dreamt of something that happened."

"Wanna tell me about it?"

"No..." *I just wanted to forget.*

56

"Are you ready to go back to bed?"

"Can we watch the end of Cinderella?"

"Sure...come on." We walked to the living room where the couch had turned into a bed. She rewound the DVD to where I stopped and we watched. She played with my hair and made me feel safe. Soon after, Snoopy and Mr. Marvin came back. Ms. Carmen gestured for him to lie down next to her so he could watch the movie with us. I felt my eyelids get heavier and heavier and I surrendered in trying to keep them open.

Eleven: Marvin

I woke up spooning Carmen. I lifted my head and right away felt the pain from sleeping without a pillow. *Damn, my neck is so stiff.* I massaged my neck and noticed Carmen was holding Keiko and Keiko was holding Snoopy. I chuckled to myself. *I bet we looked like a holding train, one spooning the other.* Keiko had a nightmare last night. Though it was inevitable that she would have one due to what she witnessed and what she's been through, nothing could've prepared me for it. I felt so helpless when she ran to me. I almost wanted to run away from her. *How can I help a kid get over her demons when I haven't gotten over mine yet?* I looked at her and Carmen lying there, and I couldn't help but wonder what I would've done if Carmen wasn't here. I wouldn't have been able to leave hysterical Keiko here while I walked Snoopy and pulled myself together. I looked over at them again and noticed Snoopy was looking at me wagging his tail.

"I bet you need to go outside, huh?" I asked as I picked him up and got off the bed. Then I put on my flip flops and went outside. The sun was beaming and the sky was clear.

"Are you hungry, boy?" I asked. If someone had told me that one day I would be taking care of a Pug, I would've laughed at their face. When I got back to the loft, Carmen was already making her famous Spanish omelets.

"Good morning," She greeted as soon as she saw me, "How did you sleep?"

"It was interesting having that many people on the bed." I admitted.

"Mr. Marvin, you snore." Keiko accused while she set the table.

"Sorry, kid. I'll work on that." I joked while I fed Snoopy the puppy chow the girls bought yesterday in my absence.

"Breakfast is served." Carmen said as she brought over the food and served hearty portions on each plate. She always makes more than enough, but I never complain. Leftovers are always welcome at my place.

"It's delicious, Ms. Carmen." Keiko complimented.

"Uh huh." I grunted with my mouth full.

"Thanks. So, Marvin, before you walked in Keiko and I were chatting." She said as a matter-of-factly.

"Is that right?" I commented not really all that interested.

"Yeah, and what we were talking about is: school. If she takes too much time off, she will lose a whole year." Carmen sounded like her mind was made up.

"Whoa, whoa, whoa, wait just a minute. She can't go back to her old school. That is out of the question." *Why don't you just shoot her yourself, Carmen? What a brilliant idea!*

"Keiko, could you go play with Snoopy in your room?" Carmen calmly said.

"I know you're gonna be talking about me, why can't I just stay?" Keiko noted.

"Keiko..." Carmen looked more serious and said her name with a stern tone.

"Okay, I'm going. Jeeze." Keiko rolled her eyes, picked Snoopy up, and slammed the door to the room a bit harder than she should have.

"I didn't mean for her to go back to her old school." Carmen said once the coast was clear.

"Then what? You want me to forge up some papers to give her a new identity just so she can go to a new school?" I sarcastically asked.

"That'd be great, thanks." My mouth dropped. *Does she know how long that would take? Not to mention, even if I pulled it off...does she not realize Keiko could mess everything up if she forgets her new name?*

"Carmen, you do realize that soon she'll go back to her old life, right? Soon, her life won't be in danger-"

"What old life, Marvin? Her family is dead and you told me her extended family was not an option. She needs stability so she can start the grieving process." Carmen cut me off. *She's right...*

"I'll start on the papers..." I caved.

"Great! Now that that's settled, I need some money to take her shopping." Carmen's big brown eyes asked along with her voice.

"Shopping?" I dubiously asked.

"Yeah, for new school clothes. You're aware that she only has that one outfit, right?"

"Yes, Carmen, I'm aware. Will you be needing anything else today?"

"No, that'll be all." She smiled victoriously. She got up, kissed me on the cheek, and started clearing the table. I went upstairs to get her some cash. I opened my money safe located under the hardwood floor, and took out three grand. *That should be enough...* I closed the safe, placed the wooden boards back where they belonged, put the money in an envelope, and went back downstairs. Carmen was already turning the bed we all slept on back into a couch.

"I still say this is a bad idea. I mean, when this is all over, she's outta here. Don't you think going to school and getting settled is a bad idea?" I asked Carmen while holding onto the envelope a little longer.

"Kids need to have their brain stimulated and they need to be with other kids in a structured environment. Why do you think drop outs are so messed up?" She asked hitting a nerve. *I'm a drop out.*

"All right," I gave up, "We'll need to seriously explain to her the situation and the importance of her new identity. She needs to know that it is imperative for her to become the new identity...and the grave danger that her life is in."

"We'll talk to her tonight. And don't worry so much...she's a very bright girl. I mean, she's giving Bram a run for his money, isn't she?"

"That's what I'm worried about. He should be getting restless looking for her and if he finds her..." *He would torture her for causing him so much trouble.*

"Everything will be okay, Marv." She gently touched my arm.

"Here, get her everything she needs. And if you want anything...you should get it, too." I said as I handed her the envelope.

"Thanks." She put the envelope in her purse and opened Keiko's door.

"Are you done talking about me like I'm not here?" Keiko asked with a hint of attitude.

"Would you forgive us if we went shopping?" Carmen lifted her spirits.

"Really?!" She squealed.

"Really, really. Now come on, put on your shoes." Carmen helped her tie her shoes. When they were done, Carmen picked Snoopy up and handed him to me. My face turned into a big question mark.

"We can't take him to the mall." Carmen said as if this was public knowledge then kissed me on the cheek. Keiko followed her lead and hugged me. As soon as the door closed, Snoopy licked my chin.

"I guess it's just me and you, buddy." I said. *How did I get tricked into this? When did I become a sucker?*

Twelve: Carmen

I was able to haul a taxi pretty easy. Keiko and I admired the scenery on the way to Manhattan Mall. I can't even remember the last time I went shopping. I was probably more excited than Keiko, who was as happy as can be. It's hard for me to see any trace of sadness in her face right now, but the image of her suffering and convulsing in my arms last night will forever be tattooed in my brain. I can't even imagine what she's going through and poor Marvin...it seems like Keiko's nightmare last night really shook him up. Maybe it stirred up some old memories of his own.

"We're here, Ma'am. That'll be fifteen even." The taxi driver read the meter. I opened the envelope and noticed they were all hundred dollar bills. *Wow, Marv, the one thing I can never call you is cheap.* I opened my wallet and gave him a twenty.

"Keep the change." I said smiling. Keiko opened the door and we walked holding hands to the mall. The first thing we looked for was a Gap Kids. I picked out everything I liked knowing that we wouldn't have to leave anything behind. *I need to thank Marvin later for his generosity.* When we were done looking, we walked to the dressing rooms.

"So, are you excited for school tomorrow?" I asked as I helped her try on clothes.

"Not really. I wouldn't mind if I never had to go back again." Keiko said looking at herself in the mirror like every woman does.

"That's a cute outfit. Do you like it?"

"Yeah, it's very nice."

"Why don't you wanna go back to school?"

"Well," She said as she took off the outfit and put it on the want pile, "The last time I went...things didn't turn out that good."

"What do you mean?" I naively asked.

"It started out like every other day until I saw...the bad man," Her face read fear and fright, "The next thing I knew...everyone was dead. Oh, Ms. Carmen, it was horrible!" Keiko suddenly embraced me and started to cry. I held her and started humming the tune my mother used to sing whenever I cried.

"You wanna know the worst of it all?" She asked wiping her tears away and looking up at me.

"What's the worst of it all?" I asked.

"The last time I saw my parents alive...I was mad at them. I didn't even tell them I love them or have a nice day or anything because I didn't know it would be the last time." She was the saddest little girl I've ever seen.

"Keiko, families fight, but it doesn't mean that they don't know they love each other..." I paused to think of something I could do to make her feel better, "Pretend I'm your mom and your dad. Say to me what you wanna say to them." She looked at me, wiped her tears away like before, and composed herself. She took a deep breath and opened her mouth.

"Mommy, I haven't lied since we had that talk, but I'm sorry anyways. I'm sorry...I wish I was a better daughter...a better sister. Sumi, I'm sorry about your CD. I didn't mean to break it...Daddy, have a nice day. I...lov---" She broke down and started to cry where she stood. She covered her eyes with her hands and I picked her up to put her on my lap.

"Keiko, even though your family is gone, they can still hear you. You can talk to them whenever you want and sometimes...they send you a sign that they hear you. I'm sure they miss you as much as you miss them. And I know that they forgive you. All they want now is for you to be happy." I said as I cradled her like a baby. She was crying as I hummed the song like before. While I hummed, I prayed. I prayed for God to shine His light on this little one, to guide her towards happiness, and to help us keep her safe.

"Is everything all right in there?" A sales associate asked.

"Yeah, we just get emotional when we shop." Keiko said making both the sales associate and I laugh. A smile flashed across her face and it seemed as though part of my prayer was answered. *Thank you!* Keiko got up and started trying on clothes again. The rest of the day was a success. We went to each store, buying whatever we wanted and everything she needed. When the mall closed, I knew it was time to go home.

"I'm hungry." Keiko said.

"Me too." I nodded in agreement. We hailed a taxi and put all our shopping bags in the trunk. Inside the cab, I called Mr. Wong's and ordered some take-out. When I got off the phone, I noticed Keiko was asleep leaning on me. Something maternal in me made me smile. I watched her sleep until I felt my heart drop. *My baby would be about Keiko's age right now...* A single tear streaked down my face and it triggered a quiet sob. I remember feeling ecstatic when the stick turned blue. I was going to tell Marvin that weekend over a dinner with a baby theme like baby carrots, baby corn, etc. But fate had a different plan because I miscarried. I never felt so culpable in my entire life. I couldn't even touch the subject with Marvin though he kept asking what was wrong. It took me a year to be able to look at a baby again.

"What's wrong, Ms. Carmen?" Keiko asked wiping my tears away with her little hand.

"Oh, I was just missing someone..." I said as something seemed to squeeze my heart.

"Is that someone in Heaven?" She asked with empathy.

"Yes..."

"Did you get to say goodbye?"

"No..."

"Why don't you pretend I'm that someone? You know, like we did in the dressing room?" She seemed so eager to help me. The cab driver was in his driving world and I turned to face Keiko.

"I loved you so much and I love you still. I'm sorry I couldn't keep you safe...please...forgive me..." My voice shook as I spoke and my heart kept being squeezed tighter and tighter.

"There's nothing to forgive because I love you too." Keiko said. Whatever was squeezing my heart let go and I breathed relief. I smiled and started crying tears of joy. *How could she know exactly what to say?* She hugged me and played with my hair until we got to Mr. Wong's. The cab driver kept the meter running while we ran in and picked up the food. On the way home, we sang along to the radio the way best friends do. The moon was gleaming just for us tonight.

Thirteen: Marvin

I took a look at Leoni's schedule again and looked up the address of where the meeting would take place this Saturday. Turns out the building is owned by Julianni and it has just been renovated, so it's still not in use. I'm sure that's the way Julianni will keep it so he could have the extra privacy when the "family" meets. I printed the blueprints of the building and laid it out on the floor. *That's a pretty big conference room. It's going to take finesse to come up with an element of surprise. How many guys are going? 16. That's not counting the bodyguards. Hm...*

I put that aside and started on Keiko's new identity. I'm rusty at forging papers, but it's just like riding a bike. I started with the adoption papers because no one would believe Carmen and I are her birth parents. Her new name will be Akemi Moreno Costa. I picked Akemi because it means bright and beautiful; very fitting. Moreno is Carmen's last name and Costa is mine; self explanatory. Then I moved on to school documents and records. I called the private Catholic school three blocks from here. They didn't have any problems with Keiko starting school so late in the school year with the donation I gave them. Anything is negotiable when you have money. We have an appointment with the principal/Reverend Mother at nine tomorrow. It's policy to meet the new student and her parents. This means, Carmen and I will have to pose as a married couple.

When I hung up the phone, I walked over to my money safe. I removed the floor boards and opened it. Behind all the cash were three velvet ring boxes; one maroon, two blue. The boxes had collected dust over the years. I remember the day I bought them. *Was it eight years ago?* I came over to pick Carmen up for a date and in the trashcan I saw a positive pregnancy test. At first I was freaked, but then something calmed me down from deep within. It was at that moment that I knew nothing else mattered; not work nor revenge...nothing. I told Carmen I had to step out for a bit and went straight to Tiffany's. I vowed that I would marry Carmen and we would run away from this wretched place forgetting my past and making a future with her and our unborn baby. When I was on my way back to pop the question, she had posted a note on the door that she was gonna take a rain check. The next time I saw her, she was distant and more depressed than when her mother died. I knew what had happened and I checked the hospital records just to make sure. She lost the baby. I felt as if my only ticket for happiness was taken from me; like I didn't deserve happiness. I put the boxes away in the safe and hid them with the money I earned from emerging myself in my work.

The day got away from me when I looked outside and it was night time. I put the ring boxes in my jeans pocket and covered them up with my shirt. I put the money back into the safe, closed it, and placed the floor boards back. Snoopy looked at me and opened his mouth looking as if he was smiling at me. I smiled back and picked him up putting him under my arm. As I walked down the stairs, the door opened and Keiko entered carrying bags from Gap Kids.

"Ms. Carmen is still downstairs with the taxi driver. We need help carrying our stuff." She said as she put the bags in her room. I followed her outside and no wonder they needed help; they bought the whole mall. Carmen smiled at me almost shamefaced. I rolled my eyes and carried pretty much the rest of the bags while Keiko and Carmen brought in the food. I just now realized how hungry I was. *Mm, Mr. Wong's.* I threw the bags on Keiko's bed and started setting the table. Carmen was taking out the food and separating each person's order. Keiko patiently sat on the table.

"So, I enrolled you at St. Joseph's today. I think you'll like it." I said.

"The Catholic school?" Keiko asked turning her nose.

"Yeah, what's wrong with that?" I asked.

"They wear uniforms. Now I won't be able to wear any of my new clothes to school. You suck." Keiko said making me feel completely incompetent.

"Keiko, don't talk to him like that. You can wear your new clothes when you go out or at home. St. Joseph's is a real good school. I went there." Carmen lectured. *I like that she stood up for me.*

"Sorry, Mr. Marvin. Thank you for enrolling me in such a nice school." She robotically said.

"You're welcome..." I didn't know what else to say.

"So, Keiko, Mr. Marvin and I have something to talk to you about."

Carmen said giving me the floor.

"Am I in trouble?" Keiko asked.

"No, kid, but you could be if you don't follow our directions," I paused, "You're aware that the bad man, as you call him, is out there looking for you, right?" Fear glossed over Keiko's eyes.

"Yes..." She solemnly said.

"We don't want him to find you and he won't if you do exactly as I say. Keiko Akashimi doesn't exist anymore—"

"But I'm right here...existing." Keiko interrupted.

"No, as of now, your name is Akemi Moreno Costa." I firmly said trying not to lose my temper. Carmen looked at me and her eyes got watery; I wasn't sure why.

"Tomorrow we have an appointment with your new principal and Ms. Carmen and I will be pretending to be your adoptive parents---"

"Why?" Keiko annoyingly asked interrupting me again.

"Will you shut up and *listen!*" I lost it. Keiko's eyes started welling up with tears. *Fuck, I suck at this.*

"Keiko, Mr. Marvin is just trying to explain your sensitive situation. Just listen for now and if you have any questions at the end, we'll let you ask, okay?" Carmen was so patient... I continued telling Keiko that in public: Ms. Carmen was mommy and I was daddy. I told her that if anyone asked, we just moved here from Florida because I got a better job offer. I gave her a piece of paper with my cell phone number, the house number, and Carmen's cell phone number. I emphasized that my numbers were supposed to only be dialed if there was an emergency. When I was done saying all I had to say, and I repeated everything twice, Keiko sat there in silence brooding over the conversation I monopolized.

"So, the bad man won't find me if I do everything you say?" Keiko asked as if she was going somewhere with this question.

"No." I sounded so sure that it became a lie. Keiko looked deep in thought for a minute and then smiled showing her cute dimples.

"Hi, my name is Akemi Moreno Costa. I was adopted when I was a baby and we just moved here from Florida. The weather sure is different up here, but I like it." Keiko said as she stood up on top of the chair. Carmen and I looked at each other like we just accomplished the impossible.

"Perfect." I said. We finished eating and they talked about their day lighting the mood. After dinner, I walked Snoopy and did the dishes while they put away the clothes in the vacant closet and remodeled my office into a princess wonderland by putting new sheets and pillows on the bed, putting posters on the walls, and toys on the floor. *I should've kissed the three grand goodbye as soon as I handed it to Carmen.* Carmen advised Keiko to get ready for bed and then tucked her in.

"She's asking for you." Carmen said as she walked toward me. I scrunched my eyebrows together and dreaded each step I took closer to her room.

"You rang?" I asked as I stood next to her bed. Snoopy wagged his tail.

"I just wanted to say good night...daddy." Keiko said making me wince at the word: *daddy.*

"We're not in public." I replied as I cleared my throat.

"I know, I'm just practicing." She smiled and turned on her side hugging Snoopy like a teddy bear. I walked out of the room turning off the light and closing the door half way.

"She's something else." Carmen said smiling at me.

"Yeah...something else." I said knowing that we both meant it differently.

"What time's the appointment tomorrow?" She asked as she sat down on the couch taking off her shoes.

"Nine o'clock." I said as I sat next to her putting her legs on my lap and starting to massage her feet. She moaned. *I love that moan.* Then, I reached in my pocket and got the two blue velvet boxes out along with the maroon one. I put them on her lap. She looked at the boxes in amazement and unexpected shock.

"What's this?" She asked not taking her eyes off the boxes, but not picking them up either.

"We're supposed to be married tomorrow." I said. She ran her fingers over the Tiffany's logo and then hesitantly opened the first box. It was her engagement ring. "A band of channel-set round brilliant diamonds enhances the classic Tiffany six-prong setting for a spectacular display of white light," the clerk described it long ago. She marveled at it and gasped. Somehow, I knew she knew how much I spent. She then opened the matching double milgrain wedding band rings in platinum; mine 6mm wide and hers 2mm wide. I watched her facial expressions go from happy to sad to nonchalant in the course of three minutes.

"What are you thinking about?" I found myself asking without realizing it.

"When did you buy these?" The sadness took over.

"That doesn't matter." I replied while I picked up the engagement ring box. I pulled the ring from the box, took her hand, and softly put the ring on her finger. I half expected her to push my hand away, but she just held her breath instead. Then, I took the wedding band and put it in front of the engagement ring holding it in place on her finger. She gasped air as if she had just been drowning and admired her left hand gazing at the shiny rings as if in a trance. I watched her watch the rings like all her dreams had just become reality. Then, she shook her head abruptly out of nowhere.

"This is just for appearance's sake, right?" She asked.

"Yeah." I said unsure if I meant it. She took the other ring box and pulled the ring off. Then she took my left hand and put it on my ring finger. She was in the process of pulling her hand away, but I held it and looked at her unable to speak.

"I should go," I was about to interrupt her, but she used her free hand to place her fingers gently on my lips, "No, don't say anything. I need to get clothes for tomorrow anyways." She retracted her legs and started putting on her socks and shoes. I wanted to say that I didn't want her to leave. I wanted to pull her close and kiss her until the sun came up...but I knew it wouldn't be in her best interest. She asked for this whole friend spiel, and as hard as it is, I need to respect it.

"I'll come over tomorrow at eight to help out with Keiko." She said.

"Don't you mean *Akemi*?" I corrected.

"Right...Akemi. Good night, Marv. Sweet Dreams." She sweetly said.

"Sleep good, Carm." I said as I walked her out the door. It's never been this hard to let her go. I never understood the saying "you don't know what you have until it's gone" until right now. I closed the door when she was completely out of my eye sight. *I hope this "friends" thing won't stick.*

Fourteen: Carmen

How the hell am I supposed to sleep with this thing on? The rings on my finger seemed to mock me as I stared at it...taunting me, saying I only have it now because I no longer have the man that gave it to me. *Why can't life for once be fair?* I got up from the bed and reached for my phone. Each number I dialed flashed a reason of why I shouldn't be doing this. I know why I chose to stay friends... be just friends with Marvin. I reluctantly hung up the phone and climbed back in bed.

I tossed and I turned all the while peeking at the rings. *How can such little things cause me so much distraught and make me feel such hostility at the same time?* I finally decided to take them off, placing them safely on the coffee table. This one single act conjured up the sand man to sprinkle the sleeping sand that sent me off to get some rest.

The alarm beat on my ear drums awaking me from a surprisingly peaceful slumber. I looked in my closet and though it is filled with clothes, I felt as if I had nothing to wear. *What does a mother wear to meet the principal? What did my mom wear?* The memories failed to come to assist me and I finally decided on black slacks and a maroon, v-neck shirt with maroon leather boots. I sat in front of my vanity mirror and looked at my under eye circles. *I thought I got enough rest...* I dabbed on some concealer under my eyes followed by foundation. Then I applied some bronzer and to finish it all off, I added mascara to elongate my lashes. My hair looked like a lion's mane leaving me no choice but to French braid it. I glanced over at the clock and started to rush as I changed purses; taking items from my brown purse and putting them in my black leather one. I looked at the coffee table and the rings were staring at me like a midget staring at a height requirement at a carnival. *Ugh, stupid rings!* I threw them back on my finger and I was out the door hailing a cab.

I paid the cabby and walked up the stairs half expecting them to be all ready just waiting for me. *I expected wrong.* They were still eating breakfast in their pajamas! I took charge of the situation at once hurrying the two hounding them like a dog. *We only have twenty minutes to get there on time!* I could finally breathe again when we were in a taxi on the way to St. Joseph's.

"What's your name again, kid?" Marvin quizzed Keiko.

"Akemi Moreno Costa, duh." Keiko said as she rolled her eyes. Though I heard her new name yesterday, I felt just as touched today. *How did Marvin remember that I wanted my last name to be my children's middle name? I told him that ages ago!*

"All right, all right. You got this." Marvin gave up. When we got to the school, Marvin paid and we walked up the familiar steps. It's strange to think that once upon a time I was in Keiko's shoes. *Well, not really. A hit man didn't kill my family or make me take on a new identity given by another hit man...* We took a seat in the principal's office waiting to get called in.

"Mommy?" Keiko asked as she smiled saying the word just as I was smiling at hearing it, "Is the Reverend Mother nice?"

"Hmm, that's a hard question for me to answer because it's most likely not the same one that I had when I was your age...but I'm sure she's nice." I replied. Marvin was staring into space like his mind was preoccupied. He looked so sexy with khaki pants and a sports jacket.

"The Reverend Mother will see you now." The sister informed us. We walked into her office and sat down on the chairs in front of her desk. Much to my surprise, it was the same Reverend Mother I had!

"Carmen Moreno, I see you haven't changed one bit." She smiled the kind smile from my past. She extended her hand for me to shake it, but I went around the desk and hugged her instead.

"I can say the same about you, Reverend Mother." And she did look the same. So much in fact that it was almost eerie!

"And you must be Marvin Costa. It's a pleasure to meet you." She shook his hand like she wanted to shake mine.

"Likewise." Marvin said smiling a smile I've never seen before... it almost seemed fake.

"I'm Akemi Moreno Costa. I was adopted when I was a baby and we just moved here from Florida. The weather sure is different up here, but I like it." She said mending her words together from saying it so fast.

"Yes, I'm sure it's not so moist." The Reverend Mother said amusedly chuckling. Then she pressed down a button by her phone and annunciated as she spoke:

"Sister Mary Florence, Akemi is ready to be escorted to her class," then she took off her finger from the button, "Akemi, you can say goodbye to your parents." Her words innocently caused Keiko to start bawling her eyes out and I knew exactly why. *She didn't get to say goodbye to her real parents. Oh, poor little Keiko.* I took Keiko into my arms and hugged her tight lightly brushing her hair with my fingers. Marvin looked completely out of his element and confused at why the tears began.

"It's all right, Akemi. Mommy will be here to pick you up right after school." I tried to comfort her and not give anything away at the same time.

"You'll like your teacher very much, Ms. Costa. Sister Bandeau is delightful." The Reverend Mother said as Keiko's tears ceased to come out of her eyes.

"Bye mommy...daddy. Have a nice day." Keiko said as she hugged Marvin and me and followed Sister Mary Florence out. My heart seemed constricted as I watched her walk away and my eyes burned as I held back tears.

"Have a seat, Mr. and Mrs. Costa." She said in a wise voice...wiser than I remember.

"I'm sorry about her; she's very attached to her mother." Marvin said trying to excuse for the tears he didn't understand.

"It's quite all right. It's not the first time I've seen a display of tears like that. If my memory's correct, Mrs. Costa was much worse than your little Akemi." She glared at me raising one eyebrow then quickly changed her glare to a smile. *I do remember my first day of school. They practically had to pry my hands from my mother's.* I smiled back almost embarrassed that Marvin heard that.

"Here are her school records. If you need anything else, just let me know and I'll bring it by for you at my earliest convenience." Marvin said handing her the vanilla folder with the forged documents. Her eyes skimmed the papers over. My heart started beating faster and faster and I took Marvin's hand squeezing it hard to let him know I was nervous. *What if she caught us? Could we trust her to tell her the truth or would we have to act as if we had kidnapped her? Would we have to run when she turned us into the authorities? What would happen to my headlining at the pub?*

"Everything seems to be in order, Mr. Costa. Thank you for coming in and meeting with me. I make it a point to meet all my new students and their parents. Carmen, it was a joy seeing you again and a pleasure meeting the Costa family. I welcome you all to Saint Joseph's with open arms and may God be with you always." She said. I let out a long, exasperated breath and smiled. *Whew, that was a close one.* Marvin shook her hand and I hugged her before we walked outside holding hands. When we were alone, he looked at me as if he was about to make fun of me...

"So, you doubted my forging abilities, eh?" He asked patronizing me with his eyes. I let go of his hand and shrugged my shoulders.

"I don't know. I guess I'm just not used to dealing with forged documents like someone I know." I pushed his chest playfully and he smiled.

"What are you doing today?" He asked changing the subject as we walked side by side on the sidewalk.

"Well, Nina gets back from Cali at eleven thirty so I'll probably be hanging with her. Why?"

"I was thinking you could come over after you pick Akemi up since Snoopy's gonna be there needing a walk. I mean, if you don't, I'll do it cuz I don't need him to ruin my floors." He said trying not to sound like he gives a damn about the dog. I smiled.

"Sure, I'll walk him Marvin."

"All right, then. See you later."

"See ya." We hugged and walked different directions. I took the subway back home and took the rings off as soon as I got to my place. I looked at the clock and saw that it was ten thirty. That gives me an hour before Nina comes over. *I should hide the rings because knowing her...they'll be the first thing she sees.* I picked them up and put them in the Marvin box. I contemplated looking through it again but abstained and lied back down on the couch that was still turned out like a bed. I closed my eyes like I just had the most hectic day...

The door knocks kept getting louder and louder and I realized I fell asleep. I quickly got up and opened the door where Nina looked angry at the time I made her wait.

"How was Cali?" I asked as I hugged her.

"I'm sorry, is someone speaking to me? I hardly recognize the voice..." She said making a point. *I didn't call her once while she was gone.*

"Aw, Nina. I'm sorry I didn't call. Come on; tell me all about your trip." She thought about giving me a hard time, but quickly made up her mind not to as she told me all about the new movie she did stunts for.

"That's great! I'm glad you had a good time." I said.

"Thanks. Well, what did I miss? Are you and Marvin back together?" She asked.

"No." Her face looked stunned. *Is it really that hard to believe?*

"What?" I asked.

"Well, I'm just surprised. I thought for sure when he came by you

76

would've gone right back to him."

"I didn't."

"Good for you."

"Yeah."

"So, what's up with the little chink girl?" She asked the inevitable question.

"She's nice and she's staying with him for a while. As a matter of fact, I gotta leave to pick her up in a half hour. You could come meet her if you want." Nina's face dropped and she gave me a look I thought I wouldn't see today. It's the same look she always gives me when I tell her Marvin and I are back together.

"Why are you picking her up?" She hissed.

"Um, because Marvin has to work..."

"Are you dumb or brain dead?"

"Neither. What's wrong with you?"

"What's wrong with me?! What's wrong with you!? You're letting him use you to help with the daughter he made while he's been messing around on you?" *I guess it does seem like that if you don't know the whole story... Damn, I wish I could tell her what's really going on.*

"He's not using me. I wanna help. Dealing with kids doesn't come easily to him."

"It just doesn't make sense, Carmen. It's like you're masochistic or something!" She was rigid and rattled until her face went blank, "Does this have anything to do with the fact of you losing his baby? You said she's...eight? That's how many years it's been...right?" Nina read me like a book. My stomach started to make hula hoops around my ass and I had to sit down. *Was it that obvious?*

"Yeah, that has a little bit to do with it." I admitted.

"O.K. so before he was just using you for sex, and now that you're supposedly just friends, he's using you as a baby-sitter. Did you find out what he does yet?"

"That's not fair, Nina." *Why is she being so mean?*

"What's not fair is that I need to be the voice of reason in your head. I'm sick and tired of you bitching and moaning about him and as soon as he gives you the least bit of attention, you throw it all out the window like he never hurt you in the first place. It's ridiculous! He's a cold man who refuses to get in touch with his emotions and pushes you away every time you get too close. Period. You shouldn't be helping him with a bastard child—"

"It's different this time." I cut her off. *It's different this time because I know the truth. It's different this time because I'm getting to know the real him...the man behind the mask.*

"Sure, it is. It's always different. It's like catch and release fishing.

He catches you like a fisherman and then releases you because you're too big or too small or not ready...or in your case because you're too needy and loving. He just doesn't deserve you, Carmen. He doesn't. And it's not like you don't have other options. I mean, if you would just give Jose a chanc---"

"Jose?! Give it up, Nina. Jose isn't my type."

"He's not your type because he's actually into you."

"Enough. I have to go. Stay, go, do whatever you want." I walked off after I picked up my purse. *Ugh, I know she doesn't know what's going on, but give me a break!*

I wish I could've told her the truth. I wish I could've told her that Keiko has sort of replaced that void I felt since the baby died; that little part of me that died with the baby long ago has come back to life. It's as if Marvin and I were in suspended animation while our baby grew from a fetus to a toddler to a wonderful little girl we both love and have finally been reunited with after eight years. It's the best gift I've ever gotten and I am thankful beyond gratitude. And the way I feel right now, taking the subway to pick up my...daughter from school, is something that even if I tried to explain...I don't think I would do it justice. It's like I finally have a purpose in this world; like it's my meaning for being put on this world. And at the same time, I feel bad. I know Nina just wants the best for me.

Fifteen: Keiko/Akemi

"Everyone, we have a new student joining us today. She just moved up from the sunshine state. Does anyone know which state that is?" Sister Bandeau asked the class while putting one of her arms around my shoulder. A red-headed girl with freckles sitting in the front row raised her hand.

"Yes Paula, go ahead." Sister Bandeau called on the eager red-headed girl with the answer.

"The sunshine state is Florida." Paula said acting all proud of herself.

"Very good. Now, why don't you introduce yourself to the class and then take a seat next to Paula." Sister Bandeau said as she sat down on her desk after patting me on the back. The whole class was looking at me before I even opened my mouth to speak. I started to feel my forehead moisten and my knees started shaking.

"My name is Kei——Akemi Moreno Costa." I said almost slipping up.

"Hi, Akemi" The class said together in one voice. I smiled and sat down next to Paula following Sister Bandeau's directions. At recess, I was ready to be alone like I always am but much to my surprise, Paula, the red-head from class, came to sit by me.

"Wanna trade your ho-ho for my fruit roll-up?" She asked.

"Sure." I replied handing her my ho-ho.

"I bet you're loving to wear normal clothes instead of these stupid uniforms, huh?" She asked as she sucked the filling out of the ho-ho cake.

"Actually, it makes me feel out of place. You know, since everyone else has it on?"

"Yeah, I guess. Just enjoy it while you can. I'm sure by the end of the day, the Reverend Mother will issue you your uniform for tomorrow...and the rest of your life!" We laughed. I never had comradery with anybody my age before. It was refreshing.

The rest of the day flew by. Just like Paula said, the Reverend Mother gave me my uniform for tomorrow. Tomorrow, I will be wearing a maroon plaid skirt with a white button down short sleeved shirt with the school crest on the left hand side. Tomorrow I will be like everyone else; something I've always failed to be. The bell rang to dismiss us. I walked toward the front of the school to parent pick-up expecting Ms. Carmen to be late like my parents always were. My eyes seemed to play a trick on me when I saw her there... on time. I lit up like a Christmas tree and ran toward her. She opened her arms and hugged me just as hard as I hugged her.

"How was your day, baby cakes?" She sweetly asked.

"It was good. I made a new friend." I confessed.

"You did? That's great!"

"Yeah, her name is Paula and we sit next to each other. Then, at lunch she sat with me. She's right over there waiting for her mom. Come on! I want you to meet her!" I pulled her hand moving fast enough for the both of us.

"Paula, this is my mommy. Mommy, this is Paula." I said a little out of breath.

"Nice to meet you, Paula." Ms. Carmen said. Paula turned up her nose.

"You don't look like Akemi..." Paula finally said after her rude action.

"That's because I'm her adoptive mother." Ms. Carmen explained.

"Oh, that makes sense." Paula commented.

"Where's your mommy?" I asked.

"She texted me saying she would be a few minutes late. You know, because of traffic?" She replied.

"Oh, ok." I said.

"We'll wait with you until she gets here. I'd love to meet her." Ms. Camen said. As we waited, Paula told us that her mommy is never late and begged us not to judge her. *Why would we judge her? That's silly.*

"Paula, darling, I'm so sorry I was late! Could you ever forgive me?" A well dressed woman said with a slight English accent...maybe with a hint of Irish, too?

"It's O.K., mother. Akemi and her mother were so kind as to wait with me. The time passed quickly." Paula replied now sounding a little like her mom.

"Hi, I'm Carmen. Akemi just started school today and Paula was the first friend she made." The two mommies shook hands.

"Oh, how nice. I'm Gina. It's so very nice to meet you. Paula doesn't have any friends, well until now that is. Nice to meet you, Akemi, is it? We simply *must* go out for ice cream. It will be my treat, of course. Come along. My car is this way." Ms. Gina spoke as if a room full of people were listening.

"That would be lovely, thank you." Ms. Carmen said as we followed Paula and her mom to their expensive looking car. She unlocked the doors and the new car scent spilled into my nostrils.

"How do you like school, Akemi?" Ms. Gina asked as she buckled Paula up with the seat belt in the front seat.

"It's nice." I replied.

"Why are you starting school so late?" She questioned.

"Oh, we just moved up from Florida. My...er..husband... just got a new job." Ms. Carmen said. Ms. Gina turned around and looked at Carmen's hands. Then she lifted her left hand up and the big diamond almost blinded me as the sun shone through it.

"Oh, I don't wear my ring all the time." Ms. Carmen said before she turned red.

"How unusual." Ms. Gina said after she turned the car on and we started driving toward the ice cream shop.

"Is the father... Asian?" Ms. Gina inquired.

"No, Akemi is adopted." Ms. Carmen replied.

"Oh, isn't that nice? I sponsor a little boy in Africa. Isn't it marvelous to help the less fortunate?"

"Well, we adopted Akemi because we fell in love with her, not because she was less fortunate."

"Right." Ms. Gina said as if she didn't understand how someone could adopt a child... She reminded me of the people who would come over to cocktail parties at our house. Mommy and daddy would act just like her... like they were better than everyone else. We got to the ice cream shop and Ms. Gina parked in a spot that read "reserved." We got out of the car and followed her in. The ice cream place was so nice that it didn't look like they would even sell ice cream. It looked more like a French restaurant mommy and daddy would insist on feeding escargot to Sumi and me. *Yuck!*

"Why hello Mrs. Notribello. Your table is ready, right this way." A fat man with an Italian accent wearing a tuxedo said. We sat down on a fancy round booth.

"I'd like four fat free soy chocolate ice creams with fresh strawberries. And Mario, *no* whipped cream this time." Ms. Gina said without even looking at the menus. I guess she comes here often. It was quiet until the ice creams arrived. I took a spoonful of the ice cream in front of me. As I tasted it on my tongue all I wanted to do was spit it out and gag, but I remembered the way mommy taught me; swallowing what's in your mouth and leaving the rest on the plate. I looked over at Paula and Ms. Gina and I couldn't understand how they were eating this brown paste. Then, I knew I wasn't alone when I saw Ms. Carmen spitting it back out onto her spoon like I wanted to in the first place. She put her index finger to her lips as if saying, "Shh, pretend you didn't see me do that." I giggled. Then we both decided to only eat the strawberries.

"So, since you two are new in town, I assume there are no plans for this weekend?" Ms. Gina asked after she finished her ice cream.

"I'd have to check to be sure, but I think you assume right." Ms. Carmen said pushing the ice cream plate away.

"My husband is out of town and Paula has been rather lonely. I was thinking we could set up for a sleep over on Friday." Ms. Gina said making Paula and I look at each other in excitement.

"Yeah, that shouldn't be a problem. Here, let me write my number on this napkin. And you could write yours on—" Ms. Gina cut Ms. Carmen off as she handed her a business card.

"Ah, thank you." Ms. Carmen said as she took the business card and put it in her back pocket.

"Well, we should go. It was a pleasure meeting you both. And thanks... for the ice cream." Ms. Carmen said as she gulped in disgust after she said "ice cream." I hugged both Paula and her mom while Ms. Carmen shook Ms. Gina's hand.

"It was a pleasure meeting you, too. See you Friday, Akemi. Ta-ta!" Ms. Gina sounded like she was singing rather than speaking.

"See ya." I replied. Ms. Carmen and I held hands while we walked toward the subway. When we got to the station, she scanned her pass twice and we walked through to wait for our train.

"I liked Paula." She broke the silence.

"Me too, but her mom is weird." I replied.

"That's not very nice, Kei—-Akemi."

"I did that in class today."

"Did what?"

"Start out with the Kei and end with the Akemi."

"Did anybody notice?"

"I don't think so."

"So, we need to practice. I'm gonna call you Akemi from now on...maybe hearing it will help you."

"Okay. But come on, admit it. Paula's mom is weird."

"She was just raised differently from you and me."

"Yeah, *real* different. I mean, what was up with that ice cream? Bleck!" I made a nasty face and Ms. Carmen laughed.

"Yeah, that ice cream was worse than castor oil!"

"What's castor oil?"

"If you don't know, you don't wanna find out! My mom used to make me take it to clean out my system and it was so nasty that I would almost throw up!"

"Ew."

"I know, ew is right."

"I miss Snoopy."

"Me too, but we're almost home." *Home.* The word resounded in the air and as much as I tried to ignore it, it kept hovering over my head. This is a better home than the elevator was, I suppose. At least here, I'm not alone.

Sixteen: Marvin

Today was just what I needed. I spent all day making preparations to strike the iron while it's hot with the Romero Mob. The last thing I need to do is stake out the building for the final details. I packed my .45 silencer along with more than enough ammo. Then I got out my Hattori dagger. I bought this dagger in Japan twelve years ago and I bought it especially for Julianni. As I admired my beautiful killing device, a fly buzzed around my ear. I took a deep breath and swiftly threw my dagger across the parking lot. *Bull's eye.* I walked toward the wall where the tip of my dagger was holding the dead fly up against it. Then I threw the fly on the floor and cleaned my dagger making it shiny as if it's never been used before. I started admiring it again; its three and three quarter inch double edged AUS-eight blade is flawless as is its Macassar ebony wood handle with a nickel silver hilt tapered in full tang. It came with a black leather boot clip sheath that's very handy. I plan on bringing both of them this Saturday. This Japanese steel will have its first taste of human blood.

I packed everything in the van and closed it. I thought it was safer to bring all weapons (not counting the .38 in my nightstand or the knife under my mattress) here since there's a kid in the house now. I felt a rumble in my stomach and realized it was talking to me out of hunger. *When was the last time I ate?* I normally get so absorbed in what I'm doing that I forget to eat. I checked my watch and noticed it was half past eight. *Just about time to get home.* I hailed a cab and ten minutes later I was home. The smell of Carmen's enchiladas was so potent that I could smell it downstairs. I floated up the way a cartoon would behind the scent of the food. I opened the door and my mouth watered. *Perfect timing. Carmen is just now serving.*

"Carm, it smells delicious!" I said with my stomach.

"Thanks, it's nice of you to finally join us." She said. I ignored her comment as I ate.

"How was your day?" Akemi asked smiling at me.

"Good, how was yours?" I replied surprised that she even wanted to know about my day.

"Good. I have a sleep over at Paula's house on Friday." *Not if I can help it, you don't.*

"Yeah, that's not happening." I said.

"Marvin, I got the mom's business card in my purse. You can do a little background check and *if* she checks out, I don't see why *Akemi* can't go." Carmen said reasoning with insanity.

"A background check? That's what you're basing this life-death decision on? Have you done a background check on *me*, Carmen? It's as clean as a whistle!" I lost it.

"Akemi---" Carmen said.

"I know, I know. Go play with Snoopy in my room." Akemi cut her off, picked Snoopy up, and went to her room lightly closing the door.

"Marvin, that little girl deserves some fun after what she's been through, doesn't she?" Carmen's chocolate eyes melted my anger away.

"Yes, but---"

"But nothing. We can't keep her hostage the rest of her life. Not everyone is a hit man. And the more you think that, the more you'll attract it. You really should read The Secret." She interrupted me angrily.

"Look Carmen, I promised I'd keep her safe, but I can't do that if I don't know where she is."

"You'll know where she is. I map quested the address and it's fifteen minutes from here. Just do the damn background check and let the girl live her life. I mean it."

"Fine..."

"Fine." We finished eating in silence and as she started clearing the table, I knew I had to tell her about Saturday.

"Carm?" I asked.

"Yeah?" She asked back.

"This Saturday will be a work night for me. I can't have the kid or the dog that day to prepare."

"A work night?"

"Yeah, I got some business to take care of."

"Oh..." She looked so worried.

"Don't worry."

"It's hard not to..."

"You can stay the night here with Akemi and Snoopy. That way you'll know exactly when I get home...safe and sound."

"Yeah, I might just do that."

"Good." I finished drinking my iced tea and put my empty glass in the sink.

"Akemi, I'm leaving! Come give me a kiss!" Carmen shouted. Akemi came running, Snoopy behind her, and she kissed Carmen goodbye.

"I'll take Akemi to school tomorrow. Just make sure she's ready by eight twenty. See ya, Marv. Sweet dreams you two." Carmen left along with her caramel scent.

Thursday went by as if it never even existed and tomorrow is Friday. Carmen just picked Akemi up for school and I'm taking the fleabag with me to stake out Julianni's building. I hailed down a taxi and told the taxi driver the address we would be driving to. He gave me a hard time about the dog being with me, but after I offered to pay more, everything was fine. It took about thirty minutes to get to the place since there was virtually no traffic. I paid the man and he drove away while Snoopy and I walked toward the building; I had him under my armpit because he walked too slowly.

I jimmied the lock of the back entrance and put Snoopy down as we walked down the hallway. I took my notepad out along with a pen. *Conference Room 101. That's on the first floor, I'm sure.* We took the elevator up to the first floor and I found the room. I noticed a large vent above the door right away. I followed the vent along the ceiling and there was another one five feet inside the conference room. *Perfect, that's my element of surprise.* I climbed up the vent and felt how sturdy and spacious it was inside. *Not bad, I certainly have been in worse.* The view into the conference room was impeccable. I started hearing Snoopy whimpering and whining. *Can't he be alone for two seconds?* I climbed back down and Snoopy stopped crying at once. Then, I inspected the rest of the building as if it was under inspection. I knew every nook and crane like the back of my hand. When I was done taking notes, I started rigging the elevator so I could control it at the press of a button; that way, if anybody left the conference room alive, I could trap them and off them as soon as I was able. I also rigged the emergency exit that lead to the stairs. There's no reason for anyone to use the stairs and well, frankly if there's a chase... *I hate stairs in a chase.* The silent alarms didn't get past me. I rigged those to ring the Domino's pizza down the street instead of the police.

After all my bases were covered, Snoopy and I hailed another cab. I dropped by my house and got Snoopy's bowls and food. I needed the place to myself to really concentrate on the task at hand, so I dropped him off at Carmen's. She wasn't there, but I used my spare key to get in. I left a note reminding her about my work day. When I got home, it almost felt abnormal to be alone. It made the silence seem loud somehow. I turned on the TV to the ESPN channel for the first time since Akemi moved in. My testosterone woke up and was ready to roar. For dinner, I had eggs and hot dogs. *Sure, it's no enchilada... but it will do.*

Seventeen: Carmen

"Hello?" I answered the phone.

"Hey, the photo shoot is booked for tomorrow." A man's voice yelled into my ear.

"Hector?" I questioned.

"Who else would it be?! So, be at the studio at noon. Don't wear any make up and make sure your hair is washed, but don't style it. See you tomorrow." He hung up before I could say anything else.

"What a silly man he is. Yes, he is a silly man." I spoke in a baby voice while I picked Snoopy up in my arms. I fed him shortly after I put my frozen dinner in the microwave. It's not fun to cook unless it's for people other than just me. Nina was still mad at me so I didn't even call her. She needs some time to cool off and when she's ready, she'll come around. After dinner, Snoopy and I cuddled up on my sofa bed while watching Breakfast at Tiffany's. The phone rang and I looked at the clock thinking it was much later than eight thirty. I paused the movie and reached for the phone.

"Hello?" I answered.

"Hi, mommy." Akemi spoke softly into my ear.

"Hi baby, how's the sleep over?"

"It's so much fun! We played in the pool today. Did you know there are such things as underwater cameras? Paula's mommy let us play with it."

"Aw, I'm glad you're having fun."

"The reason why I'm calling is because Ms. Gina was called in to do something tomorrow, like a function or something, and I need to be picked up before eleven." *Shit, my photo shoot is tomorrow. I'm sure she'll be out of the way if we bring Snoopy for her to play with...*

"That's fine then. I'll be there to pick you up in the morning."

"Thanks mommy. Sweet dreams!"

"You too, sweetie. Have a good night." I said as I blew kisses into the mouth piece and Akemi blew some right back into my ears. A smile flashed across my face as I hung up the phone. I pressed play button and finished watching the end of the movie. Snoopy started to softly snore making me smile once again. I yawned as soon as the credits started flooding the screen. Then I turned off the TV and snuggled up with Snoopy as we slept in each other's company.

The alarm went off disturbing my perfect dream. It was one of those that make you regret not being able to finish it. I followed Hector's directions and wore no make up after my shower where I washed my hair and let it air dry as I put on a jeans skirt with a red tank top along with red flip flops. Even though I'm extremely excited about today, I'm also very worried about Marvin. I know he's been doing this for years on end, but it's different now that I know about it! I changed purses from the black one to a jeans fabric one that's big enough to fit Snoopy in. We got out the door and I let him do his business before I put him in my purse to hail a taxi. I told the driver the address and we were off. When he started to veer off on a road I'd never seen before, I started looking around. Much to my disbelief, we were entering a mansion. The Notribello Mansion, to be exact. *Wow, I feel out of place already.* I kindly asked the driver to wait as I fetched my daughter and he didn't seem to mind. I walked up the doorsteps and rang the doorbell. *Is that Mozart?* The door opened and the cliché butler appeared.

"May I help you, Madam?" He said with the expected English accent.

"Um, hi, my daughter Akemi is here."

"Yes, I'll go get her. Would you like to come in?"

"Sure." I stepped up into their castle and in front of me was a beautiful staircase that reminded me of the castle in Cinderella right off the bat. *This is how the other half lives.* The butler walked off into the depths of the house and minutes later, Akemi was running toward me.

"Mommy!" She screamed out.

"Hey chickie, did you get everything?" I asked as she hugged my legs and I rubbed her back.

"Yeah, bye Mr. Rodolfo! Have a good rest of the weekend!" Akemi almost yelled.

"You too, Ms. Costa." Rodolfo, the butler, said making her giggle.

"Thank you." I said as I walked toward the door.

"Cheerio!" He rose up to the cliché even more by this farewell. Akemi and I went back to the taxi and I told him the new address. She pet and held Snoopy on the way while she told me everything she did without leaving any details out. When we arrived at the destination, I paid the driver and we got out.

"I'm hungry." Akemi admitted while patting her tiny stomach.

"Didn't they feed you?" I surprisingly asked.

"Not anything good..." We walked a little farther and on the corner of the place we would be at for the rest of the day, was a diner. I looked at my watch and noticed we had thirty minutes. We sat down and ordered a quick breakfast and ate it fast enough to cause indigestion. I paid our waitress and hurried to make it to my photo shoot.

"Now, you can't run all over the set and you need to keep an eye on Snoopy. Can you do that for me?" I asked as we walked.

"No problem." When we got there, Hector was waiting by the door.

"Hello, Hector. You look well." I said kissing ass.

"You're a minute and a half late. Time is money." He said with a serious face. Then he started pulling me by the arms, pinching my arm fat.

"Akemi, stay close by... and remember what we talked about." I said behind me in Akemi's direction.

"Okay Mommy." *Shit, I forgot to mention for her not to call me mommy on the set.* I prayed Hector didn't hear me but it was too late. He dropped my arm and looked furiously at me.

"Mommy?!" Hector yelled as he breathed out fire like a dragon.

"Hector, I can explain..."

"When I hired you, I told you about the way I feel about working mothers and you looked me in the eyes and lied to me?! No, I don't wanna hear it! As good a dancer as you are, I just can't bear to think that you have a child at home while men picture you naked on stage," He looked away with disgust, "Get out of my face Carmen. You're fired."

"Hector, come on..." I pleaded one last time.

"No, Carmen, I won't come on. Alisa will take over your show. I don't wanna see you here ever again." His words chastised me as if I had just committed the biggest sin of all. I took Akemi by the hand as she carried Snoopy with her other hand. *There goes my studio,* I thought.

"I'm sorry, Ms. Carmen." Akemi whispered with her head down as if this was her fault.

"Oh, this wasn't your fault, baby girl. I don't need that job anyways..." I tried to convince myself as much as I was trying to convince her.

"But me calling you mommy cost you a job..." She said still feeling blue.

"Honey, if anything it's my fault. I should've told you not to call me mommy in front of my boss. But you know what?"

"What?" She perked up a little.

"You calling me mommy is worth more any dumb old job."

"You mean it?"

"Of course I do."

"Then I can call you mommy even if we're not in public?"

"You can call me mommy whenever you want."

"Okay...mommy." She smiled big.

"Hey, since I have the day off now, you wanna see something great?"

"Yeah." She said without a hint of irony. We took the subway and walked to my dream studio. Every time I lose a job or I think things are bad, I come here to get inspiration to keep moving on. I took a deep breath in and breathed out a smile.

"This is it." I said; my voice was filled with pride.

"This is going to be my dance studio someday. It's really old and dirty, but can't you see the potential?" I said as we looked at the foggy, dusty windows. When I looked at this place, I saw it the way it will be when I fix it up.

"Can we go in?" Akemi asked much to my surprise. She seemed as eager to step inside as I was.

"Let's go ask Ms. Margot." I replied as I started heading up to the apartment above the studio.

"Who's Ms. Margot?" Akemi asked as she followed me.

"She's the woman that owns the studio now."

"Oh." I knocked on the door twice and Ms. Margot answered the door right away. She doesn't get visitors very often, so she's elated whenever she does.

"Carmen, darling. Come in, come in!" She invited almost pulling me in from where I stood.

"Hi, Ms. Margot. This is my daughter, Akemi." I introduced.

"It's a pleasure to meet you, Akemi. Oh, the life you have in your eyes. Amazing. And who's this?" Ms. Margot said as she marveled over Akemi's eyes and then pointed at Snoopy in Akemi's arms.

"This is Snoopy." Akemi smiled.

"Aw, he's just darling, but keep him close. I have cats that will eat him alive if you put him down." Ms. Margot kidded and scared Akemi at the same time.

"Can we have the keys to the studio? I wanted to show her around." I asked politely.

"Sure, let me go get it for you." She said as she disappeared into the big hallway.

"Will her cats really eat Snoopy if I put him down?" Her tone was flabbergasted as she half whispered.

"That's what she said." I replied while smiling.

"Here it is, darlings. Come up and see me before y'all leave, now. I'm baking cookies." Ms. Margot said as she appeared from the hallway and handed me the keys. The crow's feet on the corner of her grey eyes creased as she smiled her southern belle smile.

"We will. Thanks." I said knowing all too well that even if I declined, she would find a way for me to bring the cookies home. We walked down the steps and I stood in front of the double doors before unlocking them, marinating in what the future will hold. I sighed and started unlocking the doors before I opened them wide; a woof of moldy air came toward us.

"Do you smell that?" I kindled.

"What? Pee and mold?" Akemi asked looking at me holding her nose.

"No, silly. The future."

"The future smells like pee and mold?" I laughed.

"Come on, smart alleck," I rolled my eyes and pushed her inside, "Let's open the windows." She put Snoopy down and assisted me in opening all the windows. The sun shone the light into my future and flashes of remodeling appeared before my eyes. I went over to the stereo in the corner and blew the dust off. For a second I thought I might sneeze, but it quickly went away as I fished for a good belly dancing CD. When I picked one, I blared the stereo almost as loud as it went. Then I went in my purse to get a coin belt. I put it on around my waist and started dancing like no one was watching.

"Do you have one for me?" A tiny voice asked and I remembered I wasn't alone.

"Of course! Pick out one you want. There's several in my purse." I replied. Keiko picked out the only other one that matched the one I was wearing. Then she came up beside me and looked at my reflection as I danced on the foggy mirrored wall in front of us. Minutes after observing, Akemi started emulating me.

"No honey, you can get hurt doing it that way." I quickly corrected.

"Can you teach me how?" She asked with puppy dog eyes. *I've never taught a kid before...*

"All right, then let's start with something easy like the figure eight. Put your arms out like this. Palms down and elbows relaxed. When I say arms in second position, this is what I mean, O.K.?" The words spilled out naturally and instinctively.

"O.K." Akemi replied completely absorbed into what I was saying and doing.

"Now, for the figure eight, your feet are flat, your pelvis is tucked in, your chest is lifted, and your arms are in second position."

"Like this?" *Aw look, a mini me!*

"Yes, good job! Now we're going to push our hips backwards making a figure eight on the floor. Push back. Push back. Imagine you're making a circle with each hip on the floor. A little faster. Just the hips. Good. One, two. One, two..."

"This is fun. Teach me something else!" She was like a sponge hungry for knowledge.

"O.K., now let's learn how to isolate the rib cage. Bend your knees, tuck the pelvis, lift the chest, and roll your shoulders back. Good. Now relax your hands in front of your hips and imagine that there is a string attached to your sternum..."

"What's a sternum?" She confusedly asked.

"The sternum holds your ribs together. The sternum and ribs create a cage-like environment to protect your heart and lungs from injury."

"Oh, ok." She still looked a bit confused, but somehow I thought she understood the gist of it.

"Now push your rib cage forward and drop it down," I demonstrated and then watched her do it perfectly like a pro, "You're a natural, Akemi! Good job."

"I like this." She admitted as if I couldn't tell.

"It likes you back. I've never seen someone pick it up so fast. Now you're going to contract your rhomboids which are the muscles in the center of your back. Just imagine you have an itch in the center of your back that you can't scratch. So what do you do? You contract the muscles in the center of your back. Yes, just like that. Contract the muscles and drop your chest forward. Let's try it faster. Up and down. Forward and back. Good! Can I help you?" I asked as I noticed two women walking up behind us thanks to the mirror.

"We heard the music. Can we join your class?" The brunette asked, mesmerized by the dance.

"Sure. There's some extra coin belts in my purse. Feel free to try them on. It's easier to learn if you hear the movements. We're about to learn shimmies." I said feeling more like a teacher than ever before.

"Do you just tie it?" The blonde asked holding the coin belt.

"Yes, just tie it around your hips. O.K., now shimmies are vibrations; or a shaking of the entire body. We're going to start by putting our feet below our hips and the knees relaxed. Now, slowly start moving our knees back and forth. The pelvis is released and relaxed. Notice that your hips will start to rock as you move your knees, I want you to bring your arms out and I want you to speed it up a little bit. Relax your hips and relax your breath. Let your knees do the work. Feel and hear the movements through your coin belts. Hi everyone, I have some coin belts in my bag over there and you can just follow along. Stop me if I'm going too fast..." As I taught, women started being drawn in like the music was sirens calling off to the sailors at sea. I kept teaching until the dance studio was filled with students. When the CD finally ended, I noticed Ms. Margot was on a metal chair with Snoopy and a tray of freshly baked cookies.

"Bravo!" Ms. Margot said as she clapped starting a chain reaction that ended with everyone clapping. As each person's hand clap echoed through the insulated walls of the studio, my eyes started to water. At this moment, I knew this is where I belonged.

"When is the next class?" An African American woman interjected in on my moment and abruptly brought me back to reality. My heart dropped and I was suddenly speechless. *There won't be any classes because this isn't my studio...*

"Belly dancing will be offered every Saturday at eleven AM. We'll have a sign up sheet next week. Bring your friends. Who wants cookies?" Ms. Margot shocked the hell out of me. The women gathered around Ms. Margot like a flock of vultures on road kill. They all said they'd be back next Saturday, and they'd be back with friends. They returned my coin belts and asked where they could buy some for the next class. I gave them information to different stores and felt as if I was in a dream; a dream from which I never wanted to wake up. When the heron of women left, Ms. Margot looked my direction while Akemi kept eating the cookies.

"Carmen, I had no idea you were such a marvelous teacher. Had I known, I would've hired you long ago when I first met you!" She said making me almost faint.

"Do you teach any other dances?"

"Yeah, I teach ballroom." I said light headed.

"My dear, this is certainly the start of a fruitful friendship." She hugged me as if I was the answer to her prayers. *Could she tell she was the answer to mine?* We signed a contract stating that we were partners; 50/50. We also made a date for cleaning the studio on Sunday. Akemi and Snoopy were so sleepy by the time we got to Marvin's. I didn't have the heart to make her go shower. She was even too tired to eat the dinner I made. In my excitement, I failed to think of the danger Marvin was in until now. As I fed Snoopy and walked him, I prayed that God would keep him safe. *He will be O.K., won't he?*

Eighteen: Marvin

I woke up this morning to the empty house I slept in last night. It still felt abnormally quiet and not having any distractions started seeming more distracting in itself. *Today is the day.* I turned on the stereo to my classical CDs and the surround sound kept me company as I showered. After I dried myself, the fog flooded out of the bathroom as I opened the door. It made me think of the scene in As Good As It Gets where Jack Nicholson gets out of his extremely hot shower. I smiled to myself and shook my head as I got dressed with black pants, a bulletproof vest, a long sleeved black turtle neck, and black steel toe boots.

I reached in my closet for my dusty lie detector machine. *You'll come in handy tonight.* I put it in my duffel bag along with my laptop. Then I reached for my Hattori dagger and placed it in my boot sling. The picture of my parents called out to me from the depths of my closet. In the picture, my dad has his hand around my mom's shoulder and is looking at the camera with a big smile on his face while my mom is looking at him with googly eyes instead of looking at the camera. *They were so in love.* I put the picture standing up on my bed and I kneeled down in front of it. *I'm gonna avenge you tonight, Father. Mom, you can finally rest at ease.* I lit some incenses and sat down in front of the picture, still on my bed, with my legs crossed Indian style.

I breathed in my goal and I breathed out my doubts. I visualized my whole attack to the point where I could smell the iron in the bloods I was spilling. The alarm on my wrist watch went off and I looked down, surprised it was already five o'clock. *I need to get over to my van to drive to the building that's way across town. Rush hour traffic is gonna be hell.* I put my black leather gloves in my pocket along with my night vision glasses. I zipped up the duffel, put my duffel bag strap across my chest, and started walking toward the door.

As I walked down the stairs, I pictured Carmen, Akemi, and Snoopy. The thought made me smile and then I wondered why. *If anything were to happen to me...I'd miss them; even the kid and the flea bag.* My heart felt weird. This sensation was new to me, and I hoped it would soon go away... but it didn't. Instead, it made me start thinking that once this job is done, I can finally quit. Once Julianni and Bram are taken care of, I will have no reason to need to keep putting myself and the people I love in danger. We could get a bigger house. I could buy Carmen that studio she's been wanting and she could move out of that crappy apartment. When the time comes, I can even pay for Akemi's college. I have more than enough for three lifetimes. *What am I thinking? She's gone after all this is over... and Carmen is done with me, so why does any of this even matter?*

I arrived at the parking garage and got in my van. *What's the matter with me? I should be concentrated on the job...nothing else. Why am I thinking about Akemi and Carmen? Do I miss them after just one night away from them?* I put all those thoughts aside as I started driving toward Julianni's building. The classical music soothed my soul and calmed my nerves. Traffic was bumper to bumper; which gave me time to walk around in the van and get all my necessities packed into one duffel bag, as opposed to three. In the duffel bag with the laptop and lie detector machine, I packed in my silencer along with ammo, four tear gas grenades, and my tear gas mask. Fifty seven minutes later, I was parked two blocks over from Julianni's building.

I started walking toward the building with my duffel bag over my shoulders. It was heavier than usual, but then again, so was this job. I put on my leather gloves and the night vision glasses before I jimmied the lock like the day before. The glove hugged around the wedding band tighter than anywhere else, but I almost liked the awareness it brought to the area. I walked down the now familiar hallway and into the elevator. As the doors opened, everything seemed to slow down.

I climbed into the vent that would be my location for the next hour or so... Then I got out my laptop and made sure the control to the elevator would be fast and accessible. I then put on the tear gas mask over my night vision glasses, took out the four tear gas grenades and positioned one by the vent above the front door, and the other three on the vent above the conference room, and I also readied my silencer. *Now, the next order of business is waiting for my beloved guests; especially, Julianni Romero. He's the guest of honor today.*

My breath was even and silent as each mob member entered the conference room; each sitting in their assigned seats, or so it seemed. They exchanged pleasantries and indulged in small talk before *the Furor* arrived. In this light, they almost seemed human; asking about kid's recitals and wives' bake sales. But I knew better.

My heart almost stopped when I saw Julianni walk into the room. The side conversations ceased as he took a seat at the head of the table. *I wonder how many people's lives they've ruined and killed collectively.* The curtains started to rise. *It's show-time!* I pulled the pins from the grenades and dropped them into the conference room. Then I quickly slid on my stomach toward the vent above the conference room's entrance where I shot the two body guards as I dropped the last tear gas grenade down. Adrenaline pumped through my heart as the blinded Italian men realized they were under attack and stampeded toward the door. My gun was mounted as I shot each man in the head that exited the conference room; it was like shooting ducks in a row at a carnival booth, but the prize today would be no ordinary teddy bear. It would be the answers that's haunted me across the years; the reason my life turned out the way it did.

I kept shooting to kill and the bodies started to pile up in the hall. Two men, I left alive because I couldn't tell for sure which one was Julianni and which one wasn't. They bolted toward the elevator right into my trap. I pressed one button on my laptop and the door closed, trapping them inside like roaches in a motel. I jumped down from the vent to do the last walk through; to sweep the human carcass to make sure they were all dead. I felt as if I was walking on tomato sauce as my boots skidded on the blood; each step carefully breathing as steadily as possible to minimize any noise on my part. Suddenly, my thigh started to burn as if a snake bit me and the venom was seeping through. I looked down and noticed I was shot. Behind me, a bodyguard's angry, bloodshot eyes stared me down. I turned to him and without hesitation, I pulled the trigger. The bullet entered his skull and blew the back of his head, splattering brain matter into the wall.

I removed the empty clip and added a new one. *Ah, my leg...* I knew the bullet had gone straight through me because I did not feel it lodged in my flesh. The warm fluid started to cascade from my wound and gush down my leg. There was no time to feel lightheaded from blood loss, so the adrenaline replaced the blood in my veins. I looked in the camera that I installed in the elevator through my laptop and noticed Julianni dictating his double to fix the problem while rubbing the tear gas deeper into his eyes. I pointed my gun toward the elevator and with one click of the mouse; the door parted like the red sea as if I was Moses.

"Hands where I can see them, gentlemen." *My leg is killing me and my sock is squishing as I walk. I'm losing blood. And I'm losing it fast...*

99

"You won't get away with this, son." Julianni said with one eye open. I pointed the gun at his double and shot his neck. The arterial spray went into Julianni's open eye and mouth making him spit and gag.

"I already did. Now move your ass." I made him walk toward the room near the elevator since the air in there was clear.

"Sit down!" I said as I hit his head with my .45 making a little head wound. He winced in pain as I tied him with the rope I planted there earlier today.

"If you stop this now, I won't call the cops. I mean, you're shot and leg wounds are dangerous. You need to get it looked at. You must know you're bleeding profusely. You don't strike me as an ignorant man--"

"Cut the shit," I interrupted his blabbering, "Only talk to me if you're answering a question." I threatened.

"What do you want?" He tested my threat. I shot him in the leg to teach him some discipline.

"Shut the fuck up." I annunciated. This time, he listened. I left the room and walked toward the vent. I reached in for my duffel bag and brought it back to the room. *Can he hear that I'm limping?* I took out the lie detector and ripped his shirt open before I started hooking him up to the machine. I stood in front of him with my head in the game.

"I'm sure you are familiar with this. Now, each time you lie to me, this machine will show me. But there are consequences to lying to me, Julianni. Each time I see you're lying, you lose a finger. Capisce?"

"Why you little asshole... just who do you think you are? Don't you have *any* idea who *I* am?!" He failed to answer my question correctly, so I had to take action. I swiftly reached into my boot strap for my dagger and grabbed his hand, holding it in place. I put the Japanese steel next to his eye in a threatening manner and then I precisely struck down on his pinky. *The disciplinarian strikes again.* His scream of anguish and pain was music to my ears as he looked at his fat, bloody pinky on the floor. The dagger sliced through flesh and bone without any difficulty whatsoever. It sliced right through like it was warm butter.

"One more time, and maybe this time you will take me seriously, I ask the questions and you answer them...no more, no less. Capisce?" I tried again cleaning the dagger on my sleeve.

"Capisce." He answered like a good little boy.

"Let's start with something basic... State your full name."

"Julianni Edmundo Romero." He replied as his open wound dripped.

"Where do you live?"

"Forty second southwest fifth avenue." He tested me again. *Unbelievable!*

"Now, now Julianni. These are supposed to be the easy questions.

Is that your final answer?" I said giving him a chance to save his other pinky while gently waving my dagger in front of his face.

"Hundred seventieth northeast seventh avenue." He complied.

"Good, now that you know how the game works, let's move on to the harder questions. Why did you kill Amadeo Costa?" My frontalis muscle contracted and I found myself being unable to blink as I awaited his answer filled with anticipation.

"He was stealing from me." He chose to lie. I angrily cut his other pinky as easily as the first.

"*Motherfucker!*" His screams echoed through the vents.

"Now be nice. I'm the one with the knife... Let's try this again, why did you kill Amadeo Costa."

"I killed him because I had to." The wave lengths were stable and he was telling the truth.

"Elaborate." I demanded.

"I needed my workers to fear me. Killing Costa gave me the boost for intimidation since people automatically thought that if I could kill my best friend, I could kill anyone." As he spoke the words as-a-matter-of-factly, I turned away in disgust. I felt a frog in my throat, but I swallowed it whole. There was no time to let my feelings fuck this up for me.

"What was the reason for killing Belinda?" My voice trembled a bit as I said my mother's name, but I don't think he noticed.

"I was sick of her playing hard to get routine." *That did it.* My cool demeanor quickly turned sour, and I lunged forward getting in his face.

"Is that why you raped her in front of him?!" My breath was shallow and my heart beat was fast.

"Yeah, that and I always felt a thrill having people watch me perform." I screamed and chopped off an entire hand. I did it slow too, so he could squirm in his chair unable to stop me.

"What's the big idea?! I told the truth, kid, by your rules, I should still have that hand!" He yelled rolling his eyes in the back of his head from blood loss.

"Listen here, and listen good. I am the kid your guys couldn't catch that day you decided to make an example out of the Costa family. I am the kid you put a hit on. I am the kid that's been killing your hit men since I was fourteen. You are the reason my life turned out the way it did---"

"What? Little Marvin? Is that you?" His expression went from surprised to fear to angered in the course of a millisecond. He knew the last hit man he sent to get me was Bram.

"Yeah...that nasty scar on his lip. I gave it to him." I announced that I could read his mind.

"Hmm, it seems that our friend Bram owes me some money for an incomplete assignment then." *Even at the face of death, all he can think about is money.*

"Too bad you won't live long enough to cash anything in."

"We can work something out, little Marvin, can't we? Come on, can't we let bygones be bygones?" I breathed in the deepest breath my diaphragm could allow.

"Maybe... how do you get in contact with Bram?" I gave him false hope.

"Oh, that's easy. His business card is in my wallet. He lives in the city, you know. He has a family and everything." *Bram with a family? I can't even fathom that one bit.* I palpated Julianni for his wallet. Of course, it was in his back pocket. I opened up his wallet and looked for Bram's card. I took it out of and put it by the lie detector machine. *That's all I need you for, Julianni. You've served your pathetic purpose.* I walked behind him making him think I was about to untie him. I grabbed his forehead with my left arm to prevent him from moving too much and with my right arm, I victoriously slit his throat...nice and slow. His blood sprayed over me and it felt like the fountain of youth. *I've never felt so alive!* As the blood pressure got lower and lower, so did the angst inside of me. The death of Julianni was the birth of me. While he gurgled through his last moments, I sat down in front of him as if watching a series finale. I don't know how long I sat there staring at his dead body. I didn't even mind being drenched in his blood. I felt if I wiped it off I would insult the Gods, since they had just so kindly baptized me. I stared deeply into his dead eyes and just kept thinking, *I won.*

When the hypnotic trance lost its power, I started gathering my things and packing it back into my duffel bag. The satisfaction I was feeling was intoxicating as I limped toward the van. The night air was refreshing. The moonlight bathed over me and the stars seemed to rearrange themselves to look like the picture of my parents I have. They smiled down upon me with all their light and glory. My father winked at me and then they disappeared.

I threw my duffel bag in the back of the van and started driving toward the loft. My vision started getting blurry and my body felt weak. The further I drove, the more intense the pain was and the less clearly I could see. *That bastard must've hit an important vein.* I started to sweat cold and my hands started to shake as I parked. I parked right in front of the loft. I knew if I got a parking ticket, outsiders wouldn't be able to look into the bloody van because of the black windows. *That was a good investment,* I thought as I crawled up the stairs dragging the shot leg which wasn't working properly anymore. I opened the door and I started fading out as the room darkened. *I think I'm gonna pass out...*

Nineteen: Carmen

After leaving Ms. Margot's, we went back to my place to pack a bag of necessities. While Akemi picked out movies for our movie night, the Marvin box called out to me. I wasn't going to wear it, but it was nice to look at it every now and then... When we got to Marvin's, we pigged out and watched movies until Akemi passed out and I carried her to bed.

It's almost three in the morning and Marvin still isn't back yet. *Should I call?* No, estúpida, *you'll blow his cover. Oh God, I know he kills people for a living, but will you please protect him and bring him home to me?* I heard Snoopy's faint bark followed by the front door opening. My heart smiled. *Marvin!* I quickly dashed off the bed and started sprinting down the stairs. Our eyes met and even in the darkness, I could see him perfectly. For a moment, I really believed everything was O.K. That moment quickly vanished when Marvin fainted; his body thudding and hitting the floor loudly. I gasped and turned on the light suddenly being presented with a bloody show.

My heart started beating faster and I dropped down beside him. He was drenched in blood! I dragged his unconscious body to the bathroom and put him in the bathtub. Then, knowing the neighbors he has, I cleaned up the blood trail leading down to his van that was illegally parked in front of the building. I flew back up to the loft to tend to my bloody man in the bathtub. I started undressing him, carefully looking for the wound. *Where's all this blood coming from? There are no bullets on the vest. Shouldn't there be at least one bullet in the vest?* When he was buck naked, I turned the bathwater on. I got a sponge and started scrubbing the dry blood while looking for the source of the bleeding. *His dyed blonde hair just looks red, but it isn't his blood.* I gagged at the thought of seeing so much blood that obviously wasn't his. Then I pulled myself together and stayed true to the task at hand. *Find the wound and stop the bleeding.*

I scrupulously sponged his muscular neck, shoulders, back, chest, and stomach until I finally found the through and through wound on his upper right thigh. The bullet hole was large enough to where I could see his bone. I started sweating cold and kneeled down in front of the toilet knowing vomiting was in my near future. Marvin then moaned out in pain, and though it wasn't loud, the suffering tone to it made me get off my knees and run toward my purse. In it, was my first aid kit along with my sewing kit. I got both of them and a sudden calmness swept over me. I reached into the tub and propped up Marvin's right leg on the side. I washed out the wound heavily with hydrogen peroxide, sterilized a needle with Marvin's butane lighter, and threaded the needle. The bleeding still hasn't ceased completely and it made me nervous. *Will he slowly bleed out if I just close him up with stitches? Shouldn't I stop the bleeding? How do you stop bleeding?*

I had a flashback of my mom burning my brother's shoulder with a knife she heated up. He screamed out, letting her know how much pain he was feeling, but she didn't really care. *This will stop the bleeding,* she said once in a solemn tone. I knew what I had to do at once. I took his butane lighter and went into the kitchen. I opened the silverware drawer and reached for a teaspoon. On my way back into the restroom, I lit the spoon up with the butane flame. The spoon started to redden, and I lowered it down on Marvin's unexpected flesh. He was so out of it that he didn't make a single sound. The burning flesh smelled awful, but what else could I do? I heated up the spoon once more, and did the same thing on the opposite side of his leg. This time, he grunted without opening his eyes. The bleeding stopped and I smiled. *Thanks, mom.*

As I was sewing the burnt wound with blue thread, I reminisced of the times I watched my mom stitching up my brother. She never took him to the hospital, knowing that if she did, the police would be called and they would take her baby to jail. She was famous for her lectures, but for some reason they never seemed to work on him. *If you stay on this path, Carlito, you'll end up in jail... or even worse: dead!* He responded always in the same way by rolling his eyes. *Mom, you were right. He did end up in jail.* I haven't heard from Carlos since I bailed him out last time. *What if he's dead?*

I admired my stitches as I bathed Marvin, this time with soap and water. After I rinsed him, I dried him off. He wearily opened his beautiful blue eyes. The blue wouldn't be so special without the white crystals...

"Hey, you..." He weakly said with a raspy voice.

"Oh Marvin, you're O.K.!" I said as I hugged him not caring that his bare body was still wet. He hugged me gently and I lost my balance falling on top of him making him groan out in pain.

"I'm so sorry!" I immediately said getting up, but he held me down still holding me close. I hugged him back and seconds later, I was feeling something harden on my hip...

"Someone's feeling better!" I said as I quickly got up and out of the bathtub.

"Aw, don't be like that..." He said as he gave me the sexy look. I threw a towel at him and turned around walking up to his bedroom to pick out some blood-free, clean clothes. When I walked back to the bathroom, he was trying to stand up.

"Here, let me help you." I said as I came under him allowing him to use me as a crutch. He leaned on me and looked down at the blue thread.

"Wow." He said astounded. I reached over for his boxers and kept giving him support as I helped him put it on.

"So, is the mission complete?" I curiously asked as I helped him put on flannel pajama pants.

"Part of it." He said with a smile that sent chills down my body.

"Which part?" I gulped.

"My part." I knew he meant Julianni and we dropped the subject. I handed him a white t-shirt and he put it on, but his leg gave out and he almost fell.

"Come on, you need to get some rest." I said as I helped him walk to the couch bed I fixed up earlier tonight. He walked leaning on me, but I knew he was holding back a lot. I laid him down, and took a seat by him on the bed.

"I'm really glad you're O.K." I admitted under my breath. He looked at me with such a light on his facial features. A sort of light that comes out from deep within...

"Me too." He said as he grabbed my left hand. He brought it closer to his lips and his eyes changed expression as he kissed my ring-less ring finger. My eyes flickered to his left hand and the ring was still on his ring finger. The hurt in his eyes was almost unbearable, so I looked away. I heard him take a sharp breath and then I felt his fingers running through my hair.

"You saved my life, Carm. These stitches are amazing and I know it must've been hard burning my wounds to stop the bleeding. I guess all I'm saying is: thank you." He softly spoke the words with such intent and meaning.

"You're welcome." I turned and graciously accepted his gratitude. As we looked at each other, I almost gave in to the intoxicating feeling of love that always possesses me when I'm around Marvin. But still, something held me back. Even with him touching my cheeks so softly and looking at me with his gorgeous eyes… I knew that something would not go away tonight so I retreated and got off the bed.

"Do you need anything for the pain?" I sweetly asked.

"Yeah, um… I actually have some Percocet in my nightstand…" He said almost ashamed for admitting he's in enough pain to need a pill. I nodded and walked up the stairs. As I opened his nightstand drawer, my eyes were drawn to the picture in it. It was us the night that we first met. I ran my fingers through it and smiled, but then a sadness emerged from a place I was desperately trying to suppress. *Not now, tears… please, not now.* I swallowed down my feelings and reached for the orange prescription bottle with Marvin's name on it. I hurried down the steps only to find Marvin in a deep slumber with his left hand lying across his chest. My eyes zoomed in on his wedding band, and the tears started to flood out of my eyes. I ran to the bathroom and closed the door. The cold tiles stole my heat as I sat down on the floor crying as quietly as humanly possible.

When I dehydrated my body from tears and water no longer came out of my eyes, I got up and started cleaning the bathroom. When it was sparkling white again, I put Marvin's clothes in the wash. Then I walked in the kitchen and poured water into a glass before I brought it to the living room setting it on the coffee table next to Marvin. I put the prescription bottle next to the water glass and turned to look at Marvin sleeping. *Either commit to me, Marv, or let me go… I can't take this agony much longer.* I pulled the covers to tuck him in and then kissed him on the forehead. *Sweet dreams…*

The minute I walked upstairs, I dug in my purse for the rings. *He hasn't taken his ring off since he put it on…* I flirted with the idea before I actually slipped the rings back on my finger… *I can't wait till Marvin sees this tomorrow!*

Twenty: Marvin

"Juli, *please* don't do this!" Mom pleaded before Julianni gagged her with a pillow case. He tied it on so tight cutting off her circulation. Pops was there sitting on his favorite chair on the opposite side of the bed from the closet. Two guys were holding him down and he was gagged as well. I was in the closet witnessing this whole disaster as it unfolded.

"Ugh... Ah!" Mom grunted as Julianni roughly ripped her clothes off. He then bent her naked body over the bed.

"Hold her down, will ya?" Julianni hissed as two guys held mom down as he started to brutally rape her. The two guys by Pops held his eyes open so he could watch the whole thing. My eyes burned and I had to look away.

"NO!" Pops screamed through the gag. Julianni laughed a maniacal laugh. I heard mom's painful groans and sorrowful, scared tears, but I knew I couldn't open my eyes.

"Admit it, Belinda. You enjoyed it a little..." Julianni sang. Tears started to crawl out of my closed eyes and I abruptly opened them when I heard the gunshot. Mom's body seemed to fall in slow motion as my pupils dilated. When her body hit the floor, she looked up at me and tried to smile as the life went out of her. Pops's cries of heartache and pain echoed in my head and I was paralyzed looking at Mom's naked body in front of the closet I was hiding in. Her blood started to flow all around her and then started streaming inside the closet. Her warm blood hugged my bare feet and it felt like someone punched me in the stomach. Pops was in hysterics and I felt the exact same way, but I knew I couldn't make any noise.

"Have mercy..." Pops cried out still muffled from the gag, now sounding very defeated unlike before.

"What was that, Costa? Mercy, you say? I'm sorry to say, but I'm fresh out." Julianni cocked his gun and heartlessly pulled the trigger. I squeezed my eyes shut until they hurt and I cupped my hands over my ears until I started to hiccup. When I finally opened my eyes, I saw that Julianni and his men were gone, but a new set of men, dressed in all white, were there cleaning up the rigid crime scene. One of them followed the trail of blood and opened the door to my hideout. I instinctively started to run. I swear I ran faster than Flash Gordon himself. I kept running until my lungs felt like they exploded and I collapsed in front of the Cathedral.

I woke up to angels on the ceiling lying down on an extremely firm mattress. I looked down at my feet and noticed they were clean, but I could still feel the warmness of my mother's blood; the blood that never should've exited her body. I started to cry as I held my legs close to my chest.

"Oh, you're awake." A nun scared the living daylights out of me. I didn't respond.

"I called the cops; they should be here any second now. They'll help you..." She said standing still. *The cops? They can't help me. They won't even believe me. The crime scene is spotless.*

"Are you hungry? I'm sure we have something you like in the kitchen..." She said as she walked down the hallway. I stayed in place and started to think about my situation. I knew I needed to get out of here before the cops arrived, but where would I go? A hotel? *Churches have donation boxes,* I thought to myself. I walked toward the church and the box jumped out at me. I picked the lock with my Swiss army knife and started pocketing the money. And that's precisely when the cops showed up:

"Stop right there!" One of them yelled holding his hand over his gun on his belt. I put a few more bills in my pocket and then jolted out like lightning. The cops ate my dust and I lost them three blocks out. By nightfall, I was in the worst neighborhood I'd ever seen. The cheap motel quickly became my method of survival. I walked in and the clerk was watching a football game. His greasy appearance disgusted me, but I kept it from being apparent.

"Hi, I'd like a room..." I spoke into the glass separating the air between us.

"You eighteen?" He asked not taking his eyes off the T.V. screen.

"Yeah." I lied without hesitating.

"Thirty five even." I slid the cash into the opening and he slid me a key. I picked it up and walked fast paced to the room. Once I got in there, I locked and bolted the door. Falling asleep was hard that night. The second I closed my eye lids, flashes of my parent's barbarous murder made me open them back up. The flashes finally triggered my tear glands to overact and I cried myself to sleep. During the day, I stole from donation boxes and the days turned to weeks until one day, there was a suspicious knock on the door.

"Room service." A manly voice said attempting to sound feminine. *I didn't order room service. I don't even think this motel does that!* I peeked in the peep hole and noticed a familiar black suit. My heart started pounding in my chest and I reached over for a lamp, unplugging the chord. I then opened the locks and bolts before I hid behind the door as it opened. When the suited man cocked his silencer, I broke the lamp on his head. His tall body thudded on the ground and he dropped his gun. I quickly grabbed it before he could and he charged toward me like a tank. I pulled the trigger and my heart stopped. He fell down to his knees and gasped his last breath in astonishment. I then started to hyperventilate and the hyperventilation woke me right up. *I've never had a dream like that... so real, vivid.*

I tried to get up and grabbed my leg where the pain was insupportable. Then I looked to the coffee table and noticed a full glass of water and my pills. I reached for them and swallowed two pills, knowing my tolerance was too high. I lay back down on the bed and as my head hit the pillow, I started thinking about how if it wasn't for that horrid day, I could be a doctor or a lawyer by now. Instead, killing is all I've been able to do. *I'm an eighth grade drop-out.*

I woke up to the smell of coffee. *Damn, my leg kills.* I stood up trying to ignore the excruciating pain, I smiled at Carmen in the kitchen, and went straight to the bathroom; nature called. When I got out, Snoopy was sitting by the door wagging his tail. I bent over to pick him up immediately regretting my decision, but it was too late to stop half way. I picked him up and placed him under my armpit. I could still feel the movement of his wagging tail. *I really like puppy breath.* His panting won't be as pleasant when he's older, I'm sure. I stood by the kitchen counter just watching Carmen creating another masterpiece of edible proportions.

"Good morning, cripple." She jokingly said as she stirred the eggs on the frying pan.

"Has this dog been walked yet?" I asked as I smiled.

"Not yet. I'm guessing that's why he was waiting for you by the bathroom."

"Damn, even when I'm hurt, I gotta walk the dog?"

"Just admit it, Marv... You totally love him." The smugness in her statement annoyed me.

"Where's the kid?" I deflected.

"She's still asleep. We were up really late watching movies."

"All right, I'll be right back." I said as I limped outside and down the stairs. It took me forever, but I managed. The Percocet seemed to call me out my name by the time we were going back to the loft. As I opened the door, Akemi stole a hug after she stole Snoopy.

"Breakfast is ready!" Carmen sang.

"It looks and smells amazing. I'm starved." I said with my empty stomach.

"Did mommy tell you about her new job?" Akemi chimed in. *Mommy? We're not in public... Is she just practicing again?*

"No. New job? Do tell." I said intrigued.

"Remember Ms. Margot's studio? The one I've been dying to buy?" Carmen's eyes sparkled as she spoke in excitement.

"Yeah..."

"Well, I went to show Akemi the studio. You know I can't show the studio without dancing at least one song of belly dance... so I danced. Akemi started copying me, and I corrected her mistakes which turned into me sort of teaching her.

"Then, while I was teaching her, something amazing happened. People started coming in from the street and my class started to grow and multiply before my eyes. Ms. Margot saw all of this and offered me a teaching position. We have a meeting to iron out all the details. With that in mind, do you remember the last time I showed you the studio?" *She's about to ask for a favor...*

"Yeah..." I speculated.

"Remember how dirty and dusty it was?" She was smiling as she spoke.

"It basically smells like pee and mold. It's disgusting." Akemi said as she scrunched up her face.

"Pee and mold, huh?" I took a second to evaluate the situation and wondered why this all came out of nowhere, "So, how can you take all this on with the new promotion?" My eyebrows contracted closer together in confusion. Akemi looked at Carmen and Carmen looked uncomfortable.

"What are you guys not telling me?" I asked the room while glances were being exchanged.

"Hector fired me." Carmen finally admitted. I dropped my fork.

"Why?" I asked.

"Because he doesn't approve of working mothers." Carmen said making Akemi's body seem smaller as she slumped over the table.

"But that's ridiculous. You're not a working mother." I chuckled.

"She's my mommy and she works... If you put the two together, you get a working mother. Duh." Akemi perked up a bit, but still looked funny.

110

"Akemi—Keiko—You know this situation is just temporary, right?" I asked making me feel like a world class asshole.

"What do you mean?" She innocently asked.

"Well, you're not—"

"Marvin, can I talk to you alone for a minute?" Carmen firmly cut me off.

"Sure..." We walked outside and closed the door while Akemi stayed inside with Snoopy eating.

"Why are you trying to mess everything up?!" Carmen lost it.

"I'm not messing anything up. You're not her mother, Carmen. It's beyond ridiculous to lose a job under false pretenses." I said feeling like a bigger asshole.

"Don't you think I'd rather teach than dance for dirty old men undressing me with their eyes?" She hit a nerve, and rendered me speechless.

"I *am* her mother now and there is nothing temporary about this situation. The papers back me up on this, thank you for making that possible, but if you expect me to get rid of that wonderful little girl when this whole mess is straightened out... Well, it just goes to show that you just don't know me at all!"

"So you're just gonna keep her? What about the dog? Are we just supposed to be one big happy family now?" I sarcastically asked making my true wishes...

"Yes, Akemi, Snoopy, and I are a family," Her eyes started to water up and I knew I hurt her again like the piece of shit I am. *Fuck*, "As soon as you take care of Bram, we'll be out of your hair." Carmen looked down at her left hand and pulled the rings off her finger. *Stupid! Would I have said anything if I had noticed she was wearing the rings? Did she put them back on because of last night? Fuck!* The tears streaked down her face beautifully and the pain it portrayed was intolerable. She gently grabbed my hand and put it face up before she placed both rings on the palm of my hand. *Why is my heart breaking if I'm the one that's to blame?* She closed the door and with it, the opportunity for us to work things out shut.

I couldn't bring myself to walk back inside. My head was spinning. My heart felt like it ripped through my ribcage and fell down on the floor. As my heart looked up at me, now beating slowly, I punched the wall of the hallway with the hand that was holding the rings. *Why did I do this? Why did I not notice the rings back on her hand? Ugh, I despise myself for this!*

I walked back inside knowing that things would never be the same again. I right away noticed that the girls were packed and ready to leave. Carmen couldn't bring herself to look at me as she walked out of the

111

door. Akemi hugged me and I actually kneeled down to hug her back, fighting the tears. Holding her tiny body against mine, I admitted to myself that I loved her. It was the kind of love that I never thought I'd feel again; after the loss Carmen and I endured separately, but together nonetheless.

"Things will work out, Mr. Marvin. You'll see..." Akemi touched my face, picked Snoopy up, and left. With the light click of the door closing, I held the bridge of my nose with shaky hands. Then I felt the deserved pain as I got up and walked to the couch bed. I swallowed three pills this time. I held Carmen's rings with my left hand and involuntarily started to cry. These tears were full of reasons: Carmen, Akemi, my parents, Julianni, and even Snoopy... My eyelids started getting heavy while the wetness of the tears dried where they were. I pictured the girls with the fleabag and finally faded into the darkness of sleep.

Twenty-One: Carmen

"Mommy, he loves you. Any dumb ol' person can see that." Akemi said trying to comfort me without success.

"Sometimes, love just isn't enough, hija." I replied as I wiped my tears away with the sleeve of my jacket.

"But what about that song, All You Need Is Love?" She argued. *Maybe the debating team would be something she could be good at...*

"Honey, I don't really want to talk about this anymore today."

"Oh, O.K. Where are we going?"

"I was thinking that we could go to the studio again."

"Will Ms. Margot bake more cookies?"

"Maybe."

"They were so yummy in my tummy." She said as she rubbed her belly making me smile.

"Yes, they were. Make sure you tell her how much you liked them." We walked the rest of the way to the subway and took the Four. On the ride, I sent Nina a text saying that I would be at my studio and if she wanted to stop by, I would be happy to see her. We got out on our stop and walked to Ms. Margot's. Then we walked up her stairs and Akemi knocked on the door.

"Hello!" Ms. Margot practically screamed as she opened the door.

"Hi." We said in unison.

"Come in, come in." Ms. Margot pulled us in like we were Jack and Jill eating her gingerbread house.

"We were thinking of getting a head start on the cleaning." I mentioned.

"Splendid! I'll change and I'll join you."

"Oh, you don't have to do that." *What kind of person would I be if I encouraged an elderly woman to help us clean a big studio?*

"There's still plenty of elbow grease left in these old elbows." She yodeled as she disappeared into the long hallway. When she came back, she was dressed in some frumpy clothes. Then we got buckets of cleaning supplies, brooms, sponges, mops, and paper towels. We went downstairs and started to perform cleaning surgery on the studio while listening to music. Akemi danced as she cleaned just like me.

After the morning turned into the afternoon, we could see our reflections in the black marble floor and the reflective, un-foggy mirrors. The place smelled like lemon-lime and lavender. We even changed light bulbs and bought a new door that was more inviting. This was better than in my wildest dreams. I looked over at Akemi and she was laughing so hard at something Ms. Margot said. I smiled knowing that our lives are just beginning. We then started gathering the cleaning supplies to bring it back to Ms. Margot's place, when I saw Nina's reflection in the mirror. She was there with a man that looked familiar, but I couldn't think why.

"What's up, girl?" I asked as I started walking toward her.

"Nothing. Just replying your text message." Nina said half smiling. We hugged and it felt like we were friends again. Friends who hadn't seen each other in forever!

"Akemi, come here," I called out to her making her run toward us, "This is my best friend, Nina." I introduced the two main ladies in my life.

"Nice to meet you, Ms. Nina." Akemi politely said.

"Likewise. This is my friend, Jose." Nina introduced him and my jaw fell to the ground. *Jose?! Wow, he's come a long way from baggy jeans shorts and a wife-beater.* But here he is, standing there looking fine with a brown Armani suit. He smiled at me and I noticed I was staring.

"Nice to meet you, Mr. Jose." Akemi shook his hand.

"And everyone, this is Ms. Margot, my partner." I said filled with pride.

"Why, hello Nina and Jose, I apologize for my appearance." Ms. Margot shyly said as she brushed the fly away hairs with her fingers.

"Don't apologize. You look ravishing." Jose said full of charm. *What happened to the rude Puerto Rican I always refused to date?*

"We were gonna go grub out at Jose's restaurant. How about you guys join us?" Nina asked. *Did she say Jose's restaurant?*

"I'm starving! Can we go, Mommy?" Akemi asked in a pleading manner. I cringed when I felt Nina glare my way. I apologized with my eyes and mouthed the word "later." She nodded in agreement and smiled triumphantly.

"Oh, I've had enough excitement for one day..." Ms. Margot took a few steps back.

"No, Ms. Margot. You should come! We'll celebrate." I tried to talk her into it, but her mind was made up.

"Aw, my darlings, I must respectfully decline, but I will definitely take a rain-check." Akemi and I hugged her, and Nina and Jose shook her hand. We watched her get up safely to her apartment and I locked up the studio with my own set of keys.

"Your dream finally came true. I'm proud of you..." Nina said before she hugged me. Then we walked toward Jose, Akemi, and Snoopy who were waiting by a taxi Jose hailed. Jose took the front seat and the rest of us went in the backseat.

"Siestas De Estómago, please." Jose told the taxi driver where to go. I giggled at the title of his restaurant, Stomach Naps.

"We should probably go to my place first though, to drop off Snoopy." I commented.

"Oh, you can bring him," He winked, "I know the owner." I looked at Nina as if saying "Oh, my God!" and she looked back at me replying "I told you so." When we got to the restaurant, Jose paid the taxi not accepting anyone's contribution. As we walked inside, I immediately felt underdressed. Everyone was wearing cocktail attire except for Akemi and me. Jose led the way to a V.I.P. section in the back of the restaurant. *Wow, this is fancy...* I put my purse down on the table and started looking around at the table settings and décor.

"Jose, Carmen and I are going to the bathroom. Will you order for us and watch Akemi?" Nina said practically pulling my arm off as we rushed to the bathrooms without hearing Jose's response. I guess Nina knew he would say yes. As soon as we walked in the door, she locked it and I was trapped in there with desperate-for-girl-talk Nina.

"Mommy?" Nina's eyes were hungry for information. I took a deep breath and checked under every stall to make sure we were in fact alone. When I knew for sure the coast was clear, I took another deep breath.

"It's complicated." I quoted the king of complications.

"You've always told me everything and I've never given you a reason to not trust me with anything... you know I take secrets to my grave..." She broke down my walls. She is the one person that I can always count on, no matter what. Like let's say I pulled a bank-job and ran into some trouble, she would cover for me and never even ask for a cut of the money.

"I finally know what Marvin does for a living." I spilled my guts.

"Oh snap! What does he do??"

"He's a hit man."

"Nah ah, for real?! Like, he kills people for money?" Her voice sounded louder than it actually was, and I started to panic.

"Shh, I don't want anyone to hear us. Let's whisper."

"O.K., so where does the kid calling *you* mommy fit into all this?" She whispered.

"Marvin found her at a warehouse and then he discovered that her family was killed by another hit man... like someone from his past. And since he knows what this man is capable of, he took her in. We changed her name and forged some adoption papers so the lie would be legit---"

"But she's calling you mommy in a way that can't be just acting." Nina interrupted me.

"That's because, I'm her mommy now."

"Wow, that's amazing. I always knew you'd be a good mom and now it happened. This is your year."

"Thanks, I think so, too. Hey, I'm sorry. It was hell keeping all of this from you on the phone the other day."

"Then, why did you do it?"

"Does it really matter?"

"Not anymore, I guess. Just *don't* do it again, O.K.?"

"O.K."

"So, for the questions of the hour, drum roll please. Ba da ba da ba. Are you and Marvin back together?"

"Hell, no. And right now, I don't think we'll ever get back together. I seriously give up. I give up, Nina. It's totally over and done with." And I was surprised at how much I meant the words I said.

"Good, so what about Jose, huh? Can you believe he owns this restaurant now?"

"Yeah, that's insane. How did that happen?"

"I'm not sure, entirely, but the owner died and I think he left it for him in his will..."

"Yeah, that makes sense... cuz there's no way for a dishwasher to make his way up to owner... it's just not possible."

"You should give him a chance, though. He really is a good man." Nina made me raise my eyebrow.

"We'll see, Nina. Let's go eat. I'm so hungry that I can feel my body starting to eat me!" We walked back to the V.I.P. room with our friendship restored. When we got back, there was a wine bottle on the table along with an appetizer. We sat down on and Jose opened the wine. I reached for the appetizer; it was artichoke dip with bread. *Mm, so good.*

"So, Jose. I thought this was a Spanish restaurant because of the name... what's with all the Italian food?" I curiously asked.

"It used to be a Spanish restaurant when Paco owned it, but I was always more into Italian food and when I changed the menu, business started booming." Jose answered. During dinner, we all got caught up in each other's lives. I thought it was adorable how Akemi interacted with Jose. He was so attentive when she spoke, unlike Marvin. I looked at the corner and noticed Snoopy was eating some meat scraps from a silver dessert bowl which made me smile. Jose ordered the lobster ravioli for us all; they're one of the signature dishes. We ate in delight and ate tiramisu for dessert. *I was in Heaven!* When dinner was over, Jose wouldn't hear of us paying for our dinner. Nina didn't even try, though. I'm sure she abuses her free food privileges.

"Thank you for a lovely evening." I said as I extended my hand to shake his as we stood in front of the restaurant. He held my hand and pulled me close in order to get a hug. *He smelled so good!* His arms felt stronger than I remember and then I felt myself hugging him back. When the hug was over, I noticed Nina and Akemi looking at me which made me blush.

"I'm glad we got to see each other again, Carmen." He said still holding me by the waist with one arm.

"Yeah, me too." I said under my breath.

"Maybe we could do this again sometime, just you and I," He said as he handed me his card, "I hope you'll call this time." I took the card and slipped it in my purse.

"Yeah, I think I will. Have a good night." I said making him smile. Then I went up to Nina.

"You coming?" I asked.

"Nah, I'll stay here and girl-talk with Jose. I'm sure he's exploding with joy that you actually said you might call him!" Nina rolled her eyes and laughed before she hugged me.

"Bye, Mr. Jose. Bye, Ms. Nina!" Akemi said as she waved.

"Bye, baby girl!" Nina waved back. Jose didn't say anything, but he waved at Akemi while he smiled at me. As the taxi drove away, I smiled. *Me and Jose? It's a possibility... Nina will be so proud.*

Twenty-Two: Keiko/Akemi

Mommy dropped me off at Mr. Marvin's and I didn't understand why she couldn't spend the night here with us. Mr. Marvin was fast asleep, snoring up a storm, but it made me smile. I like that he snores. It makes me feel safe hearing him in the other room. I brushed my teeth and then I brushed Snoopy's. He didn't seem to understand that you can't swallow the toothpaste. Then we went to bed and fell asleep.

The next morning I woke up with Snoopy licking my face. I went to the bathroom and when I came out, Snoopy had peed on the floor. *Uh-oh.* I went in the kitchen, but the paper towels were too high for me to reach. I walked over to Mr. Marvin, who was in the same position he was in last night, and I remembered what he said about announcing myself before I came near him.

"Mr. Marvin! Snoopy did a boo-boo." I screamed five feet away from him. He slowly opened his eyes and then smiled when he looked at me.

"Akemi, you're home." He said making me giggle.

"Of course I'm home. Where else would I be?" He limped over to me and picked me up, hugging me in the process. *He's never done this before, but I like it!* Then, he stepped on Snoopy's pee.

"Aw, Snoopy!" He put me down and started cleaning things up. He took Snoopy outside while I started watching morning cartoons on Mr. Marvin's bed. It was still warm and cozy; it smelled like him. When they got back, Snoopy jumped up and lied on the bed beside me.

"You hungry, kid?" Mr. Marvin asked.

"Yes, I am." I replied.

"Today, we're eating cereal. I don't feel like cooking."

"Cereal!!" I cheered.

"Come on over to the table. What did you and *mommy* do yesterday?" He said the word mommy in a funny tone...

"We went to the studio, cleaned it with Ms. Margot, we met Mr. Jose and Ms. Nina and they took us out to dinner, but Ms. Margot took a rain-check. Then we took a taxi back here."

"Jose, huh?" He asked as he served me some cereal and poured the milk, "Was he in the taxi when mommy dropped you off?"

"No."

"She went home alone?"

"Yep."

"What restaurant did you eat at?"

"Stomach Naps."

"Oh, is Jose still washing dishes there?" He seemed amused.

"No, he owns it now." His amusement went away.

"Oh."

"Yeah, he's nice and funny. He made mommy laugh a lot."

"More than I make her laugh?" He looked confused and distraught.

"Kind of, but it was a different laugh."

"Ah, so it was a fake kind of laugh?"

"No, not fake. Just different. Mr. Marvin, can I ask you a question?"

"What?"

"Are you jealous?"

"Me? No. Carmen can do whatever she wants. I'm just curious about how you spent your day, that's all."

"I don't know, it kind of sounds like you're jealous. I mean, all the components are there..."

"All the components, huh?" He smiled and his smile faded away really fast when he looked at the clock, "Um, we should hurry, kiddo. Get ready as fast as you can, O.K.?" He slurped the rest of his milk and limped up the stairs. As I got ready, I wondered if Mommy will date Jose. *I hope she doesn't...*

"You ready?" He asked looking at his watch. I nodded and kissed Snoopy goodbye before we started walking toward school.

"So, if you had to pick a better looking dude, it would be me, right?" Mr. Marvin asked as we walked. Then the sidewalk ended and I was about to start holding my own hand to cross the road when he unexpectedly took my hand and held it as we crossed the street.

"Are you feeling O.K.?" I asked him once we reached the next sidewalk.

"My leg kind of hurts, but overall I'm all right."

"No, I asked if you're O.K. because you held my hand... You never hold my hand."

"Don't let it get to your head." He smiled and winked at me as he held my hand again at the next intersection.

"What happened to your leg anyways?" I asked.

"I just got hurt at work."

"What do you do?"

"Hm, Akemi, that's a hard question for me to answer." He said being honest, but it triggered a flashback of my father never telling me what he does.

"Figures." I said letting go of his hand and holding my own.

"Hey, what's the matter?"

"I'm sick of not knowing what my father does for a living. Not that you're my father, or anything, but why can't you just tell me?!" I was so angry, but the tears started coming down my face and I couldn't make them stop. I ran toward the church of the school and sat on one of the pews toward the back. Mr. Marvin took a while to get here because of his leg, but then he sat down next to me.

"Akemi, I wasn't aware that your father never told you what he did for a living..."

"Why do you care?" I said turning my head away from him.

"I care... because... we're friends, remember?"

"If we're friends, then just tell me. Friends don't keep things from each other." I turned my head to look at him and I could tell he was having an internal conflict. There was a long pause and he finally broke it.

"I don't want you to be angry with me—"

"Whatever!" I cut him off knowing he wasn't going to tell me.

"No, Akemi, listen. I promise that I will tell you someday. I just feel like you might be too young to hear this." His words were sincere and his eyes were not lying to me like daddy's did.

"When will I be old enough?" He pondered and then lit up like the answer was a light bulb.

"When you turn fourteen... that's when we'll talk."

"Fourteen? Why fourteen?"

"I'll tell you that reason then, too. Scout's honor." He said as he raised his right hand and made a "v" with his index and middle finger.

"Scout's honor doesn't really work for me. How about pinky promise?" I extended my pinky and he did the same. As our pinkies joined and intertwined, I knew I could trust him completely.

"Pinky swear." He said before he let go. I hugged him and he hugged me back like before. His chest felt hard against my face, but I didn't mind.

"Who are my choices?" I asked while we still hugged each other.

"Choices?" I heard the confusion in his voice.

"Earlier you asked me to pick the best looking dude… who are my choices?"

"Oh, er—Jose or me?" He was almost ashamed to ask, but I pushed myself off from his chest and stood on the church pew so I would be as tall as him. Then I put both my hands on his face and looked serious.

"Yeah right, you're not jealous!" I broke a smile as I giggled.

"Oh, am I jealous? Huh? Huh?" He picked me up like before and started tickling me until I couldn't breathe anymore from laughing so much. He finally put me down and we started walking to the school entrance.

"Are you picking me up after school?" I asked hoping that he would. *I like the new Mr. Marvin.*

"Either me or mommy will be here." He replied smiling with his big blue eyes.

"Hey," I said as I pulled him closer like I had a secret. He leaned close as I spoke into his ear, "I would pick you." I said making him smile before I walked into the school, excited about what Sister Bandeau would be teaching us today. When I got to class, Paula was already there reading a book. I took my seat next to her and took out my math notebook. Then I figured out how many years until my fourteenth birthday. *Six years? That's doable…*

Twenty-Three: Marvin

As soon as Akemi was out of my line of sight, I took out my phone along with Bram's business card and started dialing as I limped back to the loft. I knew walking would help me heal faster. *Pain is just weakness leaving the body...* The phone rang twice and then the female machine voice explained that he was in an out of service area. The moment I hung up the phone, it rang. I suspiciously looked at the caller ID only to find that it was Carmen.

"Yeah?" I clearly didn't want to speak to her.

"Hey, I was just calling to see if Akemi made it to school O.K." She questioned my capacity.

"Yeah, much to your surprise, I can handle things without you." I bickered like wife.

"What crawled up your ass and died?"

"Are you picking her up after school or am I?" I ignored her previous question.

"Why don't you just do it since you can handle it without me?"

"Big plans tonight?" My tone darkened and I realized that I resented her seeing Jose.

"Yeah, actually. I have my first ballroom class tonight."

"Yeah, I'm *sure* all you're doing tonight is teaching. Just make sure you give your *daughter* a call before you fornicate the night away." I hung up pissed as hell. *She doesn't even have the decency to tell me she's with Jose? I have to find out from Akemi? This is bullshit. I need to shake this off.* I pressed redial on Bram's number, and this time I got through to the voicemail.

"You've reached, Bram. I regret to inform you that I will be in

Japan for business until further notice. Leave a message after the tone stating your business and if it sparks any interest, your call will be returned. Beep." His voice sounded as arrogant as I remember. *Japan? Shit... ten to one he's there killing off the rest of Akemi's family thinking she fled there. What a disaster! Now she really will be an orphan. At least she's safe with me. We should keep her. I mean, she's settled now... Did I just say "we"? Maybe I should just forge up the papers so Carmen and Jose can have her. Would Akemi rather be with them? What will happen to me?*

I looked through my contact list on my phone, and I stopped at Milly's name; the cute girl from McDonald's that wrote her name on my receipt, hearting the dot of the "i." I gave some serious thought about calling it, but for once I was honest with myself. Now that Julianni is burning in the pits of hell, I'm ready to commit. *Why else would I not be calling sexy cashier, Milly? If Carmen knows me so well, why can't she see that I'm different now?*

When I got home, Snoopy was humping Akemi's princess pillow. *That's wrong on so many levels...* I logged on my laptop as I sat on the dinner table. I searched for a good vet, because this humping thing has got to go. I called around until I felt trust in the person that was answering my questions about neutering.

"You know what, Sir? We actually have a free slot tomorrow at ten if you wanted me to slip you in..." The nice vet technician mentioned.

"O.K., yeah, I'll take it." *I can drop off Akemi at school in the morning and take a taxi to the vet.*

"Great! Remember; don't feed your dog anything after nine PM."

"All right, see ya tomorrow," I hung up before hearing a response, "You're getting your balls chopped off tomorrow, buddy. Better enjoy them as much as you can today..." I said as I picked him up and gave him one of my feather pillows while I hid Akemi's pillow from him. He commenced humping like a marathoner. *Poor chap has no idea the thunder of pain that's coming along with a side dish of humiliation.* I gimped over to the couch, that was still open like a bed, clicked on the T.V., programmed my cell phone alarm to wake me up at two, took two more pain pills chewing them for the effects to be faster, and watched ESPN until the pills worked the way they were supposed to. *Ah, sweet Percocet...*

Twenty-Four: Carmen

"Girl, I got *nothing* to wear tonight!" I frantically said to Nina, who was sitting on the couch not helping me at all.

"You have tons of clothes, babe. Plus, I thought you said he was just taking you out for coffee after your ballroom class." Nina sedately said while looking at her nails.

"He is, but shouldn't I look nice?"

"He'd think you look good with a dirty dish towel, if you wore it."

"Shut up." I slightly blushed, turning around to face my closet before she noticed. I picked up a black leotard with a pretty "v" back along with a red dance skirt. *Yes, this will look good in and out of the studio.*

"With or without tights?" I asked as I showed her my outfit.

"With. Oh, that will look sexy, girl. Ooh, we should do your hair in a bun and really embrace this tango theme you got goin' on."

"Will you help me?"

"Sure, put your clothes on first and then do your make-up."

"I'm gonna shower first!"

"Then I'm gonna take a nap!" I chuckled my way into the bathroom, which was occupied, so I waited by the door. That's when I detected how nervous I was. The butterflies were fluttering around my insides like alarmed bats in a cave. In a way, I like this feeling because I know I really am feeling Jose as opposed to just getting back at Marvin.

The bathroom door opened and it was my turn. I went inside and turned on the hot water, patiently waiting for it to heat up. The steam started to rise, and I turned on the cold water to balance out the two for the perfect temperature. I entered the shower and closed the curtains. The water washed over me and as I washed my hair, I wondered why I was always so against giving Jose a shot. *Am I so vapid as to not date a dishwasher? I must be, because I thought I just didn't like him because he was too into me... and now he likes me the same amount, but he wears Armani.*

I finished showering, hating myself. After the shower, I despised myself as I dried my body followed by loathing myself as I walked back to my apartment. Nina was loudly snoring on the couch, which she turned into a bed before she fell asleep. I rolled my eyes and took off my towel before I walked over to my vanity mirror where my strawberry shortcake scented lotion stood erect. I moisturized every inch of my body religiously and my mind wandered to the last time I was touched by someone else; Marvin has the most insatiable touch.

I put on tonight's perfect outfit and started working on my make-up. I decided I really would embrace the tango theme, and eye line my top lids with liquid eye liner. Before I woke Nina, I caught a glimpse of myself in the mirror. The glimpse turned into a stare. *Wow, I look good!* My confidence shot through the roof and my soul smiled. I walked toward Nina feeling like a top model, then; I lightly tapped her on the shoulder softly waking her up.

"All right, Mr. DeMille, I'm ready for my close up." I said instantly making her laugh.

"O.K., Norma Desmond. Go sit on the chair. Where's the leave in conditioner?" She got up unfazed by being woken up.

"Man, we haven't watched that in forever!" *And that's true. When was the last time I watched Sunset Blvd?*

"Maybe I'll watch it while you're on your date..." I observed a hint of resentment in her voice, but I didn't shed light on it.

"Did you find a new car to restore yet?" I asked as she pulled my hair so tight that the sides of my eyes started looking like Akemi's. At that moment, I missed her.

"Not yet, but I'm on the prowl." She said as she brushed my hair with a round brush and made the top look very straight. That's hard to do since my hair is extremely curly. Then she did the perfect bun. It's big since I have a lot of hair. *I am a Spanish vision; truly my mother's daughter.*

"You look a lot like your mom tonight, Carm." Nina's eyes almost looked misty.

"Thanks," I smiled, "For the compliment and the hair."

"You should get going. Teachers aren't supposed to make their students wait." Nina deflected as she always does when things are about to get too mushy. I kissed her on the cheek and ran out the door. When I got to the studio, my studious pupils were stretching.

"Hello, everyone." I proudly said as I walked toward the stereo taking my tango CD out of my purse and putting it into the CD player. I pressed play and the Tango melody filled the room making the air crisper somehow.

"Oh Carmen, are we doing the Tango tonight?" Giselle, my most eccentric student, asked barely containing the excitement.

"Yes, we are," They gathered around me, each standing by their corresponding partner, "Now, I strongly believe that you can't learn anything in the present if you don't look at the past. With that said, the Tango originated in lower class Buenos Aires. The story of the Tango, as it was told to me, is that it started with the gauchos of Argentina. You know how they wore chaps? As they rode horses all day, the chaps would harden from the sweat of the horse's body; that's why they walked kind of bow legged with their knees bent.

"At night, they would go to the night clubs and ask the local girls to dance... without showering or changing their dirty day clothes. Hence, the ladies started having to adapt." They were right on schedule with the confusion.

"Adapt?" Giselle tilted her head like a puppy does when it hears an unusual sound.

"Yes, adapt. On contrary to the norm, the ladies would dance in the crook of the man's arm, holding their heads back so they could touch them as minimally as possible and not having to smell them at the same time," I demonstrated the dance body position with Steve, Gloria's partner, "Her hand would be held low on his hip, ironically close to his pocket, looking for payment for dancing with him; because, who would dance with a dirty, stinky, dingy man for free?" Everyone laughed and I gave Steve back to Gloria.

"Yeah, it's funny, but doesn't it look beautiful? The dance spread throughout Europe in the 1900's. Originally made popular in New York in the winter of 1910 - 1911, Rudolph Valentino then made the Tango a hit in 1921. As time passed on and the music became more accepted, the dance was finally considered respectable even in Argentina.

"The Americanized version, in my opinion, is a combination of the best parts of each. The principals involved are the same for any good dancing. First, the dance must equate the music. Second, it must comprise the basic characteristic that differentiates it from other dances. Third, it must feel natural to do so. Paul, can I borrow you to demonstrate? Jill, I promise I'll give him right back." I said with a smile to the attentiveness of the room. Then I started using Paul as my own personal robot.

"Let's have the gentlemen's arms extend like so, and ladies, your hands go inside the gentlemen's. Men, your right hand will be placed softly on the women's shoulder blade and the women's arms on the man's arm. And this is the tango embrace. Paul, go try it with Jill." They all followed my directions, repeating it over and over again until I saw everyone doing the perfect Tango embrace.

"Who's ready for some steps?" Everyone chirped with enthusiasm. Though I was completely emerged into teaching my class, I couldn't help but wonder if my mom was proud of me. *I finally made it here... doing what I've always wanted to do.* Class always goes by so fast. I knew it was over when I saw Jose's reflection by the door holding a big bouquet of flowers in the mirrors. I smiled and stopped dictating the steps. Everyone stopped and looked at me like deer caught in headlights.

"Did you forget the steps?" Giselle was concerned as she asked.

"No, I just—"

"She just got a hot date and he's right there. Mm!" Felicia said in a ghetto manner making me blush as everyone turned to look at Jose; it didn't seem to frazzle him at all.

"Everyone, this is Jose." I sheepishly said to the group as my heart beat out of my chest.

"Hi, Jose." The entire room said.

"Hello everyone, I know you still have ten minutes left, and I had no intention of interrupting your class. Would you mind if I watched, though?" Jose considerately said.

"Why don't you dance with Carmen?" Giselle pushed me toward him. I blushed even harder and there was no way to hide it. Jose looked at me, put down the bouquet on top of the stereo, and extended his hand.

"Shall we?" His deep brown eyes blazed mine. The next track began and I started dictating the steps, but somewhere along the line, I stopped because Jose was leading me a different direction. Everyone crowded around us, but all I felt was the dance running through my veins. The fluidity of Jose's and mine movements became flawless. *Who knew Jose could dance? And ballroom nonetheless!* When the track regrettably ended, he dipped me and kissed right below my collarbone in the sexiest manner I've ever felt. *Whew, is it hot in here, or is it just me?!* Everyone clapped. Jose gently un-dipped me and joined in the applause. I didn't know what to do, so I curtseyed.

"All right, everyone. That's a wrap!" I ended another successful class. Some of the girls came up and hugged me. During each hug, they whispered in my ear commenting on Jose's hotness. I wouldn't reply, but I'd smile in agreement. When the class cleared out, I looked at Jose.

"Not too shabby..." I half complimented.

"You either. And here I thought you only belly danced." He

inquired.

"Nope, I don't discriminate. If it's danceable, I'm for it. Where did you learn to dance like this? You're incredible." I whole complimented...

"My mom, rest her soul, made us all take ballroom classes when we were younger. Now I wish I could thank her for it."

"Oh, I'm so sorry for your loss." He shook his head and smiled while moving his arm like a windshield wiper, wiping away my previous statement.

"I know we talked about getting some coffee, like a pre-date, but I'm starving." He admitted changing the semi-morbid subject.

"Actually, I am, too."

"So, why don't we go eat?"

"Good idea." I locked up the studio and we started walking. I looked at the time on my cell and decided to call Akemi before it was too late.

"Excuse-me, I gotta call Akemi for a minute..." I excused myself and started dialing. I dreaded hearing Marvin's full blown attitude, but it was inevitable.

"Yeah?" His tone was almost belligerent.

"I don't have time for this. Put Akemi on." I threw it back at his face. I heard him take a sharp breath, put the phone down, and tell Akemi to come to the phone. Then I heard her little running footsteps scale louder as she got closer to the phone.

"Hello?" Her angelic voice spoke into my ear.

"Hi, baby girl." I spoke happily into hers.

"Mommy!" She elatedly said making my heart skip a beat.

"How was your day?"

"It was fun. Me and Mr. Marvin are friends!"

"Were you not friends before?"

"He said we were, but I could tell he didn't really mean it all the way. But now he means it all the way!"

"Aw, that's good to hear." *Is he using the kid to get to me? He wouldn't sink that low, would he?*

"I miss you."

"I miss you, too, hija. How about tomorrow I pick you up from school and we have a girl's night?"

"Yay! Can Snoopy come?"

"Of course." I heard Marvin's voice in the background denying Snoopy privileges.

"Oh, Mr. Marvin says Snoopy can't come because he's getting his nuts cracked open and removed tomorrow."

"Akemi! Don't talk like that!" *That's the Marvin I know...*

"What? I'm just repeating what Mr. Marvin just said."

"But you're a smart, sophisticated girl. You know better than to talk like that."

"O.K." Her voice sounded lower and foiled.

"All right, hija. Good night and sleep with the angels."

"How do I do that?"

"You pray asking God for the angels to keep you safe..."

"Will I see them?"

"Hm, probably not, but I guarantee you'll feel them and sleep great."

"Will there be enough angels for you to sleep safe, too?"

"Yeah, there are millions and billions of angels in the world."

"Then, I'll pray for me, you, Mr. Marvin, Ms. Nina, and Mr. Jose to sleep with the angels tonight." I smiled.

"I'll see you tomorrow, baby cakes."

"Bye, mommy." The phone clicked and my smile remained as I put my phone back in my purse.

"Akemi is going to pray for you to sleep with the angels tonight." I marveled.

"She's a good kid." He smiled through his response.

"She's the best kid." I corrected.

"I don't mean to pry, but you and the father adopted her?"

"Yeah, and we are separated at the moment." *I could've said divorce, but for some reason I didn't.*

"I can't really say that I'm sorry..." He evinced as he kissed my hand and made me smile.

"Where are we going to eat?" I took back my hand shyly shifting the subject.

"I'm leaning toward sushi."

"I adore sushi."

"Sushi it is." We walked to the restaurant holding hands. At the restaurant we talked without any awkward pauses. It was the best conversation I've had in years. After dinner, we took a cab back to my place and he walked me up to my door. Up the stairs, I felt dizzy from my heart beating so fast pumping nervousness through my veins. *Is he going to try to kiss me? Do I want him to kiss me? Am I bad for wanting him to?*

"I had a lovely time tonight, Carmen." Jose said as I fished my keys out of the abyss of my purse.

"I did, too." At first, it was like I was avoiding the eye contact. He broke down my defenses when he took hold of my chin ever so gently, lifting my face up toward him. Our eyes finally connected and it was like I drew him in. When our lips touched, it was docile and velvety. *The perfect first kiss...*

"Goodnight." I said with a small voice while I unlocked the door and closed it, leaning on the other side almost floating with joy. Nina's snore was competing with my happiness in filling the room; the happiness won by a landslide. I removed my make-up in the kitchen sink and brushed my teeth before I changed into my pajamas and pushed Nina toward the right side of the bed so I could get some sleep, too.

"How was the date?" She said mid-snore.

"It was good." I said not revealing any details. She's too sleepy to remember anything and I don't want to have to tell it all again tomorrow. Soon after she changed position, she started breathing hard escalating toward a snore. I, on the other hand, just couldn't stop smiling.

Twenty-Five: Marvin

"Akemi, move it or lose it! If we don't leave in the next five minutes, Snoopy will miss his appointment!" I yelled still unable to process how we fell asleep without setting the alarm last night.

"I'm ready!" Akemi yelled back and we ran out the door. There was no time for walking today, so we got a taxi.

"Here, I grabbed you some pop tarts. And here's some lunch money." I recited as I handed her breakfast and a twenty.

"This is too much. Lunch is only four bucks."

"Just use the change with Carmen." *I cannot believe I'm taking her to school late; especially because I gave Carmen attitude about being able to handle it.* The taxi stopped, Akemi hugged me, she ran into the school, and I told the taxi driver to take me to Prescott Veterinary. We got there ten after ten.

"Good morning, Sir, how can I help you?" The cute woman behind the counter wearing pink medical scrubs asked.

"This is Snoopy and he's here to get fixed today. We're a little late..." I answered.

"Oh, it's no problem. I need you to fill out this paperwork." She handed me a clipboard with three forms. I put Snoopy, who was under my arms this whole time, on the counter and he laid his head on my left arm while I used my right hand to fill out the forms. When I was done, I started to pet him as he slept on my arm.

"Aw, how sweet is that?" Pink scrubs awed.

"I'm done with the paperwork." I averted.

"A vet technician will be right out."

"Thanks." I went to sit down on a chair, trying not to be gimp while I did it. Snoopy curled up on my lap and we patiently waited; something everyone does when medical care is involved.

"Snoopy and Marvin, I presume." A gorgeous brunette wearing blue scrubs that made her bluer eyes pop, said. When she walked toward me, the wind blew her straight hair and she looked modelesque.

"Right." I appreciated her beauty even more while I shook her silky hand.

"We should be done around four. Did you want me to call you when he's ready to be picked up?" Her lips moved pluperfect and her blue eyes were the definition of beauty; yet, I thought of Carmen and felt my heart break.

"Sure." I said as I handed Snoopy to her.

"He'll be fine, you know. There's no need to be sad, you're doing him a favor." She tried comforting me for the wrong reason.

"All right. Take good care of him." I uttered under my breath. As she started to walk away, he climbed on her shoulder and looked at me like I broke his heart. That kind of got to me and I had to get out of there. I rushed outside like I was running with the bulls. Right away, I knew the pressure had changed because of my rib radar which meant it would start raining very soon. Come to think of it, it smelled like rain, too. I decided to wait the rain out at the book store around the corner. There's a coffee shop inside of it, so maybe I'll eat some breakfast; being late isn't nutritious. *Who knows? Maybe I'll read a book. What's that one Carmen's always bugging me to read? The mystery? No. It's something hush-hush... The Secret!*

I walked in the book store through the coffee shop entrance. I ordered a blueberry muffin and a latte. While he prepared the latte and warmed up the muffin, I went to customer service to ask about The Secret. The clerk handed me a copy and I walked back to get my breakfast. I sat on a booth, sipped my perfectly made latte, ate a piece of my muffin, and started reading the back of the book. *The Secret by Rhonda Byrne...* The words sounded interesting and I've always been interested in philosophy, but when I was about to open the book to page one, the most horrific sight appeared right in front of me outside the glass wall. It was Carmen and Jose walking, holding hands, but that wasn't the worst part... he stopped her in my vantage point and had the audacity to kiss her.

My whole world came apart when I saw them kiss. My hands gave out and the book dropped on the floor, closing the many unread pages that I took as a metaphor to my and Carmen's relationship. *This feels like a bad dream. Wake up, Marvin. Wake up.* When the kiss was over,

Carmen looked deep in his eyes, smiling the way she used to look and smile at me after we kissed. *What's going on? Was it really that easy for her to replace me?* They started walking away and I felt a knife go through my heart when he put his arm around her waist. I put my elbows on the table and rested my heavy head on my sweaty palmed hands. *Nothing can describe the way I feel right now. I need to go hit something.*

I threw away my unfinished muffin and I downed the rest of my latte on the way to the gym. I didn't mind the raindrops falling on my clothes or on my skin. It was as if the sky was crying the tears that I wouldn't allow to come up to surface. When I got to the gym, Derek greeted me like he hadn't seen me for years. *Maybe it has been a few months...* I nodded at him and went to the locker room. The lingering sweat odor was all around me as I taped up my hands and changed into my work out clothes from my locker.

"How the hell have you been, stranger?!" Derek clearly needed friends.

"I've been." I could hear the melancholy in my voice, but I knew Derek wasn't that perceptive.

"I hear you, brother." He sympathized with something he will never have to feel. He looked like a monster. The last time I saw him, his muscles were much smaller, but I guess when you own a gym, things like that are inescapable.

"Does anyone wanna go a few rounds with me?"

"Didn't I notice you coming in with a bum leg?" *More perceptive than I gave him credit for...*

"It's nothing. I just *need* to be in that ring." The desperation in my voice was apparent.

"O.K., I'll ask around. It's good to see you, man."

"You too." We hugged each other the sideways half hug that men often do.

Derek came through for me and found me a real wild buck for me to break. Derek told us that there was to be no hitting faces and genitals, but that everything else was fair game. When I stepped into the ring, all my technique went away. The nagging pain in my leg diminished and I was ready to raise hell; anything to get my mind off Carmen. The bell rang and the fight started. In a weird way, I knew my subconscious wanted me to feel physical pain to divert from the emotional pain, but I didn't care. Each punch felt harder and harder, but I'd much rather feel this than feeling my heart shatter inside of me. Blow by blow, I felt myself fighting less and less. That's when Derek blew the whistle and the fight was over. My ribs felt bruised, but nowhere near my ego. Derek helped me walk to the locker room and the nagging leg pain came back full throttle. He sat me down on the bench in between the lockers and started un-taping my hands.

"What's going on with you, bro?" Derek asked. I could hear the genuine concern in his voice.

"Women." I muttered as I exhaled.

"Is there one woman in particular?" He chuckled, sitting beside me and rolling the tape into a ball of trash. I looked at him, but said nothing.

"I know it can't be Carmen. You guys are like peanut butter and jelly." My body contracted when I heard the name I was trying to avoid. He noticed.

"Look, whatever it is, it will get better. There's no use in getting your ass kicked over it. And you know, when I eat too many PB&Js in one week, I start craving fluffer-nutters. I get sick of those after like two days and then the PB&J tastes better than ever." I knew he meant well, but I found no comfort in his attempt. I squeezed his right shoulder in reassurance and appreciation, and then I walked toward the sauna.

As the sweat secreted from my pores, all I saw in the steam was Jose kissing Carmen... my Carmen. It sickened me how happy they were. Sure, I've cheated on her, but I never loved anyone other than her for a decade. *Why couldn't she just get even and cheat on me?* I remembered the first time Carmen told me Nina was trying to hook her up with Jose. She told me she could never see herself going out on a date with him. She also told me that he wasn't her type. *Bullshit!* Over the years, she would have a few run-ins with him because of Nina, but she would always say the same thing to me: "I ran into Jose today. Ugh." And then she would roll her eyes or convulse her body in disgust. It blows my mind that she is with him now.

After the sweat, I took a cold shower. As the cold water washed over my warm sweat, I lowered my head down so the water would cascade down my shoulder blades. The water made me reach a conclusion, nay, an epiphany! *Without Carmen, I'm not whole.* I turned off the water and fought the Goosebumps while I towel dried. Then I heard my cell phone. I rushed to it, but I was too late. *One missed call.* It was the vet place. I got dressed and listened to the message. Snoopy was ready for pick-up and the surgery went well. I thanked Derek for the day and walked like Dr. House without a cane toward the vet. *Maybe being home with my pooch will make me feel better and maybe when I feel better, I'll be able to think up a plan to get my sweet, caramel Carmen back...*

Twenty-Six: Bram

"What do you mean the family is dead?" I asked unable to comprehend.

"Someone killed them all, Bram. They're all dead. Julianni was tortured. He's missing a hand and a pinky, but the cause of death was the slit throat. Whoever did this was a professional. They didn't leave one trace of themselves at the scene." Lissandro, my personal assistant and bitch, said.

"I want you to personally check into this. Check if anyone put a hit on the family and make me a list of suspects who would be qualified to pull off a job of this magnitude. Call me as soon as you find anything; nothing's too small." *This reeks of Azrael.* He's had a grudge on Julianni since I met him. *You're breaking our deal, guy. Then again, I wouldn't mind carving up his face like a pumpkin like he did to me so many years ago...*

"Sure thing, boss." Lissandro said withdrawing me from the past.

"How are my girls?"

"They're fine. Your wife is baking for yet another bake sale, and your daughter is doing her homework. I'm getting that film developed from the underwater camera they used at your daughter's sleepover. They had such a good time! I'll overnight the doubles for you tonight."

"All right, Lissandro." I clicked the end call button while he was still speaking, but I reached my destination. Time is money. I parked the car and took out my silencer after I put on my alligator skin gloves. I walked in the door and went straight into the dining room where the family I came here to kill was eating dinner. *All together in one room? How convenient for me...*

Twenty-Seven: Carmen

Jose brought me back to the studio after lunch and Ms. Margot was sitting on the chair by the door. I know she saw me kissing him goodbye and for some reason I sensed a tone in her eyes as I walked toward her. *Did I do something wrong? Is she going to terminate the partnership already?* I swallowed hard and smiled.

"Did you have a nice lunch?" The tone was now in her voice.

"Yeah, I did. Did you eat?" I asked petrified.

"Yes, thank you for asking, but food is not what I wanted to talk to you about."

"Oh?" I pretended I couldn't foresee what's to come next. *Carmen, it's just not working out. It was good while it lasted—*

"Now I know I'm no kin to you, but I'm hoping we are at least friends..." *Sure, we're friends. We'd be besties if you weren't about to crush my short-lived dream!*

"Of course, we're friends. What's on your mind?" I asked as I pulled up a chair next to her and dropped my purse down on the floor between our chairs.

"I am wondering what happened with that chap, Marvin." *This is about Marvin? I didn't foresee that!*

"Marvin?" My head is still spinning from the shock.

"Yes, I see you with this new man and I wonder what happened to the old one. And, is it maybe, all happening too fast?" She almost sounded motherly. I felt a lump in my throat and suddenly became defensive.

"Marvin and I have been on and off for about ten years. He's let me down time and time again, and I just don't have the strength to go through it anymore. It might be moving a bit fast with Jose, but it just feels good. I deserve feeling good, don't I?" I demanded support.

"Of course you do, my dear, but may I share some of the wisdom I've accumulated over the years?" The defensiveness left my body when I saw her smile.

"Lay it on me."

"The heart never forgets a great love. And it just seems to me that ten years worth of loving won't be forgotten by a few good times with someone that came along at the right opportune time. Just make sure you won't regret it..."

"Why do I get the feeling you know exactly what I'm going through?"

"Because I do. You see, I had someone like your Marvin and I had him for fifteen years, on and off, as you said before," Her eyes looked beyond me and I knew she was somewhere else, "For some reason, whenever he started getting things right and doing right by me, he would disappear for a couple of days looking at the bottom of every bottle he could get his hands on. Sometimes he would even have relations with other women. When he would return, I could see the shame in his eyes, though he never apologized. It was almost as if he didn't feel like he deserved a love like ours.

"I finally gave up on him after fifteen years and married the first guy that asked. I liked him, sure, but now looking back I think I did it more out of spite though it didn't feel like it at the time. Two days after I got back from my honeymoon, I got a letter saying he was hit by a bus and didn't make it." Her grey eyes seemed to turn black from the pain, sorrow, and regret as she choked through her words.

"Oh, that's awful." My heart sank and my stomach turned. *I can't even imagine what it would feel like to lose Marvin.*

"Yes, awful it most certainly is," Her time traveling eyes were back with me; intention took the place of the pain, sorrow, and regret, "There isn't a day that passes by that I don't think of him and though the times we had only resembled a dysfunctional marriage, I miss it. I remember the good times and the bad times, but the good far outweigh the bad. This is why I feel the need to tell you and try to persuade you into not giving up on your great love, Marvin." Her old hands reached out and touched mine and I noticed tears were falling out of my eyes.

"Thanks for telling me your story..." I blurted out in between sobs.

"That's what friends are for." She said before she embraced me full of comfort and understanding. When the water works stopped, Ms. Margot went back to her place. I felt overwhelmed and distraught when my students started to arrive. The whole class was stretched and ready to dance when I pressed play on the stereo.

"Places, everyone. Places." I said as I took my position in front of the class. *Teaching will be my temporary escape from this erratic existence I call: my life.*

Twenty-Eight: Marvin

"You make the most incredible tacos." I said with my mouth full.

"Thanks. It's Mami's recipe." Carmen said while she brought eight more tacos to the table.

"Your mom must be some cook."

"She really is. Maybe someday you could come with me to visit her. I'm sure she would cook us up a feast..." I chewed in silence instead of acknowledging her hint.

"I remember back when I was little, she used to work three jobs to pay for my dance classes and my brother's art classes. What amazed me is that she always made it to my recitals and that my brother and I never missed a home cooked meal. I hope that when I have a family, I will be half the woman she is today." Her eyes sparkled as she spoke of her hero.

"You are already more than half the woman she is." I made her smile and she looked at me with love in her eyes. This made me need to abruptly get up, kiss her on the cheek, and lie about some bullshit meeting. I looked back at her as I exited her apartment and noticed how sad she seemed.

I woke up from a flashback dream wanting to slap myself in the face. *Wow, what an eye opener.* Carmen's put up with so much from me over the years... I hurt her countless time, over and over again. *Maybe things are better this way. Maybe the best thing I can do for her is let her go. Jose can't fuck this up worse than I did.* I leashed up Snoopy and we walked out the door. *I need to talk to Carmen.*

It was a long ride in the subway. A little girl sat beside me and I realized that I miss Akemi. She's only spent one night away from me, and I already miss her. If she was here, she would do something that would make me feel as if everything is all right. I'm glad she's coming back home with me tonight. I got off the subway and waved to the little girl. She smiled at me and waved back. As soon as I put Snoopy back on the ground, he pissed on a bush. I laughed and said good boy. He panted and wagged his tail. He looks like a flower ready for pollination with that round, plastic thing that prevents him from messing with his stitches.

We were almost up to Carmen's dance studio. I gimped in quietly with Snoopy under my arm and sat down near the stereo watching her teach her students. *She is really in her element here.* As they went through the last combination, she spotted me and smiled. I smiled back. Her students clapped loudly and hugged Carmen when the class was over. *She looks so happy; this is the way she always looked before I became a leech, sucking all her happiness away with my selfishness.* Though she was a few feet away from me, I could still feel her positive energy. When the studio became vacant, I put Snoopy down on the floor to wander and got up leaning on the wall for support.

"I thought 'those who can't do teach.'" I half-assed a compliment.

"I always hated that saying. It's kinda mean." She scrunched up her face as she spoke making me smile. My smiling face became solemn and serious as I exhaled in preparation to what I came to tell her.

"I came over to apologize for the attitude I've been giving you lately." Her mouth opened and looked like a snake hole.

"Yeah, I just found out about Jose and though I have no room to be jealous...I was insanely jealous." I replied to her facial expression.

"Oh, Akemi told you?" She said uneasy.

"She wasn't ratting you out or anything, but yes."

"I'm so sorry you found out that way."

"Hey, I'm the one that came here to apologize. Just let me do what I came here to do... please?"

"Oh, O.K." She was shocked but intrigued at the same time.

"Not only did I find out from Akemi, but I also saw you guys kissing in front of the bookstore I was in," She was about to interrupt me, "No, just let me finish. You guys looked really happy. I'm not saying that for you to feel sorry for me. I'm just saying that so I can gracefully bow out. You'll hear no more attitude from me.

"You are an amazing woman, Carm, and an unbelievable friend. All I want is for you to be happy and if this guy is making you as happy as I saw, who am I to stand in your way? I would still very much like to be your friend, and from now on, I will be the best friend anyone's ever had.

Would that be something that you'd be interested in?" Her eyes lit up and she jumped up at me throwing her arms around my neck.

"That's something I'm very interested in!" She squealed into my ear. My heart soared when I saw how happy I just made her.

"The only thing I ask is that Akemi be with me if he's—er-gonna spend the night." I gagged a little at the thought of them having sex, but I masked it with a smile.

"I can comply with that. Marvin, you just made my day!" She kissed me on the cheek and my instinct was yelling at me to kiss her, but I opted against it. I looked at my watch and came up with the perfect excuse to get out of here.

"Um, I gotta go pick up the kid. I'll see ya around, Carm." I ended the hug by kissing her forehead and picking Snoopy up. I paced on the sidewalk and made my way toward Akemi's school with Snoopy under my armpit. *I did the right thing.* I remember once my father told me that you should set them free, and if it's meant to be, they will come back. I set Carmen free and now I just have to wait and see if we're meant to be the way I think we are; however long the wait might be...

Twenty-Nine: Carmen

"Hello?" I answered my cell phone.

"Hi, sweetie, I was just calling to see if you wanted to go to a restaurant opening with me tonight." Jose sweetly asked.

"Sure, that sounds great. What do I have to wear?"

"I actually bought you a dress and it should be delivered at the studio sometime soon."

"What if I had said no?"

"Then you would still have a brand new dress. I saw it at a window display near my place and I thought it would look great on you."

"Aw..."

"Aw," He kind of mocked me, "I gotta get going, though. I'll pick you up around nine."

"O.K., see you then!" We barely hung up the phone and the delivery guy arrived. I signed for the most beautiful box I'd ever seen and opened it up. *It was a strapless yellow dress that was so me!* My mouth opened when I took it out of the box and saw how the fabric flowed. I put it in front of me facing the mirror to picture how it will look when it's on. I put the dress back in the box, still feeling the fabric as I dialed Jose's number.

"Hello?" Jose answered.

"I know you can't talk, but I just wanted to tell you how much I love it!"

"I'm glad. See you tonight, bonita." I was smiling so big that I didn't mind the fact that he kind of hung up on me. Then, out of nowhere, Marvin's face popped in my head. In my mind he looked much like he did today when he surprised me with maturity; his dark roots were showing since it's been a while from the last time he dyed his hair blonde, and his demeanor felt different. I couldn't put my finger on it, but I knew something had changed and I'm not sure if it changed for the better yet.

I picked up my dress box, turned off the lights and stereo, locked up the studio, and banged three times on the pipe so Ms. Margot would know I was leaving. She popped her head out the window and waved as I hailed a taxi and told him to drive me to the spa where Nina and I have appointments for manis and pedis. Nina was waiting by the front and opened my door when the cab stopped. I paid him and got out. Nina's eyes bugged out at the sight of my big box.

"What's in the box?" She curiously asked.

"Only the best dress I own!" I screeched.

"Oh, the red one? Did you have it dry cleaned or something?" Her curiosity dimmed a little.

"No, Jose bought me this for the restaurant opening we're going to tonight." Her curiosity sparked back up.

"Is that right? Well, open it up! Don't I get a peek?"

"I'll show you in the spa. I don't wanna get it dirty." We walked into the spa and put the box on top of the magazines on the table in the waiting room. Nina, the receptionist, and I fawned over the dress and both of them told me how lucky I am to have a man like Jose. Then we checked in. Nina and I went in the back and got lockers for our stuff. In the lockers, were our robes and flip flops to wear while we were getting our services. Now, I don't understand why we need to get naked to get manicures and pedicures, but whatever. We were then brought over to the massage chairs where they had put purple salts that smelled like lavender in the water in front of the chair. We sat next to each other and moaned when we put our feet in the perfectly temperatured water.

"So, after we're done here we gotta go to your place to get you smokin' hot for your date!" Nina excitedly said almost yelling.

"I know! Are you gonna help with my hair?" I asked knowing she would insist anyways.

"Is the sun dying?" *What?*

"I don't know...is it?"

"The sun is a star, isn't it? And stars die...so, yeah it's dying," She looked at me defeated and confused, "That didn't work out like I planned. You know how someone asks a question and then someone else asks a rhetorical question with an obvious answer that answers the question the other person asked?"

"Oh like: 'Will you help me with my hair?' and 'Does it rain in Seattle?'"

"Exactly." We laughed.

"So, guess what?" I asked.

"What?" She asked back.

"Marvin found out from Akemi that I'm seeing Jose."

"No! How did that go?"

"Well, he was giving me attitude for a while but today he came to the studio and told me that he's sorry for giving me the 'tude and that all he wants is for me to be happy. And oh!"

"What?!"

"He saw me kissing Jose in front of a bookstore and he said he could tell I was happy with him, so he thinks he should bow down and just be there for me always as a friend. Isn't that so nice of him?"

"Yeah, it's *really* nice of him... I guess you guys really *are* over. Did that kill you?"

"No, it moved me."

"Wow! Then let me be the first to congratulate you in growing up."

"Thanks, it felt good."

"Hey, what's gonna happen to the kid if you and Jose get married?"

"Married? Oh, I am so far from that right now, it's not even funny."

"Got it, moving on."

"Hey, quick question. Why haven't you gotten with Jose after all these years? Like, is there a reason you were always pushing him off on me?" Nina looked at me drenched with apprehension.

"Um, you know when you land in the friend zone too quick?" She confessed.

"Oh." *Damn, I must be a horrible friend. How did I never notice the way she always dresses up when she sees him? Or the way she smiles when she sees his name on the caller ID?*

"Oh, I'm totally happy for you guys though! So don't even try to throw guilt or pity my way. I kinda have a crush on his meat guy, anyways."

"Nina! Why haven't you told me? I'm sure we could hook you up!"

"I'm not ready for a hook up yet. I'm only gonna flirt with my body language for now..."

We talked for the remainder of the mani/pedis. *I'm gonna keep a look out for the meat guy next time I'm at Jose's restaurant. I need to see if I approve.* After the treatments, we got dressed and checked out. Then we took a Nina's car back to my place. She had another ticket on her windshield. *What else is new?* I don't even say anything anymore. There's no point to it. I do think someday she's going to have a warrant out for her arrest! As soon as we got to my place, I got in the bathroom to bathe. Nina was heating up the straightening iron and getting out the hair supplies she was going to use. In the shower, I started getting butterflies. A restaurant opening gets so much attention that there is always like a red carpet scene before you get in filled with photographers and paparazzi. After the shower, I went straight back to my apartment and started the moisturizing process.

"What time is he coming?" Nina asked wondering if we were scrunched for time.

"He said he's picking me up around nine." Her eyes bugged out and I knew she was gonna have to hurry.

"If there isn't enough time, I can just wear it curly." I tried making things easier on her.

"No, there's time. I'm a magician, remember? Just do your make up while I do your hair and it will be O.K." I sat down in front of my vanity mirror and as I did my make-up, she did my hair. It's amazing to watch her work. First, she blow dries small amounts of hair with a round brush, and then she runs the straightening iron through it once making it perfectly straight. My hair is very curly and very long, so for her to do it less than forty-five minutes shows impeccable skills.

"So, have you and Jose...you know?" She asked as she worked her one woman salon.

"Nina! We just started dating; do you think I'm a tramp?"

"No, it's just that with Marvin..." she hinted at my "one night stand."

"Marvin doesn't count. You've known me longer than the whole fluke that was Marvin."

"A fluke that lasted ten years?" She raised one eyebrow and looked at my reflection in the mirror.

"Do you think I'm making a mistake, too? I'm getting this from all angles! I thought you of all people would be happy that I was with Jose!"

"Carmen, I am happy. The only thing I worry is that all your feelings for Marvin aren't resolved and that you'll break Jose's heart. And that wouldn't be fair for him." As she finished saying this, my mouth seemed to glue itself shut. I didn't have a reply because she's right. My feelings are nowhere near resolved. I like Jose and I could possibly love him in the far, far future, but the truth of the matter is that I'm in love with Marvin still... *What am I doing? Should I just end this sort of fling I got going on with Jose and not give up on Marvin like Ms. Margot advised? There is something different about him, right? Or am I seeing things because I've wanted it for so long?* Nina finished my hair fifteen minutes after I finished my make-up. It looked like movie star hair! I quickly put on my dress and shoes and immediately felt like a princess.

"You look beautiful." Nina stated making me smile.

"Thank you for doing my hair and making me beautiful!" We hugged and then heard the knock on the door. I motioned for Nina to answer it for me while I changed purses. She opened the door, and my prince walked in. *He was wearing a tux!*

"Are you sure you don't wanna come? There's gonna be lots of rich, single guys there tonight." Jose spoke to Nina not looking my direction.

"Yeah, I'm sure. You kids have fun." She patted his arm and I noticed the look. I know that look all too well because it's the same look I often gave Marvin when he left me for bigger and better things. *Is this a sign that maybe I shouldn't go tonight? I can't contribute to hurting Nina like this or any other way. She's my best friend.*

"Wow! You make that dress come alive!" His eyes looked me up and down before he tried to kiss me on the lips, but I turned my cheek and got kissed there. He looked confused, but he was a gentleman about it.

"Hey Nina, you should come tonight. We can wait for you to get ready real quick." I tried to save Nina from hurt, but it was no use. Even if she went, I would still be with the man she loves.

"When have you ever seen me get ready quick? Plus, I have a date with my TiVo tonight." She joked, but I knew better.

"I don't have to go..." I semi-whispered, looking her dead in the eyes.

"Go." She firmly whispered back with fire in her eyes. I realized this wasn't the time or place for this type of selfless act and took Jose by the arm. Nina watched us walk away and I felt so bad. When we got downstairs, there was a white limo waiting for us. I tucked the bad feelings away and decided to get swept away into the night. Jose opened the door and put his hand out to help me get in the limo. I lifted my dress before I took his hand and stepped in. He got in and shut the door. The limo driver was wearing those driver's hats that you think they only wear in movies. We were in motion and I was ecstatic!

"Care for some champagne?" He asked motioning toward the limo's bar where a bottle of champagne was chilled with ice in a silver bucket.

"I'd love some." I said smiling. He popped the champagne and served it in the two glasses that were by the bucket. My instinct almost made me take the cork to start a Jose box, when he:

"I'd like to make a toast to your beauty, your soul, and your persona. To you, Carmen." *Does he ever say the wrong thing?* I blushed and we clinked our glasses together before we sipped the sweet champagne. It felt cold as it ran down my throat and into my stomach. The limo slowed down and I looked out the window. This is so much more than I could ever imagine. I felt like I was going to a movie premier, not a restaurant opening! There are lights and cameras everywhere, not to mention the people crowding around the ropes wanting to get in. He got out of the limo first and then helped me out.

"Jose, I don't fit in there!" I said all nervous.

"Sure you do! You fit in right here." He said as he put his arm around my waist and pulled me close as we walked the red carpet path inside the restaurant. I don't know how many people took our pictures, but I made sure I was smiling the whole time. Inside, we got seated right away. Everyone knew Jose and I was surprised at how he didn't forget to introduce me to everyone; not even once.

"I hope you brought your appetite tonight. We're trying portions of every dish on the menu." Jose said as he placed his napkin on his lap. Course by course, the waiters brought us the food. Each plate had its own wine that went with it and each was more delicious than the next. Then, for the desserts they served tiny portions into espresso cups. *Tasting them, I was in seventh heaven, mm.* When it was all over and done with, I was so full I couldn't even stand up if I wanted to. Jose went to the kitchen to compliment the chef which happened to be his cousin. As I sat there smiling, my phone rang.

"Hello?" I answered without looking at the caller ID.

"Mommy?" My angel softly spoke into my ear.

"Hija, what are you still doing awake?"

"I can't sleep until you say goodnight..."

"Oh, I didn't know that or I would've called you a long time ago. Goodnight and sweet dreams, my adorable little girl." *I swear I heard her smile...*

"Mommy?" Her voice sounded a bit shaky.

"Yes?" I curiously asked.

"I...love...you..." She managed to get out with pausing increments. My heart started to soar and my soul smiled.

"I love you, too. I'll see you tomorrow, babe." We hung up and minutes later, Jose came back wearing a facial expression I've never seen on his face before.

"I'm gonna have to stay and help clean up, unfortunately. I'm also gonna have to help with the inventory and the books. My point is: my driver can take you home..." He looked down and kissed my hand. Most people had already left and the people that remained, looked like they were ready to go. My eyes were feeling heavy and wanted to close, so I didn't mind about leaving.

"O.K., sounds good to me." I responded. He helped me out of my chair, not because I needed it, but because he was a gentleman through and through. We walked to the limo, right away noticing the difference in activity from the photographers. The red carpet scene had died down, and I was relieved. *There was no way I could smile right now.* The limo driver got out to open my door, but Jose waved him off and did it himself.

"I had a lovely time with you tonight, Carmen." Jose said as he helped me in the limo.

"I did, too. Your cousin is an unbelievable chef."

"I'll make sure he gets the compliment." He kissed me and I don't know if it was because of all the eating, or the exhaustion, but I didn't feel any sparks... He slammed the door shut and pounded three times on the roof of the limo before we drove away.

"Ma'am, will I be driving you back to the same place I picked you up from?" The driver asked as he lowered the center glass, separating him from me.

"Yes, please." I said after yawning. He nodded once and rose up the glass between us again. I surrendered to the tiredness and melted into the seat as I fell asleep. In my dream, Marvin and I were lying on a picnic blanket gazing into each other's eyes. Wild flowers were all around us and the spring breeze cooled the sun's temperature bathing our skin.

"Ma'am, we have arrived." The driver pulled me from paradise.

"Oh! Thanks. You have yourself a good night." I said as I walked out the door that he had opened for me.

"You do the same, Ma'am." He said before he closed the door. *Marvin.* The stairs never felt so strenuous. The last step almost felt like an achievement. When I unlocked the door, Nina was sleeping on the bed. I was so tired that I didn't even take off my dress or shoes. I just plopped down beside her and hoped my dream would pick up right where I left off.

Thirty: Marvin

As I reached the school, I took my place among the mothers. One mother in particular took it upon herself to stare at me like a slab of meat. She looked me up and down, ripping my clothes off with her eyes. I uncomfortably smiled at her and picked Snoopy up to use as a shield. Smiling was the wrong response because she took it as an invitation to start up a conversation.

"No way you're the father to a child that goes here." She said with a sultry voice.

"Actually, I am." I replied.

"What grade?"

"Third...I think."

"You think?"

"Well, I know for a fact that she goes to school here... I'm just uncertain of the actual grade." *What kind of "father" doesn't know what grade his kid is in? I'd be a terrible father anyways... it's better for me to just be friends with Akemi.*

"If he or she is in the third grade, they probably know my Paula."

"Paula, huh? May I presume that you are Gina, then?" I remembered the background check I performed before Akemi's sleepover.

"Yes, I am. Akemi is yours? I just adored her! The girls had a lovely time."

"Good."

"They even played with the underwater camera in the pool." *Camera? Akemi can't be caught on film at this point in time! I knew this whole sleepover thing was a bad idea from the get-go.*

"They took pictures?" Though I was angry, furious, scared, and worried, I tried to sound nonchalant.

"Yeah, a whole roll!"

"I'd love to get doubles. Kids grow up so fast, you know. Maybe I could even chip in to get the film developed? Where do you get yours done?"

"Oh, I don't know. My husband's assistant gets these small things taken care of. I'll be sure to send you copies through Akemi."

"An assistant, huh? Your husband must be an important man. What does he do, if you don't mind me asking?" I investigated.

"Not at all, he is a business man specializing in trades worldwide. I just had a marvelous idea! Why don't you and Akemi join us this afternoon? We have a big pool that's rarely used..." *Perfect. While I'm at the house I could do some digging on the husband... the job description she gave was way too generic and vague. Plus, I need to figure out if Akemi's cover had been compromised.*

"That sounds lovely."

"This might sound silly now, but what is your name?"

"Marvin and this strapping young man, is Snoopy." She bypassed the pooch and focused solely on me.

"Marvin...what a manly name," She squeezed my biceps and came closer to me, "Now tell me, Marvin. Just between us, are you and Carla having problems?"

"Carmen." I corrected.

"Right, Carmen. I noticed both of you don't wear your rings..." *I'm sure she asked Carmen about this... How did she deal with the question? What did she say? She doesn't believe in separation or divorce so...*

"Oh, we don't need to wear our rings to remember our vows."

"What a shame." She flirtatiously winked at me as the bell rang. *This woman must cheat on her husband every chance she gets.*

"Daddy!" Akemi yelled as she ran toward me knowing full well that she needed to sell the fact that we were family in front of Gina.

"Hey kiddo, how was your day?" I asked as I picked her up mid-jump with my left arm while holding Snoopy with my right arm.

"It was good. So, you met Ms. Gina?"

"Yep. Hi, there. You must be Paula."

"Hi." Paula shyly said.

"So, Ms. Gina invited us to go swimming at her place." The girls looked at each other and squealed, jumping up and down holding hands. We got in Gina's car, and while she was driving, she'd look my direction and smile. *Women.* When we got to their house, I was stupefied. It was a mansion. *I'm having trouble believing that the husband is just a business man. This reeks of blood money.* The fact that there were no surveillance cameras intrigued me and backed up my theory. Gina parked the car in the circular driveway in front of the door, and a personal valet drove it off toward the garage. The girls went directly to the pool with Snoopy while Gina started giving me a private tour, hoping it would end in a seduction in the bedroom.

"And this is my husband's den..." She said as we walked into the den. The mahogany desk called out to me where the wedding photo zeroed me in. I picked the picture up and as my mind processed who the groom was, I was quickly transported into the past. The room around me became the organic grocery store I used to shop at sixteen years ago...

"Thanks, Rick! I'll see you next week," I said to my organic grocer after I paid for my groceries.

"All right, Marvin boy. Take care." He said smiling and reminding me of my late grandfather. As I was walking with my grocery bags down the sidewalk toward my place, a stupid guy booted one from me. He just grabbed one of my bags and started running for dear life. *What a joke!*

"Hey!" I yelled out after I started running after him. *This guy is extremely fast!* Luckily for me, he's stupid, because he got hit by a taxi when he was crossing the road. His body rolled off the mustard hood and on top of the grocery bag breaking the eggs with his fall.

"What the hell is wrong with you, kid?!" The taxi driver yelled out of his window.

"Nothing." The "kid" said as he got up from the asphalt. He looked about sixteen, just like me. He noticed that I caught up to him and flicked me off.

"How are you gonna give *me* the finger, guy?" I was appalled at the unprovoked insult.

"If you didn't chase me, this wouldn't have happened, asshole." He dared to say to me.

"Asshole? You just stole *my* groceries! And you do realize that organic food isn't cheap, right?"

"I know, but that's all I eat. If I carry your groceries back to your place for you, will you give me some dinner?" He asked. My mouth opened at the audacity that my ears just heard. *This guy stole my food, made me chase him, flipped me off, called me an asshole, and now he expects me to consider feeding him?* The thought angered me, but then the anger switched to understanding since two years ago I started fending for myself. I remembered what it was like to steal to eat and it softened my actions.

"O.K., if you carry my food to my place, I'll feed you." I said while I handed him my remainder two bags. He smiled at me and we started to walk together. Not even a minute of walking later, he turned around and started running away with my groceries. I felt surprised at first and then

I just laughed it off, unwilling to chase after him. That night, I ordered a pizza and the next morning, after finishing a job, I went back to the grocery store. Rick started ringing me up, looking confused.

"Didn't you buy all this stuff yesterday?" He finally asked before telling me the same total he told me yesterday.

"Yeah, some punk jumped me and stole all my food." I half lied.

"Oh, one of these days the cops will catch this fella. He's been terrorizing my customers for two weeks now. He must really like organic food or something. But enough about that, when am I gonna meet your parents?"

"Soon, Rick. Soon," I paid him and started walking out the door, "Hopefully I'll only see you *next* week." We chuckled. The minute I walked outside, I noticed the "kid" leaning up against the wall beside the exit doors.

"So, I feel kinda bad about yesterday..." He said as he walked beside me. I clenched the bags closer to my body and sighed.

"Don't, but you're high off your ass if you think you'll be able to do it again today." I said as I walked toward my place not really acknowledging him with eye contact.

"You're pretty fast. You could've caught me if you chased me yesterday. Plus, I was running with two full bags of groceries while you had nothing. Aerodynamically, you'd be faster." I stopped walking and faced him, still firmly holding onto my grocery bags.

"What do you want, guy?" I hissed.

"I followed you last night. Where are your parents?"

"What's it to you?"

"How do you do it?"

"Do what?"

"Live by yourself... afford all of those weapons." He lowered his head and looked at me through his brow line making him look deranged and somewhat evil. *I was cleaning my guns while I was watching T.V. last night, but how could he have seen that? I live on the eighth floor and I have no fire escape. Weren't my blinds closed?*

"We're one and the same, guy."

"What's it gonna take to ensure your silence?"

"Teach me what you know so I can get a place of my own and make enough money to stop stealing from civilians."

"Why would I do that?"

"Because, I can teach you things, too."

"Like what?" I scoffed.

"Like how to protect yourself... how to know when someone is running up behind you to take your groceries from you," He smiled as he paused for dramatic effect, "I can teach you things you can't do with your fancy guns..."

"How do you know I won't kill you in the middle of the night for causing me so much trouble?"

"Because, I am assuming you're smart. I can help you be better at what you do, and you can help me get what I need. Just give it a shot. What do you have to lose?" *My dignity, but what could I do?* I embraced the saying "keep your friends close, but your enemies closer," and we walked to my place.

Over the next six months, he crashed on my couch. I found out that he escaped an academy that trained boys into becoming killing machines for armies all over the world. He taught me all the combat stuff he knew and vice versa. I made him a fake I.D. that made him eighteen years of age. Another six months passed and we became friends. I even told him what Julianni did to my family and that I intended to kill him someday. For some reason, I felt as if he admired Julianni after I told him the story.

"How did you come up with your alias?" He asked me one night after dinner.

"After all that happened with me and my family, I started reading up on all kinds of religion. In ancient Muslim and Jewish belief, Azrael is the angel who parted the soul from the body at the moment of death. I just liked the way it sounded. And since I deal with death..." I replied and shrugged my shoulders.

"Have you ever heard of the raven that has historically stood for death and destruction?"

"No." I swallowed my food looking across the table at my roommate and friend thinking I don't know him at all.

"Well, I think my alias is going to be Bram." It gave me chills that he wanted to stand for death and destruction. A year after living together under the same roof, he asked for me to give him one of my clients, so he could start saving some money to get his own place. I unfortunately agreed. He was supposed to kill an abusive, cheating husband; only him. But when it came to doing his job, his training came to surface and he ended up killing the mark, the woman he was cheating on his wife with, and her two kids. Names can be too fitting, and in Bram's case... I kicked him out after that.

Fast forward to my eighteenth birthday: I went to a club and got hammered since my I.D. said I was twenty-one. I was seeing this girl named Olivia back then. She was an Italian beauty with short black hair and dark black eyes as big as black olives. We went back to my place and she was giving me my birthday present when she was shot in the back. The bullet went through her naked body and her blood sprayed my drunken face sobering me up. The ricochet hit the wall. She kissed me softly on the lips before her body gave out and death glared over her face. I looked up and I saw him. My blood boiled until I took the knife I had stashed under my mattress and lunged at him.

I was aiming for his throat, but the alcohol messed with my perception, making my knife go into his mouth instead. The blood gushed as I retrieved the knife back making him scream out in pain and drop his gun. I kicked the gun under the bed, where Olivia's body resided. Still naked, I jumped on top of him going in for the kill when I felt his knife go into my shoulder from the back. *He's stabbed me in the back physically and metaphorically. That wound meant business.* We wrestled on the floor wounding each other all over our bodies with our knives until we reached a point where each of us had our knives in the other's throats.

"Why, Bram?" I asked basking in betrayal.

"Julianni sent me, Az." He betrayed me even more; something I couldn't fathom though I was trying. I knew if I slit his throat, he would slit mine and that would be the end of me. *Before I die, I need to send Julianni off to hell.* I put my knife closer to his skin and he did the same.

"We're both pretty messed up here, Az. We should really reassess and look at what we're doing here. I know you don't want to die because of your little revenge and I don't want to die because there are just too many things I haven't experienced yet. Like the sex you were just having? I'm still a virgin here. Why don't we consider this a tie?" He said moving his bloody, ripped mouth.

"A tie?" I felt myself starting to fade out from blood loss, willing to listen to an alternative plan.

"Yeah, how about I go back to Julianni and tell him you're dead? You get yourself a new life and I'll go on with mine as if you are dead?" I considered what he was saying and then I felt him pull his knife away from my neck. I could kill him right then and there, but I didn't. Instead, I agreed to his terms and he left.

I hadn't seen him again until right now in his mansion where I am holding his wedding picture in his den. I always knew our paths would cross again. It was inevitable due to our history. I just never expected our paths to cross because of a little girl...

"Happy couple." I stated as I smiled and put the picture back down where it was on the desk before my flashback. Bram's desk was immaculate. Nothing was out of place and I could tell that his book shelf was the entrance to a secret passageway. I almost bought one just like it two years ago. I wonder what he has hiding back there. I now knew why he had no surveillance cameras in the mansion. In the academy, he was taught never to leave incriminating evidence behind. *I could use this to my advantage...*

"Thanks. That was the happiest day of my life. I was so proud to be Mrs. Marcus Notribello. Isn't it crazy how things change over the years?" She raved putting her hands on her chest in a sensual way reminding me of a bad actress.

"Yeah, but such is life." *I need to go through her purse and find her day planner; rich broads always have day planners.*

"Did you want to go swimming? You could borrow one of my husband's trunks." She said looking at my package.

"Sure..." She smiled at me and she made her way up the stairs. I almost felt tempted enough to go into the secret passageway, but I knew that I didn't have that kind of time. I regressed, and went to the purse to where her palm pilot was. Luckily, I never leave the house without mine. I transferred all of her information with a sort of USB cord into my palm pilot. I put her stuff back into her purse and then put everything back into one of the many pockets of my cargo pants. *They really do come in handy.* I walked toward the kitchen and Gina got there seconds later. She raised the swimming trunks over her head and smiled.

"These might be a bit bigger on you, but if you tie the strings it should work." *I'm sure she got the biggest pair of trunks so she could see my junk.* She was wearing a two piece that was so minuscule. I honestly don't know how some women find those things comfortable. *And has she no shame? Her daughter is here with a guest...* I went in the bathroom and changed. When I walked out, Gina was right in front of the door and she looked me up and down once again. *She could use some finesse.*

"Shall we?" I said as I tied the strings extra tight and knotted it twice. We walked outside and the pool was round, ever so blue.

"Come on, Daddy! The water is great!" Akemi yelled while floating on a pink noodle.

"Watch out then! Geronimo!!" I yelled before I ran and dropped as a cannonball on the pool, splashing everyone. The girls giggled and Snoopy barked while Gina turned up her nose. *Maybe now she'll back off...* She lay out by the pool while I played with the girls. If someone had told me that someday I'd be a having a hell of a time with two little girls, I would've never believed them.

"Who's hungry?" Gina asked.

"Me!" The girls and I raised our hands as we screamed out. I helped the girls get out of the pool and handed them each a towel before I started drying off my body. She watched me like a hawk watches its prey. *She needs some action, pronto.* She rang a bell and her butler came right away. *This all seems like a bad movie.*

"Rodolfo, will you get the pastrami out and make us some

sandwiches with the rye bread?" She demanded.

"Yes, Ma'am." He said before he lurched into the kitchen.

"So, do you know when your husband's assistant will bring you the pictures? The girls were telling me all about the pictures and I just can't wait to see them." I inquired.

"I'm not sure. He will send the doubles to my husband before he brings it to me, but I'll call you as soon as they are in my possession." Gina replied.

"I appreciate it." I said as I winked at her allowing her to believe she has a chance. Akemi and I changed back into our clothes before we all ate our fancy sandwiches on gourmet bread on the kitchen table.

"Hey Rodie, will you call us a cab?" I asked Rodolfo, giving him a nickname he automatically hated. As I saw him go call the cab company, I noticed the employee work schedule by the refrigerator on the door.

"Who wanted more sweet tea?" I asked the room. The girls raised their hands without stopping to chew to kill their appetite. I took out my digital camera from my cargo pants and took a picture of the work schedule. I put the camera away and then got the sweet tea out of the fridge. I brought it back to serve the girls and they drank it thankfully. After our early dinner, Akemi and I kindly said goodbye after Rodolfo said our cab had arrived. I picked Snoopy up, who was dry from being too scared to get in the pool with us which was for the best because of his stitches. Every time we would splash, or Akemi would squeal he would bark up a storm. We had a lot of fun, given the situation.

In the cab, Akemi passed out on my lap. I couldn't stop staring at her sleep and it made me smile. She was so peaceful. As I watched her, I started thinking about how much I enjoyed hearing her calling me "daddy" today. Then my thoughts darkened when I thought of the close proximity to danger she was in when she was at Bram's mansion without me. I knew I couldn't allow for her to come back until he was no longer a threat. *I can't let anything ever happen to her...*

Thirty-One: Bram

I disposed of the gun I used in the neighborhood garbage bin. I took off my gloves and put on my sunglasses when I got back in the car. *Where is Keiko?* I drove back to the hotel feeling content that I only had one more family to kill before returning home to my girls. I miss them so much when I'm away. When I got to my hotel, the concierge told me I had a package waiting for me. I picked it up and went to my hotel room. I put the package down on my bed and the keys on the armoire. I turned on the water to take a shower after I turned on the bathroom radio to a Japanese station.

I removed my clothes and put them on the bidet before I got in the shower to relax before I called my girls. I call them every night. My sweet Paula can't sleep unless she talks to her daddy and I know Gina only cheats on me to get a rise out of me. *That woman loves me and she couldn't live without me; I'd kill her.* After my shower, I air dried while I opened Lissandro's package. I felt myself grinning when I saw that Paula's new little friend was no other than the little girl I've been killing the entire Akashimi family tree to find. I got out my cell phone and dialed home.

"Hello?" Gina answered.

"Hi, baby." I could hardly contain the sense of irony. *My own daughter did my job for me by making friends with the one girl I need to annihilate.*

"Hey, let me put you on speaker phone. Paula is right here." She said before I heard the beep of her pushing the speaker button.

"How are my girls doing..."

Thirty-Two: Carmen

"I just felt humiliated! Why did you have to make everything so awkward before you left?!" Nina yelled pushing away the omelet I made apologetically, especially for her.

"I'm sorry; it's just that I felt awful that I was going out on a date with the man you obviously love!" I yelled back, shoving the plate back in front of her.

"I don't need your pity, Carmen Isabella Consuelo Moreno!"

"I wasn't pitying you, Antonia Garcia Vargas!" I took a deep breath and held her hand gently, but firmly at the same time, "I just know how it feels. It's excruciating to be in love with an unavailable man." She looked at me and her hand softened.

"You can't make me feel like an ass in front of him, Carm..."

"I didn't mean to embarrass you, Nina. I was just trying to help..."

"I know, but just don't help me like that ever again!" We laughed and finally started eating breakfast together.

"How was the date, anyways?" Nina asked.

"Um, it was...nice." I hesitated.

"Come on, girl. Spill. Don't hold back or I'll have to start yelling again."

"I'm not holding back, at least, not in the way you think. I had these dreams last night and Jose's kisses didn't feel like they used to..."

"Look at me," Nina held my head and looked into my eyes, "Marvin." She said as she let go of my head and went back to eating.

"How do you do that?!"

"It's been ten years. You get this Marvin haze and I just know."

"A haze?"

"Yeah, and come on. Who did you think you were fooling? I knew you'd go back to him eventually..."

"Really?"

"Duh."

"I can't believe we slept till five in the afternoon..." I changed the subject.

"I can. You've been working like a dog at the studio and then you had a late night. And my excuse is that I love to sleep."

"Still..."

"Well, just let Jose down easy. Maybe this will be my window to get out of the friends zone," She put her dishes in the sink, got her purse, kissed my cheek, and winked at me, "See ya later!" She left me smiling in the apartment while I did the dishes. Minutes later, my phone rang.

"Hello?" I glittered as I answered, knowing it was Marvin.

"Hey, you," He said as I sat down so I could give him my undivided attention, "I just made an amazing discovery."

"Wow that sounds good. What kind of discovery? And how amazing is it?"

"I'll let you be the judge of that. So, remember Akemi's sleepover?"

"Yeah..."

"Paula's father is Bram." My heart sank as the information entered my brain through my ears. *I put my daughter in so much danger! I could've killed her...just like my other child! What kind of mother am I?*

"Carm? You there?" He sounded concerned.

"I...could've...killed--" The tears were emerging from a familiar place.

"Don't do that to yourself, baby. This is good news, sweetheart." His voice calmed and soothed me.

"Why is this good news?"

"Gina invited Akemi and me over to go swimming after school today. There, I saw their wedding photo and you know what? I'm glad Akemi didn't see it. She would know it was him right away," My stomach churned and my heart felt constricted, "Anyways, I copied Gina's palm pilot and he is coming back from Japan in three days. Now, I need you to do me a favor..."

"Anything." I blurted out almost regretting it.

"Bram knows Akemi is friends with Paula, so I need you to take her out of town."

"How does he know that?"

"The girls played with an underwater camera and his assistant sent him the doubles of the film..." My heart constricted even more and fear washed over me.

"Man...this is bad." I uttered under my breath.

"It won't be bad if you and Akemi get out of town. I've lost too many things in my life already and I can't bear to lose you guys, too. As long as I know you're both safe, I can concentrate on my work." He said as if pulling the strings of my heart and playing a beautiful melody.

"O.K., I'll call Ms. Margot and tell her I have a family emergency or something."

"That's my girl. Pack a bag and come on over. I want you two to leave first thing in the morning." I didn't say anything because I felt frozen.

"Babe, he has an assistant that he can call to start making arrangements. Who knows if he's already made some?"

"I'll be over in two shakes of a lamb's tail."

"Be safe, and call me if you need anything." I hung up the phone and immediately dialed Ms. Margot's.

"Hello?" She answered.

"Ms. Margot, I'm so sorry to do this to you..."

"Carmen, what's the matter?"

"I have a family emergency and I have to leave first thing in the morning, so I won't be coming in to work tomorrow."

"Oh, that's fine, dear. You take all the time you need. I'll cancel your classes for you."

"Thank you for being so understanding."

"My prayers will be with you, child."

"Thanks." *We'll need them...* I hung up the phone and started packing. After I packed, I wrote Nina a note knowing that she would come over and use her key if I didn't answer after two days. In the note, I told her that I would explain everything to her when I came back to my place, not mentioning that I'd be out of town. After I finished everything, I walked outside, locked my apartment behind me, and hailed a taxi. *Stop fluttering, butterflies. You know, Marvin, and you know him well. You haven't fluttered for him in so long...*

Thirty-Three: Marvin

After mine and Carmen's phone call, I checked in on Akemi. She was fast asleep from being tuckered out at the pool with Snoopy, dormant right beside her. I gathered her clothes and underwear so I could pack it into one of my duffel bags. I also got Snoopy's water and food bowls, his food and treats, a rawhide bone he's been working on since we got him, and his leash. I went upstairs with the duffel bag and opened my safe up. I put two thirds of all my cash in the duffel bag and then I came across the rings that I put away after our last fight. I wrote a letter for Carmen and enclosed it in an envelope along with the rings. I kissed the envelope and shoved it under all the cash. Good thing my duffel bag has wheels, because it would be too heavy for Carmen to carry. I booked them on a charter bus to Canada at nine tomorrow morning and printed their confirmation page; Snoopy needed to be in a crate or a purse. I set the page on top of the duffel bag and then went to the bathroom.

I looked at myself in the mirror and noticed how long my roots had gotten while I ran my hands through it. I opened the cabinet and looked at the unopened box of hair dye, contemplating on what to do. *I only dyed my hair to make myself look different; an occupational hazard. Now that Julianni is gone, do I really need to keep doing it? I've been hiding from myself long enough...* I took out my hair clippers and started shaving it all off. Clumps of hair started populating my bathroom floor and I started to see myself clearly for the first time since my childhood tragedy. In my ear, the buzzing sound seemed to vibrate. When I was done, my eyes really popped, looking bluer than ever.

I swept the hair and compacted it into a plastic bag. It was almost as if the weight of the years stopped affecting me as I threw the trash away down the garbage shoot. There was a package in front of my door, so I brought it inside, knowing it was the fake passports I ordered for Akemi and Carmen. I closed the door and started opening the package. The passports were better than perfect. Then I went upstairs and brought the duffel bag down, so I could put the passports on top of it. I heard the door open, so I reached for my gun. I walked behind the door as it opened. I stood silently until I noticed it was only Carmen, so I put my piece away.

"Hi." I smiled as I said.

"Hi back." She said as she put down her briefcase and peeked into Akemi's room. If there is a way to look motherly, that's the way Carmen looked right now. When she looked at me again, her face was shocked.

"Oh my Gosh! Your hair..." She said as she felt my buzzed head.

"Oh, you noticed," I said as I hugged her. I smelled her hair and almost got lost in the scent, "Let's sit down, though. There's a lot you need to know." I pulled out the chair for her. Then I got the bus confirmation page and the passports before I put them in front of her on the dinner table.

"These are your tickets. They are bus tickets because those are harder to track. Snoopy needs to be in your purse the whole time. Once you get to Niagara Falls, take your pictures and have a little fun, but I want you to rent a car and start driving to a place you pick on the map; a place I won't know about unless you tell me at a later time when the danger is no longer a threat, you know?" I spoke trying not to stare at her beauty.

"How will I know when it's safe for me to tell you where I am?" She was on top of her game.

"We should come up with some code words...code words that will prove that everything is all right. What would you like yours to be?"

"Um...crazy eights?" She giggled. *I missed her laugh so much...*

"O.K. My safe words are going to make up a phrase."

"A phrase?"

"Yeah, when you hear me ask you 'what's your answer?' that's my safe code."

"Oh, O.K." She said acting a little confused. *I missed her facial expressions, too...*

"I packed Akemi's and Snoopy's stuff in this duffel bag. There's cash inside for when you need it. But here, put this grand in your wallet." I reached in my pocket and handed it to her.

"Thanks..." She sounded overwhelmed.

"No, Carm. Thank you." Our hands touched when I handed her the money and we were captivated by each other's eyes. I started to lean in to kiss her, but I caught myself and pulled back. I was about to look away when I felt her hand on my face. She moved from her chair to my lap and pulled my jaw up before her lips met mine; fireworks and fanfares went off all around us. I closed my eyes and buried myself into this moment. Passion flowed from her mouth to mine and from mine to hers again. The elongated kiss ended when we started smiling, rejoicing in our reunion.

I carried her upstairs like grooms carry their brides across their threshold, kissing her as if it was the last time. *What if this is the last time?* I gently put her down on the bed and pressed play on the CD player. Our song, This Year's Love by David Grey, started to play and Carmen's eyes welled up with tears as she smiled. We didn't have to speak, because our eyes said it all.

I took her hand and we started to slow dance. As we danced, it seemed like the world stopped existing and we were alone in the universe. I was feeling it more than realizing that she was everything that perfect meant. As the song kept playing, I closed my eyes and kept her close. The rain started to heavily pour outside, and the lightning kept making the room flash. Nothing, not the lightning nor thunder, or a sudden door knock on the door could stop what was occurring between Carmen and me.

Her arms cupped around my neck and I pulled her closer holding my hands on her waist. Her gentle hands started roaming over my back from my neck. That's when I slowly started to undress her. She, in turn, started to undress me. Each time she unbuttoned a button, she would kiss my chest all the way down to my stomach. The next song that started to play was Unchained Melody by the Righteous Brothers. We kept on dancing bare naked. Our skin touched one another and it was like being in the middle of the fireworks of feelings. My heart was beating love through my veins and I felt truly alive. In her eyes I saw the reflection of my own thoughts and feelings. I kissed her once more with all the passion I had from deep within my core. *I shouldn't have denied our love all these years. We could've been doing this everyday and night over the last ten years.*

"Where did you go?" Carmen asked, knowing me all too well.

"Nowhere, I'm still right here..." *I'm more here than I've ever been...*

"No, you're far away. What are you thinking about?" The curiosity in her eyes started to spill out.

"Honestly?"

"Yeah."

"I'm thinking about all the years I wasted by being an idiot. We could've been doing this all these years, Carm." *I felt like I was about to cry!* She smiled and kissed me passionately. All my thoughts, fears, and regrets just faded away and again there was just us in the universe with nothing being able to part us. When passion absorbs you in like this, there is no way you can resist it.

"Better late than never..." I've never seen her so happy. We kissed our way into the bed. I licked every inch of her skin, kissing the most sensitive parts; the taste of caramel seeped through every one of my taste buds. The blood was pulsing inside my member and then I finally felt her intense, wet warmth like a cave drawing in light. I was enchanted and in a trance. I've physically felt the warmth of her body, but it's never felt so open, so strong. As I slowly started thrusting my pelvis gently kissing her and maintaining soulful eye contact, time ceased to exist. I've never given myself to someone the way I am right now. There are no barriers or complexes.

The air was shaking between us. Since the CD had been long finished, her moans were filling the room and it was the sweetest music of them all. Her hands were leaving hand prints of touch as her body was burning, calling as my body was melting onto hers as if it was made of wax.

We reached orgasm at the same time and then closed our eyes emerging ourselves in the pure delight of extreme ecstasy. As we opened our eyes, she hugged me with her legs keeping me inside of her. I pressed my forehead against hers knowing that from this moment on, I would never hurt her again. Our bodies were wet with perspiration when I finally lay beside her. The rain was lightly touching the roof and windows with a calming effect. She lay down on her stomach and looked at me with her amazing brown eyes. I ran my fingers through her beautiful, silky, curly hair with my fingers until she closed her eyes; the lightning outside created beautiful dancing silhouettes on Carmen's body. She went off into the sleep world with the remembrance of a smile on her face while I stayed awake softly caressing her body. I felt the velvet of her skin under my finger tips soaking it in like a blind person, as if trying to remember her for the rest of my existence.

I heard Snoopy whimper downstairs, so I got dressed to go walk him. I looked at the semi starry night sky outside. I felt the light sprinkle of the rain and felt as if nothing would ever be as perfect as it is right now. That's also when I noticed; I hadn't had a cigarette since Akemi came into our lives. *I guess quitting is easy when you're so preoccupied with keeping people alive or coming to terms that your soul mate is happier with someone else.*

When Snoopy was done, we went back upstairs. I took my wet clothes off, and dried off with my towel before I climbed back into bed with my sweet, dormant caramel Carmen. I programmed the alarm clock for seven tomorrow morning. Then I spooned her and held her as close as I could before our bodies meshed together creating one massive body. I breathed Carmen in, and breathed us out until I finally fell asleep without any reservation as to whether or not I should.

The alarm clock beat on our ear drums, waking us up to start the dreadful day of saying goodbye. We were in the same position we fell asleep in last night. I kissed Carmen's shoulder and embraced her closer to me, ignoring the annoying alarm that was still angrily beeping. We fit together so perfectly as if we were professionally tailored to do so. Carmen squeezed my forearms before she interlocked her fingers into mine.

"What does this mean?" She asked as she kissed my hands with her soft, plump lips.

"This means you, Akemi, Snoopy, and I are one hell of an unconventional family." I chuckled into her ear. I felt her skin pull and heard her smile. She turned her body toward me, wrapped her arms around my neck, and kissed me. Neither of us minded having the morning breath. We had one last quickie in the shower before we started getting ready to go to the bus station. After the shower, Carmen went downstairs to get started with breakfast and to wake up Akemi. I stayed upstairs to get dressed and after I did so, I opened my safe back up. I reached in for the ring box with my ring in it and took it out of the box before I slipped it in the tiny pocket above the regular pocket of my jeans. Then I locked it back up and joined the girls downstairs, smelling the eggs and toast.

"Are you coming with us on our trip?" Akemi asked as I picked her up and carried her to her chair on the dinner table.

"No, but only because I have to work. Will you take a bunch of pictures so I can pretend I was there with you guys?" I asked while I helped Carmen bringing the breakfast to the table.

"I suppose I could do that..." Akemi said making Carmen and I look at each other and smile. We ate our eggs and toast together, now more like a family than ever before. Then they got all of their stuff ready for me to take them to the bus station. I called the cab company yesterday so the taxi would be here to take us to the bus station at eight twenty. On the cab ride, Akemi and Snoopy sat between Carmen and I. Carmen and I held hands the whole way. I paid the cab driver and we went to the customer service desk to exchange the confirmation page for the actual tickets. The bus number got called and we brought the bags to be checked. The last call for boarding came over the speakers. Carmen looked at me and I knew both of us weren't ready to say goodbye. I, in turn, kneeled down in front of Akemi and put my hands on her tiny torso. She put her little hands on my shoulder and waited for me to say something.

"Take care of your mom and Snoopy for me, will ya?" I uttered.

"Only if you do something for me too..." She bargained, surprising me.

"If it's in my power..." I replied. She said leaning in and putting her hand over her mouth and my ear as if she was about to tell me a secret.

"Don't die." She whispered with such authority and then glared at me making my heart skip a beat. *How does she know?* I cleared my throat and noticed her glare started to gleam as the water filled up. I looked at Carmen searching for an answer. Carmen nodded her head and I knew what to do.

"Akemi... I can't die," I paused to gently wipe her tears away, "We still have an important talk coming up in six years." She smiled and hugged me so tight that I started getting misty eyed.

"I love you... Daddy." Akemi whispered making my eye cavity burn until my tear glands joined in and created tears I couldn't hide.

"I love you, too, Kiddo." I stood up still holding Akemi and hid my head on her small shoulder. When I finally put her down, Carmen handed Snoopy to her. I pet him once and turned to Carmen.

"Carmen..." I reached for her and as soon as she felt my touch, she broke out in tears in my embrace, "I've always loved you and I always will. Know that." I said as I rubbed her back while holding her close.

"I love you, too, Marv," She pulled back from the hug halfway and looked into my eyes, "Promise me I'll see you again." She looked deeper into my eyes as if trying to hypnotize me into saying the right answer.

"I promise." I said knowing that I would do my best to keep it. We kissed as Akemi and Snoopy watched and then they boarded the bus, looking out the window at me. They waved to me as the bus drove away, both crying. Though I wanted to cry, I knew it wouldn't help, so I just waved.

Once the bus went off into the horizon of the road, I hailed a taxi. In the taxi I reached into my tiny jeans pocket, getting out the ring and slipping it on my ring finger. I smiled as I admired it, knowing I would never take it off again. When I got home, I felt the relief of knowing the girls are safe. Now I can focus on my last mission: Bram. *I need to keep my promise to Carmen, so this has to be as flawless and perfect as I can make it be.* He is smart, and has much more training than I do, but I am driven by a force that men like him can never truly know; the force of the meaning of the word "good." *He's the bad guy. He has to lose...*

Thirty-Four: Bram

I woke up this morning feeling refreshed and rested. Things always work out in my favor. I know that the family I have to kill tonight is coming home around ten after their benefit dinner. I'm going to wait until they go to sleep, that way there won't be any screaming. Until then, I'm going to the spa and have some services done. *I think a manicure and pedicure would be nice. Gina loves it when my hands are soft when I touch her. Maybe I'll even get a Shiatsu massage. Who knows? A happy ending might be in order...* I called the spa and booked my treatments before I called my airline and I rescheduled my flight to a day earlier. Then I dialed Lissandro's number.

"Hiyah boss, what can I do for you?" He chirpily answered the phone.

"Lissandro, I am coming home a day early. Make sure you are at the airport at seven AM on Wednesday." I said rolling my eyes at his chirpiness.

"Sure thing, boss. Anything else I can do for you, Sir?"

"Yes, I need you to get me my usual list of weapons, but include another silencer."

"Why do you need another silencer?"

"Because if I get home and Gina is fucking the mail man again, I'm going to shoot him."

"Oh."

"And Lissandro?"

"Yeah, boss?"

"I won't remind you again to mind your own business and stop asking me questions to fill your frivolous curiosity."

"Sorr—" I hung up on him before he could pathetically apologize. I got dressed and went down to the spa to receive my first treatment. The lovely Asian receptionist showed me to my locker and opened it for me. I flashed her a fifty dollar bill. She bowed before she took it and put it away before she undressed me. Then she unfolded the robe that resided inside the locker and put it on me, tying it around my waist on her knees. Still on her knees, she untied my shoes, took my socks off, and put the flip flops on both my feet. She folded my clothes and put them neatly in the locker for me before she locked it and handed me the key. She motioned for me to follow her down the hallway and we walked all the way into a room with a massage table. She bowed and closed the door for me. I took my robe and flip flops off and got under the sheets on the massage table.

When the door opened, I instantly smelled the Jasmine scent on my masseur's skin. I flashed her two one hundred dollar bills and she knew exactly what it meant. She started on my back, massaging me with her firm hands. *Killing, though it happens to be a job I enjoy very much, takes a toll on my body; especially when I have to drive long distances in between hits.* When she flipped me over, I closed my eyes and anticipated where her hands would be going next. She massaged my entire body before I felt her now gentle hands on my penis. She gently massaged it until I was hard as a rock. Then she quickened her pace, rapidly moving up and down suavely gripping until I unloaded several loads of stress all over my body. She then took out a warm bowl of water and with a cloth started to clean me off. When she was done, she bowed. I flashed her another fifty and she got my flip flops from under the massage table while I sat up. She put the flip flops on my feet and then when I stood up, she put the robe on me and tied the belt around my waist. I followed her to the manicure and pedicure room where I enjoyed two cups of green tea and listened to Oriental music until they were done doing my hands and feet.

After my treatments, I went to my locker and dressed myself feeling rejuvenated. My hands and feet were as soft as baby's skin. I paid for my services at the front desk and then went back up to my room to get ready for my last kill. I ordered dinner, ate it, and then went to my car to start driving to the last Akashimi family's house, not counting the little girl I will kill back in the States. When I got to the house, all the lights were already off. I disarmed the alarm with its rightful code and went in the kid's room first. *One shot to the head.* Then off to the parent's room. *Two shots. How easy.* I heard the dog start barking, so I shot it, too. *The dog knew my scent. No reason leaving behind any witnesses.*

Thirty-Five: Marvin

Within the hour, I'm going into the Notribello mansion. Gina and Paula have dinner at the grandparents and it's the workers' one night off of the week. I'm going to confiscate any weapons I find. That's why I'm bringing a huge crate to throw the weapons in it. If, by an off chance, Gina left her palm pilot, I'm going to take a look to see if anything new has been penciled in.

I locked up my loft, and started walking to my van. The crate was already there along with all my tech equipment. I'm also going to set up my own surveillance cameras to know exactly when the right time is to attack. *I don't want Gina or Paula to pay for any of Bram's shortcomings.* I might even bug the place if I have enough time. It would be nice to hear what Bram is saying.

As I got in the van, I started feeling pumped up. I blasted my radio when I put in my Michael Bubble CD. The first song is Feeling Good and that's exactly how I feel. I put it on repeat for the rest of the way. I even sang along and danced to it, not feeling silly in doing so. I shut my engine off when I parked a block before the mansion. I reached in my duffel bag, and got a GPS locator. Then I climbed out of the car and started walking toward the mansion. The lights were all on, so I had to creep around the front yard like a ninja cat. I got under Gina's car and plugged the locator in under the carriage. This way I'll know when she's on her way home. *Shit, the front door is opening and it's Gina!*

"Darling, did you get your report card to show grandma?" Gina asked as they walked toward the car that was above me.

"No, but you didn't get the vase you bought for her either. I thought we were just putting our purses in the car and going back in together." Paula said saving my ass. *I knew I liked that kid!*

"Oh, well let's do that then." They put their purses in the car and then went back in. I crawled from under the car the fastest way I knew how and then sprinted back to the van. *Boy that was close! Too close, in fact... I need to be more careful.* I watched them drive away from inside my van, and then I saw the workers leave. I only counted six of them, though. So I had to wait for the seventh to get out, too. When the last worker got out, I noticed he stood out front and quickly realized he was waiting for someone to pick him up. *I don't have time for this!* Ten wasted minutes later, his ride showed up. *Now it's go time.*

I drove up with my van and parked in the back. Then I picked the lock to get in and carried my crate and duffel bag inside. The first thing I knew I had to do was set up my cameras. I set one up in every room inside of a vent. Lucky for me, they have those wall vents that you can see everything that goes on in one room from. As I set up the cameras, I looked in each room meticulously to see if there were any hidden guns. I found a few knives and daggers, but that was it. Then it was time to see inside the secret passageway and set up a camera in there. *How do I activate the mechanism to open up the door?* I checked to see all the books to see if they were the triggers...no luck. I looked behind the paintings and on his desk, still no luck. Then I looked closely to the floor. One of the tiles was a bit off, so I decided to step on it. *Eureka!* The whole bookshelf came forward and then moved to the left. I was disappointed to see how small it was inside, but the way he has the room organized made it look like a gun warehouse; mainly collector's weapons in glass boxes under lock and key.

I decided to steal all the keys, but leave the weapons intact. He would never use these since they hold too much sentimental value. I did find one gun in his desk, though. I installed a camera in the secret weapon room along with a bug for sound. I closed the passage door and then started looking through his files. Turns out, he started a killing academy of his own, but instead of the pupils being young boys, they were all eighteen or older. Then, one file and its picture drew me in. I've never met Carmen's troubled little brother and I know that Moreno is a popular Spanish name, but he looks *exactly* like her. *This explains why she hasn't heard from him in so long...*

I put everything back exactly the way it was, and then set up a bug in his den, the kitchen, and their bedroom before my laptop started beeping that Gina was eight miles from home. I packed everything up and got out of there as fast as I could. Minutes after I pulled out, Gina pulled in. It was close enough to make me start sweating. Overall, going there was a success. I didn't get information from Gina's palm pilot, but a lot of other stuff was accomplished. Plus, not only do I have visual of every room, but I also have sound in the important rooms.

On the drive home, I felt as if I really could keep the promises I made to Carmen and Akemi. This whole ordeal with Bram will be nothing but a speed bump on the road to a better life with my family. In no time, I'll be reunited with them, never to leave them again.

Thirty-Six: Carmen

Nine hours later, we arrived in Niagara Falls. The bus driver unloaded the bags and the passengers claimed their rightful ones. I was grateful that our duffel bag had wheels since it was so heavy. The air was colder up here than back home, but it felt nice. It also felt cleaner as I breathed it into my lungs. Before Akemi, Snoopy, and I could enjoy the view, we rented a car as per Marvin's directions. Overall, the trip wasn't so bad. It was long, but we made stops and Akemi was a real trooper. We bought mad libs, cards, and lots of junk food. They even showed a movie, but since we were sitting in the back, it was hard to see so we just played and talked instead.

She doesn't seem to be tainted by any of this, but she's always been a really strong kid since I've met her. I mean, her parents were brutally killed, but she still found a reason to smile and light up my and Marvin's life. I, on the other hand, am extremely tainted by everything and extremely scared. *What's going to happen if Marvin doesn't come out alive on the other end? Is Bram going to come after us? Are Akemi and I going to be on the run for the rest of our lives? I don't think I'm strong enough for all of this.* Here I am at one of the most breathtaking wonders of the world, and I'm too scared to even be able to enjoy it. I also know we have a lot of driving to do tonight, and I'm not looking forward to doing that. *The last time I drove was when I rented a car to take care of my mom. That didn't turn out good...how do I know this will?*

"Come take a picture with us, Mommy!" Akemi yelled out and I put on a fake smile before I walked toward her. We used a whole disposable camera taking picture after picture which surprisingly made my fake smile turn into a real one. I even started having a little fun. We asked a couple to take a picture of the three of us. I was holding Akemi and

Akemi was holding Snoopy. *I bet it came out really cute.* When the film was done, we went to the bathroom and walked Snoopy so we could drive longer without making a stop. When we got to the car, we put Snoopy in the back seat and Akemi sat up front with me.

"I miss him." Akemi stated while she fastened her seatbelt. I looked at her and I knew she was talking about Marvin.

"I miss him, too, hija." I said as the tremors of never seeing him again took over my body. I turned on the radio after I ignited the car and put it in gear, driving toward the open road.

Thirty-Seven: Marvin

Being back home without the girls felt so wrong. I feel empty and incomplete. I set up my laptop on the coffee table and I kept a close watch on the Notribello house. Gina had sex with the mailman three times just today. She's also been baking up a storm in the kitchen. *I bet the house smells sweet. I should probably order something to eat soon. I'm pretty hungry.* That pastrami sandwich Roldie made for us would hit the spot right about now... Rodolfo is the head of the workers. He doesn't really work...he's more of a supervisor. When Gina calls him, he takes her order and goes to someone else to tell them to do it. I also saw Gina look at the pictures and it made me so glad that I did all of this because you can really see Akemi's face in all of the pictures. Bram is probably thinking that it's going to be so easy to kill her. *Oh, is he in for a treat! This is going to be anything* but *easy for him.* The phone rang at the house.

"Hello?" Gina answered, "Yes, I know the bake off is tonight..." She said to the person on the other end with a slight attitude, "I have been baking like crazy. I bet my table will be the one that raises the most money...

"All right, Mandy. I will see you tonight. Ta-Ta!" She hung up the phone and went back to icing the cup cakes. *I've never seen icing without a Betty Crocker sticker.* I watched her make it herself and I was tempted to make some at the same time as if I was watching a cooking show, but I didn't. My stomach growled and I knew I couldn't wait any longer. I programmed the laptop to record everything that went on at the house so I could go get some food.

I walked to the supermarket on the corner. *They say not to shop hungry, but I disagree.* This is when you really find out what kind of things you have denied yourself from having over the years. Like right now, I have coffee ice cream, chips and dip, soda, cream cheese jalapeno poppers, mozzarella sticks, and two frozen pepperoni pizzas in my shopping cart. *I can't recall the last time I ate any of these items! My feast will be delicious, and whatever I have left over I'll eat later on tonight.* I paid the cashier and grabbed my bags. I walked fast paced back home and ran up the stairs.

I put the pizza, jalapeno poppers, and mozzarella sticks to bake in the oven, served myself a big glass of cola soda, and opened the bag of chips and the container of dip after I put the ice cream in the freezer. *I need to figure out how to get Gina and little Paula out of the house so they don't get caught in between the cross fire. I couldn't handle it if they got hurt; innocent bystanders are not on my list.* I watched the tapes from the twenty minutes I was gone until I caught up to the live feed. The phone rang again.

"Hello?" Gina answered, "Actually, the prize hasn't been established yet. I don't think they're going to have a prize this year. And anyways, it's not about the prize. It's just about being the best, and we all know who the best is," She smiled and took off her apron, "All right, Helen. I'll see you tonight." As she hung up the phone, I got a brilliant idea. *She wouldn't be so conceited about being the best baker, if she wasn't.* I hacked into the school mainframe and researched how the school gets their prizes and who's been the winner for the last few years. *My hunch was right.* She's won the bake-off since her daughter started this school which was seven years ago. And the school gets the prizes as donations. This year, no one donated anything. I quickly went on the web and purchased a cruise package for a family of three for tomorrow, non-refundable knowing that Bram wouldn't go because of his unfinished business with Akemi. Then I called the school and said since I wouldn't be able to go on my cruise, I wanted to donate it to the bake-off. They accepted and said they would send a bike messenger to come pick up the online tickets. *My plan is becoming more and more flawless each passing moment.* The oven timer went off and my mouth watered. *Ah, my food is ready...*

Thirty-Eight: Carmen

We're somewhere in Manitoba, Canada in a hotel. I told Akemi to go take a shower and get ready for us to go out to dinner in the restaurant that's inside the hotel. It seemed like a pretty nice place to eat. I went in the duffel bag to get Akemi an outfit to wear. *Man, Marvin. This is so much money! I've never seen this much money in my entire life. And it's all one hundred dollar bills!* Under the money, there was an envelope with my name on it written with Marvin's handwriting. I put it in my pocket and kept on looking for an outfit for Akemi to wear. I got her yellow overalls with a bumble bee embroidered on the chest along with a black tank top. While she showered, I fed Snoopy. Then I decided to pack her clothes with mine so they wouldn't smell like money. *Our shoes can go in the money bag with Snoopy's pet supplies.* When she got out of the shower, I dried her off and wrapped the towel on her head.

"Now it's my turn to take a shower. I laid your clothes right there on the bed. Is that outfit O.K.?" I wondered if I should've let her pick out what she wanted to wear.

"Yeah, I like the bumble bee. Mommy, can I watch T.V.?" She asked as she put on her underwear.

"Sure, let's find you something. Oh, they have the Disney channel. Do you wanna watch that?" I said as I turned the T.V. on with the remote and flipped to the guide channel.

"Yeah." She said as she put on her tank top and the towel fell off her head.

"If you want to change the channel, come ask me if what you're going to watch is O.K." I said as I wrapped the towel back on her wet hair knowing that there are movie channels and the movies might not be suited for an eight year old.

"O.K. Mommy, will you braid my hair after you get ready?" She asked as she put on her overalls and sat on the bed holding her towel wrap as she got comfortable. Snoopy jumped up on the bed and sat down beside her.

"Sure." I answered, smiling at her. I went into the duffel bag and picked out a pair of jeans and a tank top to wear after my shower. I went in the bathroom and turned on the shower. As I took off my clothes, I remembered the envelope that was in my pocket. I opened it, took out the letter, unfolded it and a ring fell on the floor making a clinking sound on the bathroom tile. Reading it, happy tears ran down my face:

"I'm not getting any younger waiting for you, you know. Will you marry me already?!" Marvin wrote with a sharpie on a plain white computer piece of paper. I looked at the floor and noticed the rings that I wore on my finger not too long ago. I bent over and picked them up. I kissed them before I put them on my ring finger, remembering the way Marvin did it the first time; engagement ring followed by the wedding band. I got in the shower and the happy tears kept on flowing. *I never thought this day would come! I also never thought that the day the man of my dreams proposed to me, I wouldn't be able to give him my answer. I hope in a couple of days, I can... God, you will protect him, won't you?*

Thirty-Nine: Bram

My flight landed in the LaGuardia Airport on schedule. I picked up my suitcase from the compartment and waited until I could get off the plane. As I walked toward the passenger pick up, I looked for Lissandro. I spotted him and walked toward him, handing him my suitcase when he was close enough to grab it.

"You're looking well, boss. Did you have a nice flight?" He asked like a kid needing his father's approval.

"Lissandro, why do you feel the need to ask me absurd questions? How can any twelve hour flight be a nice flight?" I scoffed as I rolled my eyes.

"In my book, any flight that doesn't result in death is a nice flight."

"Then, by your standards, I had a splendid flight as I am standing right before your eyes." My tone was drenched with sarcasm.

"I'm glad you had a nice flight, boss. I parked the car this way." He was completely unfazed, and I wondered if my patience was wearing thin or if he was getting stupider each passing minute. We got in the car and started driving towards the house I have missed the last fourteen days. "Did you get the weapons?" I asked.

"Yes, sir. They are in the garage in the crate like always." He said as he looked at me in the rear view mirror.

"Must I remind you to watch the road every time you answer my questions?"

"No, boss. Sorry, boss."

"Just drive." I shook my head and rubbed my temples. As we pulled up to the driveway, I felt exhausted. I got out of the car and walked into the door. The aroma of baked goods invaded my nostrils. *Is the annual bake off here already?*

"Honey, I'm home!" I yelled into the house. I heard running footsteps upstairs, then down the stairs. I walked toward the bottom of the stairs and Gina jumped into my arms. *This is the best part about being away; coming home to a welcome like this.*

"I missed you so much!" Gina squealed. She kissed all over my face and neck while I carried her up the stairs. As I walked us to our bedroom, I closed the door before I threw her on the bed. *I've loved Gina since I laid eyes on her.* I started to undress her perfect body with curves in all the right places. She looked at me with desire in her eyes and then undressed me. After she undressed me she lay back on the bed and opened her legs. I climbed on the bed with her and kissed her before I inserted my manhood all the way inside her. I made sweet love to my wife for almost an hour before she had to start getting ready for her bake-off. I was completely ready to fall asleep and I did. I felt her kiss me before she left, but the sleepiness was too strong to open my eyes. I didn't wake up until the house phone rang. It was probably Gina calling to tell me she won like every other year since she started in this nonsense.

"Hello?" I spoke into the mouthpiece.

"Daddy!" Little Paula said making me smile without opening my eyes.

"How's my peanut?"

"I'm good. Mommy and I want to know if you want us to pick up something on the way home to eat. Did you bring me a present?"

"Of course I did! And tell mom to pick up some sushi."

"Yay, sushi! O.K., I'll see you at home. Love you, dad."

"Love you, too, peanut." I hung up the phone and got in the shower. *Boy, it feels good to be home.* When I got out of the shower, I got dressed and went to the garage to see if Lissandro got everything I asked for. *Surprisingly, he did. No mess ups this time.* I closed the crate, and went to my den. I sat down on my chair and looked at the messages I had on the machine. Thirteen messages all together. *There's never a day off.*

As I sat in my den, I felt as if something was off in here. Something I can't quite put my finger on. *Maybe Gina hired a new maid or something.* I saw the lights of Gina's car as she pulled up the driveway. I'll ask Gina about the den after Paula goes to bed. The front door opened and Paula started running towards me.

"Dad!" She yelled before she jumped up and I caught her in mid air. I kissed her on the cheek and embraced her tight.

"You're getting big, peanut." I said. Gina carried in the food as I carried Paula into the kitchen behind Gina. I put Paula down on her chair and then went to the refrigerator to get the sweet tea. Then I warmed up the sake for the grown-ups.

"How was the bake-off?" I asked as I kissed Gina's hand.

"I won!" She yelled as if it was the first time she's won.

"Big surprise." I made her hit me the way she usually does when I don't take her seriously. Then I tickled Paula and made her laugh the laugh I missed so much in the two weeks I was gone.

"No, babe. This time the prize was a cruise! A cruise!!" She said as she excitedly showed me the tickets.

"Whoa, this leaves tomorrow." I noticed the date.

"I know. I already called the airline and bought us tickets to go to Fort Lauderdale, Florida. We gotta pack because our flight is at ten in the morning." Her face glittered with happiness as she spoke.

"Gina, I can't go." I knew this would start a fight. I noticed her whole body show the disappointment she was feeling.

"You can go to Japan for two weeks, but you can't go on a cruise for ten days with your family?" She composed her disappointment and turned it into anger. I looked at Paula and she rolled her eyes.

"I know, I know. Go to my room to watch T.V. and eat my dinner." Paula said as she took her dinner plate and sweet tea filled glass.

"Gina, I went to Japan for work. You act like I took a vacation without you."

"You're always gone! I get lonely here without you and I just won a wonderful little vacation and you're telling me you can't go? When are you going to take time off to be with us?!" She hissed with the familiar tone I know all too well.

"Look, why don't we plan something around Christmas time? We can go to Europe...I just can't take the time off right now."

"I'm sure you'll have an excuse when that time comes, too. One day, you're going to regret not spending enough time with your family. I just hope that when you realize it won't be too late. You know what? I'm not hungry anymore. I have to go pack." She said as she left the kitchen holding back tears. I ate my dinner alone and started to really hate and resent that little Asian girl. *I should've been done with this assignment over a month ago. If I was, I could've avoided this fight with Gina. How can one little girl be so hard to kill?*

Forty: Marvin

The cruise worked like a charm. As I watched Bram eat his dinner alone, I noticed the rage come out of his eyes. Then, I saw Gina crying while she was packing. *I feel bad for her.* Even though she is an adulterous woman, I think she only does it because she's lonely. She really does seem to love Bram and all she wants is for him to have more time with her and Paula. She deserves better than a low life like him. I looked at Paula eating her dinner and watching T.V. Then the door to her room opened. I didn't put a bug in her room, but I can tell Bram and her are really close. He sat down next to her on the bed and brought her a present for her to open. It was an authentic Japanese dress most likely tailored just for her. She hugged him and then they watched T.V. together until Gina came in to start packing a suitcase for Paula. To avoid arguing in front of Paula, Bram left the room after he kissed her goodnight.

Bram went to his living room downstairs and watched T.V. on his big screen. The girls got ready for bed and slept. I decided to make the other pizza and then I heated up the rest of the jalapeno poppers and mozzarella sticks. *I'm glad Bram is watching Live Free or Die Hard. I hadn't seen that movie yet.* I finished the rest of the food and felt pleasantly plumped. Then Bram paused the movie to go into the kitchen and to get the leftover baked goods Gina brought home. I thought it was the perfect time to get my coffee ice cream. We got back on our different couches at the same time and he pressed play. *Bruce Willis kicks so much ass in all the Die Hards.* After the movie was over, Bram went upstairs to go to bed. I decided it was a good idea for me to do the same. I pressed the record button so I wouldn't miss anything that happened during the night. Then I put my ice cream back in the freezer and went up to bed. *The real work begins tomorrow when Bram's girls are gone.*

Forty-One: Carmen

"Wake up, angel. We gotta get back on the road." I spoke softly almost singing in Akemi's ear. She was asleep on my arm and Snoopy started licking her face.

"Are we doing anything fun today?" She asked as she rubbed her eyes.

"We can ask the front desk lady if there is anything fun to do on the way." I said feeling a little bad for driving the whole day yesterday without scheduling anything fun for Akemi. *In my defense, I had a lot on my mind. That's no excuse. Be a better mom, Carmen!*

"Can I pick what we do?"

"Hm, I'll give you the choices to pick from...deal?"

"Deal." We got ready and packed everything back into our duffel bags. Then, before going to the front desk to check out, we walked Snoopy. We put him in the car with the windows cracked and then went to get our continental breakfast. We ate and then threw our trash out before we went to the front desk to return our keys and check out.

"Hi, we're not from here. Is there anything to do around here, tourist wise?" I asked the receptionist.

"There are a couple of things you can do. We're pretty near Churchill where you can go on a polar bear excursion. Here's a brochure. There's also a place where you can go snorkeling with beluga whales, but that's in Hudson Bay. Here's the brochure for that one. It just depends how much you want to drive." She replied as she handed me the brochures.

"Thank you very much."

"You're welcome and I hope you enjoyed your stay with us."

"We did." I affirmed while turning to walk toward the front door smiling.

"Mommy, can I see the brochures?" Akemi asked.

"Sure. Then tell me which one you would like to do."

"I can pick from these? Oh boy!" We walked out to the gift shop and I purchased some snacks, drinks, and a Canadian map so we could know where we were going. Akemi was studying each brochure as if it was going to be on the most important test of her life. I paid the cashier and we walked to the car. Snoopy was crying until he heard the key go into the key hole. We got inside the car and then I turned the car on.

"So, what's the verdict, little one?" I asked, waiting to put the car in gear until I looked on the map to see where we were going.

"Beluga whales sing, but polar bears are cuter..." She indecisively weighed her options.

"Meaning...?"

"It means I would be happy doing either one. Which one is closer?"

"Let's see," I opened the map and looked at both locations from the brochures; "The Polar Bears are closer." I finally said.

"Yay! Polar Bears!" She said as she got out of the car and threw the beluga whale brochure out in the trash can in front of our car on the parking lot sidewalk. I smiled as she came back in the car and put her seatbelt on. When I put the car in gear and started backing out, I felt content; especially with my left hand clearly shouting to the world that I am no longer a single woman. *Polar bears, here we come.*

Forty-Two: Bram

I woke up today with Gina's alarm in order to eat breakfast with my girls before they leave for the airport. I called Lissandro last night and told him that he was driving them. During breakfast, Gina didn't even look at me. It's not unusual that she would act this way, but I wish she wasn't leaving so angry.

"We'll take lots of pictures for you, dad." Paula said as if that was the root of the problem. I smiled.

"I'm always there with you, even when I'm not. If you miss me, just feel me right here." I said as I poked her where her heart is. She smiled and finished eating her buttered croissants and drinking her orange juice.

"Mr. Lissandro is here, Sir." Rodolfo announced.

"Thanks, Rodolfo. Can you tell him to load the suitcases in the car?"

"Certainly, Sir." He said before he left.

"Are you done, peanut?"

"Yep."

"Go brush your teeth, then."

"Aw dad, do I have to?" She whined.

"Go on." I said with a more stern tone. I heard her little foot steps going up the stairs proving she was doing as I said.

"I hope you have a lovely time on your cruise, darling. You deserved to win. Those cookies and cupcakes were simply irresistible. I ate all of them last night." I attempted to make up with my wife.

"I'm glad you enjoyed them." She dryly recanted not looking up from her magazine. She finished her coffee and went upstairs to put the finishing touches on her make-up and to brush her teeth.

"Fifteen minutes!" Rodolfo called up the stairs to keep Gina punctual. They came rushing down the stairs thirteen minutes later. Now it was time to say goodbye.

"Have a good time, peanut. I love you to the moon and back." I said as I hugged her. She was wearing the dress I brought back for her from Japan and looked simply adorable.

"Well I love you to the moon and back and to the moon and back again." She said as she kissed my cheek and walked to the car.

"Whether you believe it or not, I love you, Gina." I said as I touched her face. Her eyes welled up with tears, so she walked away without saying a word and got in the car. I waved the car off. Paula waved back, but Gina didn't even turn her head. *I hate feeling like shit before a job.* Normally, things are my fault when Gina gets this mad at me. But this time, it's Keiko Akashimi's fault, not mine. If she didn't run, she'd already be dead and maybe I could've gone with my family on a cruise. I have devoted too much time into the Akashimi family. *I'm ready for them to be all extinct.*

I went back inside and went into my den. I hacked into the school mainframe and looked up the new student records. *Oh, this is too good. Marvin Costa decided to resurface at the wrong time with the wrong little girl.* I printed his address and looked it up on map quest. *I knew that Julianni's death smelled too much like Azrael. But you've gotten careless, old friend. It was simply too easy for me to find you.* I touched my lip scar and closed my eyes. *Azrael, this time I won't be so merciful. Consider yourself as dead as Keiko Akashimi. Or maybe you haven't been careless. Did you pick up your little girl from the sleep over? Did Gina give you a tour of the house? Did she even show you my den, where you saw our wedding photo?* I started looking through my files and I noticed that the keys to my collectable weapons were gone. I quickly opened my secret room to see if they were stolen. They were all still there. *This makes me angry. Azrael knows I would never break the glass boxes.* Now I'm enraged. *He dared go through my things?* I closed the door and went into the kitchen. *Azrael was in my house. Not only did he break the deal, he disrespected me in my own home by going through my things. And he stole from me!* I picked up a chair and I threw it as high as I could as I let out a roar of rage. When the chair fell, so did the vent cover and I saw a camera.

"Everything all right, Sir?" Rodolfo peeked his head in and asked.

"Yes, Rodolfo. Everything is better than fine." I said as I climbed on top of the table, reached for the camera, looked in it to make sure Azrael knew I found it, and then smashed it into a million pieces. *This means war...*

Forty-Three: Marvin

Man, he is relentlessly searching his entire house looking for my cameras. And I must say that he is taking his anger out on my poor, defenseless surveillance devices. The last one that he has yet to find is in his room. *This all just sucks royally since I was thriving on knowing his next move so I could plan mine.* All isn't lost though, for he hasn't found any bugs yet. I spoke too soon. He found the first bug in the master bedroom. *Shit. Now he's going to be looking for those, too.*

"Azrael! Not only have you been watching my family, but you've been listening to us, too?! You've stooped so low, guy. I'm actually stunned and shocked. This isn't like you, Az!" He hissed into the bug before he broke it and made it screech a feedback that hurt my ears. He ravaged through his room full of animosity until he found the last camera. *Now, I have no visual and limited sound.* I have only two bugs left: one in the kitchen and one in his den. I'm pacing back and forth trying to strategically come up with a plan when I heard a knock on the door. I picked up my silencer and walked over to answer the door thinking it was going to be someone Bram sent over to roughhouse with me. I looked in the peephole, and much to my surprise, it was Nina. I hid the gun in my jeans on my low back and then put my shirt over it before I opened the door.

"Hey Nina, how's it going?" I asked, incredulous, and opened the door just enough to where she could see me, but couldn't come in.

"I'm looking for Carmen. She left me a note that she should be back at her place in a couple of days and it's been a couple of days..." Nina said.

"All this trouble for a kid you just met, Az? You big softie. I do give you mad props for offing the whole family, though. How did it feel finally killing the man that's responsible for killing mommy and daddy? I wonder how Keiko would feel if she knew that her father figure is a monster...I guess I'll just have to tell her before I kill her, huh?!" Bram said before destroying the bug and making it feedback like the last one. Since the bugs projected voices crystal clear, Nina heard the whole thing including the banshee scream feedback that made us both wince in pain.

She pushed the door open and went straight to my laptop. She looked around in my messy kitchen, upstairs, in both bathrooms, and in the spare bedroom which now looked like an office again. She looked at me with a poker face that I couldn't read, and then sat down on the couch. I couldn't read her body language either. I decided to stay quiet until she opened her mouth. I closed the door behind me, and then went in the kitchen to get a glass of water. I drank it knowing that she was watching me. I could feel her eyes burning a hole on my back. When I was done, I put the glass in the sink and then went to stand by the wall in front of the couch she was sitting on. I leaned on the wall and then sat down with the wall supporting my back. We were staring at each other, not saying a word, when Bram found the last bug.

"Az, I'm starting to respect the balls it took to infest my house with bugs and to install the peeping toms. Bravo. I looked at the school attendance records and it turns out, little Akemi hasn't been in school for the last three days. I've also checked airlines, trains, and buses and you were smart enough to give them aliases. You've angered me enough to where I want to kill you before I go on the search for the little bitch. Stay alert and sleep with one eye open, because I'm coming for you. Bram, over and out!" Another loud, insupportable feedback screech made us squint our eyes and cover our ears.

"How many more times is this guy gonna talk?" Nina asked, watching the laptop like a reality television show.

"That was the last time." I stated.

"Where is Carmen and Akemi...or Keiko...whatever her name is?"

"They're safe."

"What's your plan?"

"Nina, you already know too much. It's not really safe here for you."

"Listen, I'm here for the long haul. I'm not going anywhere. Consider me your partner, because no one is hurting those girls."

"Excuse me?"

"Carmen told me everything. I know you're a hit man, and I'm guessing this Bram dude is the one looking for Akemi." *Man, what is this? I told Carmen not to tell anyone!*

"O.K., do you feel special or something?"

"Marvin, stop being a smart-ass. What are we going to do?"

"There is no *we*. *I'm* going to wait until he comes to me or calls me. You wanna know what you're gonna do? You're gonna go home and forget any of this is going on. I work alone."

"Are you naive enough to think he's coming for you alone?"

"No, I'm expecting a lot of company." I said as I got up from the ground and stood in front of her.

"Then don't you think it would be wise to have some company on your side?"

"Nina, I appreciate the gesture, but I can handle it. Plus, I can't be worrying about you when the going gets tough..." I barely finished talking when she stood up from the couch and threw a punch. I blocked it with my right arm and then she flipped me by my arm, took my gun, let my arm go making me lose balance and fall down on the floor before she pointed the gun in my face.

"Don't worry about me. I can take care of myself." She winked at me as she took the gun apart and let the parts fall on the ground in front of me. *What is she?* That just blew my mind and made me thankful she was on my side. Her movements were so precise and sharp. I watched the tape of it back in my mind in slow motion to see if I could've stopped it from happening if I saw it coming. *Maybe, maybe not.* And the way she took apart that gun without breaking a sweat or looking at it...

"Who *are* you?" I blurted without thinking. She laughed at my question and my shocked facial expression.

"I guess Carmen never told you I was in the Marines with full intentions of changing their minds of letting a woman be a part of the U.S. Special Forces. When I had no luck with that, I became a bodyguard. After my first car chase, I fell in love with the adrenaline rush and became a stunt driver which is what I do now. You can close your mouth, Marvin."

"Whose bodyguard were you?"

"I'd rather not say."

"I understand. It's all very secretive... So, is racking up tickets of traffic violations a way of sending a 'fuck you,' to the government?"

"Um, I never thought of it that way..."

"Well, either way, I'm sorry about the Special Forces. It would be my honor to fight beside you. Welcome to the team." I said as I stood up and extended my hand for her to shake it, knowing that Bram is now rounding up criminals to make it harder for me to get to him. My whole view point of Nina changed as soon as I saw what she could do. It doesn't even matter that she is a woman.

"All right, partner. Tell me all the details about your arch-nemesis..." She picked up the pieces of my gun and started putting it together while I told her everything I knew about Bram. *This is going to work.* We both love Carmen very much and we also both know that if we don't pull this off, the girls are as good as dead.

Forty-Four: Bram

"Rodolfo, I need all of you to get going. When y'all come back tomorrow, clean everything up. I want you to throw out and replace the broken things with exact replicas. Here's a credit card. Now, scoot. I don't wanna see any of you until tomorrow!" I heard the intensity in my voice and scared myself. *I can compose myself better than this. Focus!*

"Yes, Sir." Rodolfo took the credit card and calmly left the room, though he smelled of fear. Then he rounded up all the workers and they all left as per my directions. After they left, I dialed Lissandro's number.

"Hello?" He answered.

"Round up he troops and come over to my place. We're going hunting." I hung up the phone before he had a chance to answer. I went upstairs and took a long cold shower to cool off my boiling blood. In a way, I am ecstatic about carving up Marvin the way he carved me up years ago. But on the other hand, I am worried about the way he's changed the way he does things. *He broke our deal. That is very unlike him.* After my shower, I put on my signature black Armani suit that I wear every time I have blood to spill. The only different thing about this time is that my victim knows I'm coming for him, hence the bulletproof vest under my shirt and blazer. As I finished tying my shoes, Lissandro appeared in my peripheral vision.

"The boys are downstairs ready to go." He said after he knocked twice on the open bedroom door.

"Good, I'll be right down." I said. I knew I had to make sure my will was in order. I opened my night stand drawer, and there it was staring me in the face. I picked up the notepad that was beside it, and started writing Gina a note:

"To my beautiful wife, Gina;
If you are reading this note, it means I'm dead. Gina, I never meant to put my work before my family, but those were the cards I played. I left everything to you, not including the trust fund Paula will get when she turns eighteen. You will never need to worry about money, darling. I have every faith that you will find someone worthy of you, for in many aspects I was not. Just promise me you'll end things with the mailman. Men are stupid, but we know when our wives are unfaithful. Tell Paula how much I love her everyday, and remember me only by our good memories. Please, forgive me for the bad ones. I will always love you.
Forever Yours,
Marcus."

As I signed my name, I felt things fall into perspective and I got a reality check. *He's been to my place and is very familiar here. And he is too familiar with his place. The only logical solution is to go to neutral ground. But where is that?* I placed the note back inside my night stand drawer on top of the will where Gina knows it's located. Then I started walking down the stairs still trying to figure out what has to happen tonight. When I got downstairs, the boys were raiding the fridge.

"Hey boss man, what's shakin'?" Claudio asked before he took a big bite out of his pastrami sandwich.

"Sit down, boys. We have a lot to talk about." I said ignoring Claudio's greeting. I call them boys, but they are men. With the exception of Lissandro, they were all trained at my academy and graduated at the top of the class. *Naturally, I would take the best to work for me.*

"You all have seen my heinous scar and have asked me about it some point in time. Tonight I will tell you the story to serve as inspiration for things to do to the man we are going to annihilate." I said while calmly walking back and forth in front of the dinner table my men were sitting at giving me their undivided attention.

"I knew this was gonna be good!" Vinnie said, full of excitement.

"Quiet. Long ago, I thought I made a friend in Marvin Costa, also known a—"

"Didn't Julianni kill a cat named Costa some odd years ago?" Giordano interrupted me. *I don't like to be interrupted!* I walked up to him and laid a solid punch on his cheek bone.

"*Quiet*," I sternly said, "Yes, Julianni did kill a 'cat' named Costa long ago, Giordano. Marvin Costa was his son. His alias is Azrael, and I'm sure all of you here have heard of him. He is the one that gave me this." I said while touching my lip scar and then took a deep breath.

"Azrael is responsible for the death of the family, so go into this knowing that he is dangerous. I want him terminated, so shoot to kill.

202

I'm going to phone him in a couple of minutes telling him I want this to be a gentleman's fight, just him and I on neutral ground. When we figure out what the neutral ground will be, we'll get the blueprints and figure out where each of you will hide for sniper shots. There is no room for mistakes, and whoever fucks this up will be killed on site. Does everyone understand what I need them to do?" They all stood up and saluted me.

"Sir, yes, Sir!" They yelled in unison. *Good boys.* I went into my den and dialed Azrael's cell phone number in which I had to dig deep in the web to find.

"Bram, old chap, to what do I owe this pleasure?" He answered, knowing I would be calling.

"Az, I was just sitting here thinking that we are gentlemen and we deserve to have a gentleman's duel. What say you to that?" I sneered a smile, picturing him dead and leaning back on my leather chair.

"I say you're full of shit, but I'll bite. Where do you want this gentleman's duel to take place?" *He knows me too well...*

"That's what I was calling for. We need a neutral place where neither of us knows the surroundings in order for it to be a fair fight."

"How are we to know if the other is lying about knowing the place? Plus, when did you start believing in fair fights? Just pick a place and a time and I'll be there."

"Oh, why do you think so little of me, friend?"

"Just pick a place, guy."

"How about the warehouse at the marina?"

"What time?"

"They close at eleven. Let's say... midnight?"

"O.K."

"Why don't you make up a will for your loved ones? Oh yeah, your loved ones are going to die soon after you...so there's no point really. Unless you'd like to leave me everything you own, I mean we did use to be really good friends before you stabbed me in the face." I rubbed my scar and my hand started shaking with anger.

"I say that's better than being stabbed in the back. At least you saw it coming."

"Potato, potah-to."

"Till the duel."

"Till the duel..." We hung up. I know the marina pretty well and there are lots of vanish points for the boys to set up in. I looked up who built the marina warehouse, and then who the architect was that designed it. His name was Jean McDonough. He worked for one of the best companies in New York. I hacked into their mainframe and printed up the blue prints before I went into the kitchen to start making plans with my boys. *This couldn't be more perfect if I wanted it to. Azrael is history…*

Forty-Five: Carmen

The polar bear excursion was amazing! It was basically a car that was equipped to get up close to the bears and still be safe. We got so many good pictures! Akemi named the bears and it was so cute. Snoopy had to stay in the hotel, but I don't think he minded too much. He really likes sleeping and being on beds. We left the T.V. on so he wouldn't feel so lonely. After the excursion, we went out to eat and then went back to the hotel to shower and sleep. While Akemi was in the shower, my phone rang. I answered it, wholeheartedly thinking it was Marvin.

"Baby! What's the safe phrase?" I squealed.

"The safe phrase? Hm... you're beautiful?" Jose answered very unsure of himself. *Why didn't I look at the called ID?*

"Oh. Hi Jose." I disappointedly said.

"You didn't know it was me?"

"Um, I thought you were someone else..." *Crap.*

"Who else do you call 'baby'?" *Shit.*

"Oh... Jose, we need to talk..."

"Are you cheating on me with your ex?"

"Well, you see..."

"Carmen, I think I deserved to know before you did anything. This is unacceptable."

"I know, but you just don't understand the circumstances..."

"I don't care about the circumstances. You should've at least called me. I better get off the phone before I say something I regret. Goodbye!" The phone clicked and I knew he hung up on me when the dial tone started to hum. *He's right.* Even though things just happened and I had to leave town...I should've broke it off with him before anything happened between Marvin and I. *I did owe him that.*

"Who was that, Mommy?" Akemi asked as she walked out of the bathroom soaking wet.

"Jose." I said while I took one of the towels in the bathroom and started drying her off.

"Did you break up with him?"

"More or less."

"Good, because I think daddy would mind if you had a boyfriend on the side when you guys got married."

"What do you know about us getting married??"

"Mommy, I'm not stupid. You're wearing the rings again, aren't you?"

"How did you get so smart, huh?" I said as I tickled her. Then I put her pajamas on her, and went to take a shower. After my shower, we watched T.V. in our pajamas, snuggling against each other until we fell asleep with Snoopy between us.

Forty-Five: Marvin

"What did he say?" Nina asked when I hung up the phone with Bram.

"We're meeting him at midnight at the marina warehouse. You have to stay out of sight. I'm thinking he will have five or six guys there. They won't be civilians; most likely graduates of his academy. I need you to take them out. Can you do that?" I asked, now knowing what the game plan would be.

"Piece of cake."

"Do you have your own weapons, or do you need to borrow some?"

"Yeah, I have an M40A3 that should do the job…"

"Nice. Have you ever been to the marina warehouse?"

"No, but it shouldn't be a problem for you to get the blueprints, right?"

"Why don't I just do that now?" I walked over to the laptop and started googling.

"All right. Well, I'm starved. I'm feeling like some Italian food. What do you want?"

"Surprise me."

"Will do. I'm gonna go get my gear and then the food. I should be back within the hour." She said as she gave me some dap and left closing the door behind her. I finished retrieving the blueprints and then I printed it so I could study it close. I was looking at the blueprints as if I was Bram trying to figure out the best vanish points to put his men when I heard a door knock. I reached for my gun, and looked in the peephole. It was only Jose so I hid my gun the same way I did when it was Nina at the door. I opened the door and I got a punch right in the nose which made me groan and cover it up with my hands. I felt the warm blood start to flow out of my nostrils and the involuntary tears come out of my eyes.

"What the fuck, Jose?" I said as I sat down on my couch, tilting my head back still holding my nose as if to make the pain go away.

"You stole Carmen. Just be glad that I feel much better now. I came here with the intention of killing you." He said so angry which made me chuckle to myself. *Amateurs. He couldn't kill me even if he tried. Some people have it, and most people don't. He's in the 'most' category.*

"I didn't steal Carmen, dude. She was never yours."

"Oh, she wasn't?"

"Nope. Hey, can you get me some ice?"

"Sure..." He walked toward my freezer and I heard him get the ice. As he was about to hand it to me, he threw it; it went all over the couch and floor.

"What the hell?" I asked in disbelief.

"I'm not gonna give you ice to nurse the pain I want you to feel!" He flipped out.

"O.K., then sit down. Make yourself at home, I guess. I'll get the ice myself." I got up and walked toward the cabinet and reached for the packet of zip-lock bags.

"Thank you."

"So, other than almost breaking my nose, is there anything I can do for you?" I said as I opened the freezer and filled the zip-lock bag with ice cubes.

"No, that was basically it."

"O.K." I said as I sat back down on the couch with the zip-lock bag full of ice on my nose. *I wonder how long he's planning on staying.*

"This is a nice place you got here..."

"Yeah." *Does this guy have schizophrenia?*

"Where's Carmen?"

"Not here."

"Yes, I can see that. But where is she? I need to talk to her."

"I'll tell her you stopped by." I stood up to go look at my nose in the mirror and then Jose jumped on me making me land hard on the wooden floor. *That's it.* I reached for my gun and then noticed he was pointing it at me standing over me. I swiped my legs under his making him fall beside me, took my gun back, and pointed it on his face. His eyes were terrified, so I put the gun away and stood up.

"Man, are we done with all the horse play? I'm not in the mood for any more." I said putting my hand out for him to take it so I could help him up. He pushed it away and stood up by himself.

"Why do you even have a gun? Is Carmen O.K.?!" I could tell he was picturing horrible scenarios in his head.

"Yeah, dude. Carmen is fine."

"I'm calling the police. Something just isn't right!" He said as he reached for his phone and started dialing. I was too far from him to take the phone with my hands, and I wanted to take it before he dialed the two ones and the nine, so I shot the phone off from his hand with my silencer. He screamed like a little girl as loud as he possibly could almost sounding like the feedback from Bram smashing the bugs. *The last thing I need is the neighbors coming in to ask what is going on...* I decided the best thing to do was knock him out, so I ran toward him and hit him on the neck on the acu-pressure point that causes people to pass out immediately. He fell on the ground, unconscious, and Nina walked in.

"Are we under attack already?" Nina asked, reaching for her gun with her right hand and holding a large duffel bag and take-out food on her left arm.

"No, it's Jose. When I opened the door, he punched me and then he jumped me when he saw the gun, so naturally I had to fight back... and this is the result." I stood up and pulled myself together.

"Seriously? That's Jose?"

"Yeah."

"And he did that to your nose?" She started to laugh hysterically.

"I guess Carmen didn't break up with him before she left."

"Yeah, I guess not. I only knocked him out because he was gonna call the police."

"Um... why didn't you say you *were* the police?"

"That would've definitely been a better way to handle things. When I saw him dialing nine one one, I shot the phone off his hand."

"Oh. No way he'll believe you're a cop now."

"Oh well, what'd you get me?" I changed the subject.

"Lasagna!"

"Nice!" I took the take-out bag from Nina and placed it on the dinner table. Nina put down her duffel bag and her gun before she took out the containers from the bag while I got the soda, two glasses, and silverware. I sat down and started eating. After I took the first bite, I got up and got the blueprints for her to see.

"I put an 'x' where I think Bram is going to put his guys..." I pointed at an X and sat back down to eat some more with the blueprints in front of us as we ate.

"O.K., I was thinking that I should get there around ten so I could see exactly when they get there and where they are. That way I could take them out one by one with no one being the wiser."

"Nina?" Jose asked in a daze.

"Yeah, papi. How you feeling?" She answered with affection flowing through her voice.

"Sleepy... and I have a weird headache..." He said as he yawned. Then he saw me and a scared look washed over him.

"Hi, Buddy." I winked at him in a patronizing way while I put a forkful of lasagna in my mouth.

"Nina, he has a gun and he shot my phone. I bet he killed Carmen and the little girl! We have to get out of here before he kills us!!" Jose stood up as he flipped out much like before.

"Jose, how did you know to come here?" Nina patiently asked.

"I dropped off Carmen and Akemi once..."

"Jose, Carmen and Akemi are fine. They're just not here."

"How can you be so calm around this hoodlum?"

"Because we're working together."

"Doing what?"

"It's complicated."

"I'm so sick of people telling me things are complicated. Tell me, or I'm going straight to the cops." Nina looked at me. I looked at Nina. We both knew we had to tell him the truth. Then we looked at Jose. After we told him everything, he sat down in shock.

"Do you want some of my dinner?" Nina asked Jose.

"Oh, you got take out from my restaurant?" Jose asked when he noticed his logo on the bag.

"Yeah."

"Did they make you pay for it?"

"No. They never do."

"Next time you get food for *him*, I expect you to pay." He dryly said looking my direction. *I didn't say anything. I don't mind paying. I got the girl...*

"Will do. Are you O.K. with all of this?" Nina asked him.

"Yeah. Sorry for freaking out." Jose said to me.

"No problem. I probably would do the same if I was in your shoes." I attempted to be nice.

"So... you won't go to the cops, right?" Nina asked the question lingering in my head.

"No, I won't. Just be careful. Can you call me when you're done with your 'mission' so I know you're O.K.?" Jose asked obviously concerned with Nina's safety.

"Sure thing, Papi." Nina's eyes sparkled and I finally caught it. *She loves him...*

"I'm gonna get on out of here so you guys can get to it." Jose stood up, kissed her cheek, and waved at me. After he left, we finished eating. We formulated the plan and we had an understanding of what kind of body language I'd be giving so she could read me easily. When we were done talking shop, I gave her a look.

"What's that look about?" She asked as she threw out the trash.

"Jose and Nina sitting by a tree. F-u-c-k-i-n-g..." I sang making her blush and punch me hard.

"Is it that obvious?" She wondered, lowering her head.

"Not to him..."

"Well, let me skedaddle. Be safe, and just know: I got your back." She said as she hugged me and then picked up her duffel bag surely packed with lots of heat. As she left the apartment, I started to meditate. I knew things could go wrong tonight, but I had to visualize it all go right. *May the force be with us...*

Forty-Seven: Nina

As I drove to the marina, I wished I still had the '68 Dodge Charger. *The Honda Civic just doesn't do this moment justice...* I got to the marina around ten. I looked over at the sign and read their business hours. *This is the first lie that I've caught Bram in.* The marina closed at nine, not eleven. I shut my engine off and started feeling excited. *This is as close to the Special Forces as I'm gonna get.* I opened the trunk and reached for my duffel bag. It was hella heavy, but I can't make it lighter. I'd much rather have more weapons than I need than running out when the going gets tough.

I went to the highest point of the marina warehouse in the darkest corner. I got out my bulletproof vest and put it on over my shirt. I got out my dagger, and placed it on my belt. I also got out my forty five and put it in my gun slinger. Everything was loaded and ready to go except for my sniper weapon. Then I put my M40A3 together and laid down on my stomach to get into position to wait for the bad guys. That's when I started thinking about how there's always a chance I won't make it. *What if tonight is my time and I never told Jose how I really felt?* Staying in position and keeping a watchful eye, I got my phone out and dialed Jose's number.

"Nina?" He asked with a surprised voice knowing that my mission just couldn't be over yet.

"Hi." I said as my heart started beating out of my chest.

"Hi..."

"How are you doing?" I stalled.

"I'm O.K. Aren't you on the way to the marina?"

"I'm at the marina."

"Well, get off the phone! They're gonna hear you! Do you have a death wish?! Are you insane?!" *I love it when he freaks out like this...*

"They're not here yet."

"Oh, then what's on your mind?"

"If by the off chance this is my time to go into the afterlife...if there is an afterlife. My mom always said that there was, but my dad said that we just become the dirt that grows the grass that feeds the animals that feed the hum—"

"Nina, you're babbling. You only babble when you're nervous. What's up?" He interrupted my rant.

"Well, here's the thing: I love you. I have for a while now. I realize that it's weird for me to tell you this now, but I might not have another chance and I didn't wanna die never telling you the way I feel." There was a pause of silence and my heart stopped beating.

"Why did you fix me up with Carmen?" He wondered.

"Because you liked her..." My heart started beating again.

"I did when I first met her, but when she never gave me a shot and we were always hanging out, I developed a huge crush on you. I never thought you'd give me a chance, so I dated Carmen." *Is he for real?!*

"You settled for Carmen because you thought you couldn't have me?"

"Pretty much." I was elated beyond elatedness. Then I saw headlights driving in toward the building.

"Shit, I gotta go. There are cars pulling up."

"Wait! Nina?"

"What?" I whispered.

"Don't die so I can take you on a real date." He whispered back though he had no reason to.

"A real date? I like the sound of that..." I whispered before I hung up and turned off my phone.

I heard indistinct voices outside until they came in trough the doorway. All of them looked like army personnel except for one chubby, short guy. I immediately picked Bram out of the pack when I saw his hideous scar on his lip that Marvin told me to look out for. *The second lie I caught Bram in was that he wasn't alone for the gentleman's duel, and the third was that it was only ten thirty, not midnight when he said he would be arriving. Marvin was right about the quantity and the quality of men Bram brought.*

"All right, boys. All of you have trained for a night such as this. You all know which position I want you in and what I want you to do. So go do it." Bram said, sounding like he has already won.

"Sir, yes, Sir!" The men said while saluting him before they fanned out to their rightful positions.

"Shouldn't they inspect the building before going to their positions, sir?" The short, tubby man asked making my stomach drop.

"Lissandro, stick to driving and leave the heavy lifting to the big boys. Now drive the extra car out of sight and *stay* out of sight." Bram patronized the only man that could've saved him from the Nina storm.

"But sir—"

"No buts, Lissandro. Go!" Bram said as he terminated the conversation. Lissandro left probably feeling very small.

"Lorenzo, get down here!" Bram yelled. I heard his heavy footsteps going down the metal staircase before he saluted Bram and stood in attention position.

"I want you to give this warehouse a clean sweep and then go directly to your position without reporting to me. Understood?"

"Sir, yes, Sir!" Lorenzo saluted and then started sweeping on the bottom level. *Ah, my first kill will start early, then. I need to be extra quiet as to not stir up the others.* I hid my duffel bag out of sight after I put my sniper inside of it. Then I hid in the corner, waiting for Lorenzo.

I heard his footsteps clanking on the metal getting louder and louder telling me he was getting closer and closer. He looked around for almost a second and I saw the perfect opportunity when his back was turned to me. I jumped up and wrapped my legs around his waist; then I wrapped my arms around his throat. He pulled my hair and bit my arm, and though it hurt, I didn't scream out in pain. Then he took out his dagger, and stabbed my left hip. The pain shot all the way up my spine into my brain causing me to get angry, so I took out my dagger from my belt and slit his throat. The arterial spray showered my arm and his body started to get weaker and weaker much like the strength in my left leg from the puncture wound to my hip. I held onto him so I could control the way he fell and how fast. It was as if we were moving in slow motion. When his massive body was gently lying on the metal floor, I got up victoriously. Even though I know I was alone up here, I heard my audience applaud and saw them all give me a standing ovation. I bowed to them and reached in my duffel bag for some pants to tie around my bleeding hip.

As I tied the pants tight around my wound, I knew it wouldn't stop the bleeding. It was bleeding so fast that I probably won't be able to make it to my and Jose's date. I decided to kill the rest of the men while my adrenaline was pumping, making Bram and Marvin have an actual gentleman's duel after all. I quietly limped to the next man, who was lying on his stomach with his sniper set up. I crept around like a slick cat, quiet but agile. He didn't see it coming when I was standing with my feet beside him and then I kneeled down on top of his shoulders before I slit his throat effortlessly fast. He shot one bullet that went straight through the open window since his finger was on the trigger, but no one seemed to notice since it was a silencer. *Two down, three to go. My hip was really starting to sting. Come on, Nina. Work through the pain. Hut, two! Hut, three!*

I limply crept to the next guy, who was in the same position as the one before. He was wearing a turtleneck, but my dagger sliced right through that. *Three down, two to go.* I was starting to sweat cold due to my blood loss. I just wiped it off and kept going strong. As I was creeping to the next man, I got dizzy and leaned on the metal box which clinked, alerting the unsuspecting guy who would be easier to kill if he didn't know I was coming. He saw me as soon as he turned around, and immediately turned his sniper weapon toward me. I kicked him on his unprotected balls, and he dropped the gun on impact making a loud noise on the ground.

"Giordano?" A man's voice whispered from the abyss of darkness.

"Argh." The guy in front of me groaned until he swiped his legs under mine trying to make me fall down beside him. I jumped up and then landed on his legs breaking one of them which resulted in him letting out a loud grunt of pain. His bone was exposed, and he was wiggling on the ground in pain. I kneeled down on his side and violently stabbed him in the neck to silence him for once and for all.

I heard footsteps coming up behind me so I immediately turned around with my forty five drawn. He smiled at me and kicked the gun out of my hand. I swiftly swept my legs under him and he fell flat on his back. I drew out my dagger and stabbed him in the eye. Before he could scream, I shot him in the temple of his head with his silencer that I took from his gun slinger as I laid down beside him. As I lay beside two dead bodies recently killed by me, I smiled with deep content. *I just killed five men with only one semi-serious wound. Women can't be in the Special Forces? Phooey. I know now more than anyone that a woman can do anything she puts her mind to. Women are just as tough as men, though men refuse to believe so.* I reached in my back pocket, turned my phone on, and texted Marvin: YOU'LL HAVE YOUR GENTLEMAN'S DUEL AFTER ALL.

I dropped my phone when the pain turned up the intensity. I started feeling warm and when I tried to get up, I slipped in my own personal pool of blood. *At least Jose knows.* The room started turning and I felt myself drowning in a whirlpool, spinning into the black hole of my unconsciousness...

Forty-Eight: Marvin

As I dressed in my black suit, my phone beeped. It was a text from Nina. Her mission is done and she will hang out, staying hidden, while Bram and I have our fair gentleman's duel. She'll back me up if I need it. The bulletproof vest felt strange against my skin, but I knew it would be frivolous not to wear one. I put my dagger in my boot sling and my .45 in my gun sling across my torso. Driving to finish this madness and finally retire almost felt like an aphrodisiac. It was ten to midnight when I parked my van beside Bram's car in front of the marina warehouse. As I got out of my car, Bram got out of his. He was sitting in the driver's seat, but I doubt he actually drove himself here.

"Bram." I said as I looked into his soulless eyes.

"Azrael, you look well." He said with a smug smile.

"This gentleman's duel of ours: what kind of weapons are we aloud to use?"

"No guns." He dryly said as he started to remove his guns from his wardrobe. I, in turn, did the same. *I know he will leave a gun somewhere the naked eye can't see.* One of those extremely small ones, no doubt, is in his shoe. *Things with Bram are never fair. And I know that fair is just a joke to him.*

"After you." Bram said as he motioned for me to walk towards the warehouse with his arm like a waiter does before he shows you to your table.

"Thank you." I said as I walked into the warehouse without any fear or doubt that we would be there alone, not counting Nina who wouldn't interfere with out duel because she knew I had to do this alone. Bram walked two feet behind me anticipating that one of his men would shoot me. When we were both in the middle of the warehouse, I faced

Bram who was covertly looking around for his men.

"They're dead." I said. Bram looked at me as he never had before; with a hint of fear in his eyes. He lowered his head and looked at me with his eyebrow eye line which made him look satanically deranged. Then he quickly took out freakishly small gun and shot me in the chest five times knowing that this would hurt like hell through the bulletproof vest.

He threw the gun on the floor before he attacked me with a combination of punches and kicks. I blocked all I could, but the years seemed to have made him faster. He kept punching me and kicking me until I went to a place that felt no pain. I blocked hard and rough surprising Bram with a knock out uppercut that threw him on his ass. He then took out his ninja Shurikens and threw them at me one after the other. I escaped three of them, but two got me. One was halfway into my shoulder, and one skinned the side of my face. I tried taking the star out of my shoulder, but Bram came forward to attack me again. He pushed the star deeper into my right shoulder making me scream out in pain. Then I ducked down his next punch and reached for my trusty dagger to stab him in the kidney. I did so successfully making him drop to one knee and look at me with hate in his eyes. He got up, touched his back, looked at his hand which now had blood on it, and laughed.

"You're gonna have to do a lot better than this, Az." Bram snarled.

"I'm just getting warmed up..." I said before I attacked in full force with my dagger. Every time he would block with his hands or arms, I stabbed him in different spots until both of his arms and hands were dripping blood. He fought as if nothing was different until I stabbed him on his side, between two ribs. He fell down to the floor and lied down with his eyes closed.

I took what felt like two seconds to catch my breath and then I heard metal clinking together. He took out three more ninja stars, and threw them at me getting one on my other shoulder and one on my right knee. I was only able to escape one. Though the throws were not as strong as the first time because of his wounded arms, it made no difference. I lost balance and fell down to the floor. We were laying down perpendicular to each other, both trying to catch our breaths. *Now, I have no use of my right leg because of the star being deep in my knee. I also have only limited use of my arms because I have two stars in each shoulder.* Both of us are in pain, and losing blood fast.

"So, how did you hook up with Keiko Akashimi?" Bram asked, breathing as hard as I was.

"I found her hiding out in a condemned warehouse." I muttered through the pain.

"Isn't life funny?" He nostalgically asked.

"Hilarious." I sarcastically answered.

"No really. Think about it: if your path hadn't crossed with the girl's, I would've already had found her and completed my task. You would've killed Julianni and the family, and most likely retired. If it wasn't for the brat, we would both not be lying here. We would be out there enjoying life instead of fighting to keep it." He said. Though some of what he said was true, I can't picture life without Akemi even if I tried. I now know that without her, it would probably have taken me ten more years to get in the place where I am with Carmen now.

"I think things turned out the way they were meant to." I said as I gathered up all the strength I had left in me to stab Bram in the throat. I watched him gurgle and struggle with his breathing.

"I'll... see... you... in..." Bram pulled out the knife from his throat and looked at me deep into my eyes while the blood started pouring out of his open neck, "Hell." He hissed as he let out his final breath. I closed his demonic eyes and reached in my pocket for my phone before I dialed Carmen's number.

"Hello?" She sleepily answered.

"So... what's you answer?" I weakly managed to ask.

"Marvin?!" She squealed in happiness when she figure out it was me. I could tell by her voice that she was smiling.

"My answer is yes, yes, yes!" She squealed some more. As she told me her answer and I knew nothing else could go wrong, I passed out. It was weird. Most of the times when I pass out, I see all black. This time, I saw all white.

I woke up in a white room with no furniture. I looked at my shoulders and they were completely healed. I looked further down to my knee, and it was healed, too! *How long have I been here? Too long, if all my wounds are all healed. Was I in a coma? Is this a hospital? Where's the bed? Or the button you're supposed to press if you want the nurse? Oh shit. Am I dead?*

"No, son, you're not dead." I heard my father's voice after I saw him walking through the white wall beside me. I took two steps back and felt extremely freaked out. *He just walked through a wall! And I know for a fact that he's dead! Damn it! I am dead!*

"No, son, I promise you. You're not dead." He repeated himself walking closer to me and since I was backed into a wall, I couldn't walk farther back from him. Technically, I could've moved to my right, but I'm freaking out so much that I feel paralyzed.

"I was told you'd be happy to see me. They didn't say you'd react like this." Pops said as he looked deep in thought trying to figure out what went wrong.

"If I had died, which you say I haven't, and you were where I am, seeing your dead son telling you that you weren't dead even though you don't have any of the wounds you did a second ago... wouldn't you freak out, Pops?" I made myself talk.

"Yeah, I see what you mean." He nodded his head. Then he sat down in mid air until a chair appeared out of nothing.

"If you're trying not to freak me out more... you shouldn't do things like that!" I spoke in an unnatural high tone.

"Things like what?"

"Um, sitting in the air and then making the chair appear as your ass touches it!"

"Oh, sorry. Did you want one?" He asked before another chair appeared beside me in front of his. Both of them were the wooden chairs we had back at home. *I remember when mom used to cook an amazing dinner, and we'd sit on these chairs on the dinner table...*

"Who's 'they'?" I asked while I surrendered control and sat down on the chair.

"Not important. What is important is that you are in surgery right now. We have about fifteen minutes, give or take a few, until you have to go back into your body. Your mother and I are so proud of you, taking in that little girl like you did. And Carmen is exactly the kind of girl we always wanted to welcome into our family."

"I'm in surgery?" *What kind of surgery?*

"Yes." He said not really elaborating in which kind of surgery I was in.

"Are you and ma in heaven, Pops?" I asked thinking about what Bram said before he died.

"Don't you worry about that. You'll see your mother and I again when your time comes."

"I never thought I'd hear you say you were proud of me..."

"We are, son. We always have been."

"Thanks, Pops."

"One last thing, we love you with all our hearts, Marvin. We're always watching. Till we meet again, son." He said as he stood up from his chair and started walking backwards into the wall.

"I love you guys, too." Tears started falling out of my eyes. I think it's because I was overwhelmed with emotion. I opened my eyes, and I was lying on a hospital bed crying.

"Your surgery went just fine, sir." The nurse said as she adjusted my morphine drip.

"Exactly what kind of surgery was I in?"

"Removal of the ninja stars and repair of the surrounding tissues and veins, sir."

"Thank you." I said before the morphine caused me to fall asleep.

The next time I woke up, I looked beside me and saw Akemi and

Carmen passed out on chairs to my right, and Nina and Jose passed out on the chairs to my left holding hands. Then I felt a warmth on my legs and noticed that Snoopy was lying between them. I moved a bit, and he woke up and came to lick my face. As his collar and name tag jingled against each other, Akemi woke up.

"Daddy!" Akemi yelled before she came toward me and gave me the warmest hug I've ever felt. My chest was extremely sore where I was shot by Bram, but I didn't care. I hugged her back with all my heart. Then Carmen woke up and kissed me passionately.

"*Never* scare me like that again!" She said after the kiss. Nina and Jose woke up. Jose shook my hand and then helped injured Nina get up to give me a hug.

"What happened to you?" I asked Nina after our hug.

"Nothing some stitches, a blood transfusion, and painkillers can't fix. They just discharged me." She winked as she spoke.

"So, how did I end up in a hospital?" I asked, wondering how everything worked out after I passed out. I'm feeling elated, but worried at the same time. *There were a lot of dead bodies. Am I going to jail? What's going on?*

"Carmen, do you wanna get a snack with Akemi?" Nina hinted.

"Sure, do you want anything, baby?" Carmen asked me. I shook my head, she pecked me, and then they both left the room so Nina could speak freely with only Jose and I in the room.

"Lissandro turned out to be an FBI agent. He had been wanting to bring Bram down for a long time, but never had enough proof for the arrest to hold. Then you and I came along, and he turned his head. He brought us into the hospital, and took credit for all the kills. He's getting the medal of honor and a big promotion." Nina informed.

"So, we're in the clear?" I asked not really believing my ears.

"Yup, clear as sparkling water. Honey, will you get me a drink so I can take my pain pill?" Nina asked Jose.

"Sure." Jose kissed her forehead and left the room.

"Honey?" I chuckled.

"Yeah, we're an item now." She said smiling big and blushing at the same time.

"Why did you make Jose leave the room?"

"Very perceptive, my friend. I think I saw Carmen's brother talking to Lissandro in the car when he was driving us to the hospital. But, since I was very out of it... I don't know if I was seeing things or what."

"Is that right?"

"Yep."

"Well, we should definitely keep an eye on things because I saw his file in Bram's desk. He got trained in Bram's academy."

"So... I'm not crazy?"

"No, far from it. Do we know if Lissandro's a good guy?"

"Do we ever know if the good guys are as they say they are?"

"Good point. Like I said before, let's just keep an eye on things. I think what we need to focus on now is the wedding."

"It's about time you marry that girl."

"I know. Are we to expect wedding bells on your end soon as well?"

"Who knows?" She said as she shrugged her shoulders and smiled big. Jose came back and then the girls.

I stayed in the hospital for two more days after that. When the hospital released me, the girls took me home. Carmen moved in and the three of us remodeled Akemi's room so she had a room that was just hers. I never dyed my hair blonde again, and Carmen really dug that. I needed to do something for work, so I started helping out with the studio. I was responsible for all the billings and ordering of equipments. I guess you could say that Ms. Margot hired me on as the dance studio's manager. When she passed on, she left the studio and the apartment above it to Carmen. Three months after that, Carmen and I got married. Akemi was the flower girl and Nina was the maid of honor. Akemi and Snoopy stayed with Nina and Jose while Carmen and I went on our honeymoon in Spain. Shortly after we got back, we found out Carmen was pregnant. We sold the loft, and bought a house outside the city. We got rid of the van and bought Carmen an SUV. We bought me a jeep since it's the type of car I've always wanted. Nina and Jose got married one month before our beautiful baby boy was born. I named him Giovanni after my father. I'm never going to truly know if I just had a dream about the conversation with my father, or if it was real. I guess when my time comes, I'll find out for sure. Nina and I still keep tabs on Lissandro and Carmen's brother just to be safe. You never know if we'll have to come out of retirement...

THE END
...or is it?